Love on Pointe

Love on Pointe

A Novel

Tiffany Odekirk

Covenant Communications, Inc.

Published by Covenant Communications, Inc.
American Fork, Utah

Printed in the United States of America
First Printing: June 2017

23 22 21 20 19 18 17   10 9 8 7 6 5 4 3 2 1

ISBN: 978-1-52440-200-6

For Kevin,
my forever

Acknowledgments

It takes a village to raise a baby and a tribe to complete a novel. For this reason, I will forever be indebted to my LDStorymakers tribe: Melanie Jacobson, who, when I e-mailed her questions about how to write a book not only answered my questions but offered to meet with me in person. You're my mentor but also one of my best friends. Ellisa Barr and Kristen Arnold, it was your love of Emmy and Rhys that helped me push through revisions. Thank you for your invaluable feedback and friendship. Natalee Cooper and Wendy Jessen, my cheerleaders, thank you for being my shoulders to cry on, my sisters in writing. Thank you, Jenille Isakson, Carrie Crosland, and Rebecca Toronto, for watching my babies so I could write and for letting me monopolize our conversations about writing. And all of my beta readers, and there are many, thank you: Raneé S. Clark, Kaylee Baldwin, Jolene Perry, Laree Ipson, Jen Mosier, Susan Auten, Candice Toone, and Jennifer K. Clark.

Thank you to my new family at Covenant. Samantha, your guidance, encouragement, and attention to detail has made this story what I dreamed it would be. Toree, thank you for creating a beautiful cover that so perfectly captures the feel of this novel. And to the many others working behind the scenes.

My extended family and in-laws (who are the best in-laws ever), your support means the world to me, and I couldn't have written a single word without you. Thank you.

Mom, thank you for dancing ballet in the kitchen. When you thought no one was watching, I was.

My children: Lexi, who shares my love of reading and writing; Jaxon, who first offered to publish my book; Xaley, who shared her mommy every other Tuesday for critique group and way too many hours in between with writing; and baby Brexden, who is the happiest newborn editing partner a mommy could ever wish for—thank you. You've made so many sacrifices to allow me to follow my dream, and you each deserve to have all your names on the cover too.

And my husband, Kevin—you encouraged me to write before I even had the guts to call myself a writer. It's because of you that I understand what love is and how to get my characters from "once upon a time" all the way to "happily ever after." This book and all others that may one day follow are possible only because of your support. I love you, Bug.

And always, I want to thank my Heavenly Father, who makes weak things strong. Thank you for giving me this talent and for the many doors you've opened. Truly, I am humbled.

Part I
Fall Semester

September

Chapter One
Rhys

The BOM [thuh / book / uhv / mohr-mun] n—the Book of Mormon, not "the bomb," as in "cool"

I'VE BEEN DREADING THIS MOMENT since I first signed the honor code and made BYU my alma mater. RelA 121: The Book of Mormon—one of two religion classes left on the docket before I graduate in the spring. Not a big deal for most students attending school here, but for a nonmember like me, it's torture.

Before coming to class this morning, I Googled *BYU Book of Mormon class, how to survive.* Surprisingly, there was an article in the digital *Daily Universe*, BYU's on-campus newspaper, that made a few suggestions:

1. Hydrate. Not sure how this helps me do anything except have to pee, but whatever.

2. Bring a snack. I actually like this one. Too bad I forgot to pack something.

3. Sit in the front row. I'm more of a back-row kind of guy.

4. And 5. Take notes and ask questions. Duh and duh.

6. Use the buddy system. Highly unlikely.

7. Find a class crush. I'm beginning to doubt the validity of this newspaper.

8. Have a mint handy. This one goes hand in hand with number seven. Only at BYU.

The door clicks shut behind me, and I reluctantly move forward, searching for a seat in the mammoth auditorium. I thought I'd give the front row a try since *The Daily Universe* recommended it and all, but with only five minutes before class starts, all the seats are taken. I sit in an empty middle row two seats from the door in case I need to make a quick getaway, and I pull out my notebook.

There are other Book of Mormon classes offered, but they don't fit my schedule. And since I've procrastinated taking this course until the last possible semester, I'm stuck.

My problem with this class isn't so much the subject matter though; it's my peers. I may have read the entire Book of Mormon this past summer to prepare for today, but I'll never know the scriptures like they do. I'm not good with the -ites or remembering which Nephi did what.

My other problem with RelA 121 is that I look like a Lamanite—dark hair, dark eyes, dark skin. It wouldn't be a bad thing if I were taking the second half of the BOM when the Lamanites are the good guys, but that's next semester. I'll likely have to deal with questions about "my people" and comments about how cool it is that my ancestors are in the Book of Mormon.

"Good morning. I'm Brother Clark, and you're the luckiest students on campus because this class is going to be the bomb!"

With my elbows propped on the armrests, I slide low in my chair to get comfortable. This is going to be a long semester.

Brother Clark is halfway through his opening monologue when the door opens. My gaze slides to the right, and my jaw nearly hits the desk in front of me. Girls at BYU are good-looking, altogether unbelievably hot, but this girl is . . . wow.

With her blonde hair piled on top of her head like a halo and a white cotton dress hugging her curves, she all but floats into the room. I turn my attention back to my desk and scribble in my notebook so it looks like I'm taking notes.

A sweet fragrance teases my nose a second before she whispers, "Is this seat taken?"

Without looking up, I shake my head, and she sits next to me. Guess I found someone to fulfill suggestion number seven. *Find a crush.* Stupid.

"Have I missed much?" she asks quietly.

When I glance up, she's biting her lower lip. I force my eyes back to my notebook. "No." I'm going to have to find another seat next time. This isn't going to work. To have any chance at passing this section, I need to focus. And right now, I am definitely not focusing—at least not on the Book of Mormon.

"While you may be familiar with the subject matter," Brother Clark says, "this class will be among the most challenging courses you take at BYU because it will require you to not only think spiritually but critically as well." Brother Clark picks up a stack of syllabi on his desk and hands them to his teacher's assistant to pass down the rows. "Due to this fact, you will be working with a partner for the rest of the semester. Please turn to the person next to you, exchange phone numbers, and get to know each other."

What? No. I have one goal in this class: pass. I plan to accomplish that by keeping my nose down, studying hard, and trying to blend in. I can't do any of those things with a partner. Especially a partner who looks like *her*.

I turn to the blonde next to me, and she's straightening her already straight iPad—clearly avoiding eye contact with me. Apparently neither of us is happy about this arrangement. Bet she's wishing she'd gotten to class a little earlier. "I guess we should get to know each other," I say. *Smooth, Rhys.*

"Yeah. Sure," she says with a tight smile, her fingernails tapping a frantic beat against the desk. "I'm Emelia. But you can call me Emmy."

Emmy. Half the girls in this school are named some variation of Emma. Emily, Emory, Emmy.

"Great, Emma." I purposefully call her by the wrong name, curious to see how tight she's wound.

"Just Emmy," she corrects, stiffening her posture as she angles toward me.

Apparently pretty tight. "Right. Emmy."

Her smile relaxes a fraction. "And you are . . . ?"

"Rhys. Spelled r-h-y-s but pronounced *rise*. Like BYU's fight song . . ." I cringe, wishing I hadn't just compared my name to a song.

"Cool name."

It's as random a name as my Mexican-Caucasian pedigree. Not sure whether I should thank my earth-loving mother for giving me such an eccentric name or my absentee father for not being around to stop her. "Solario," I add, letting the *r* roll off my tongue to be sure she hasn't mistaken me for a Pacific Islander or something more exotic.

"Jennings. Emmy Jennings."

"Nice to meet you. Where are you from?"

She picks at her pink painted nails. "California."

Not surprising. Wait. Jennings from California. "Any relation to UCAL's quarterback?"

She shifts in her seat. "Yeah, he's my brother."

I laugh under my breath. Of course this angel is related to college football's god.

Emmy touches her face as if trying to hide her blush. "Where are you from?"

"Other side of the Rockies. Denver." At least that's where I grew up. Though I did spend the first year of my college career in California."

"Do you have family in Utah?"

"My mom." She moved here three and a half years ago, right after Cami graduated, to start up a network-marketing business—just before her relapse.

Emmy nods that she's heard me, and then our conversation comes to a standstill, the lull magnified by the animated conversations around us.

"Should we keep asking each other questions?" Emmy asks.

I can guess what she's going to ask. It's always the same: *Where'd you serve?* "Sure. You can go first." Might as well get this out of the way. I tug on my shirt collar, adjusting my white undershirt. It may be pathetic to wear camouflage, but I don't feel bad about trying to blend in.

"Oh, uh, okay." Her brow scrunches when she pauses to think. "Do you play the guitar?"

I guess if she isn't going to investigate my spiritual status, then my talents, or lack thereof, are a good place to start. "Nope." I run a flat palm over my chin. Despite my having shaved this morning, it's already rough with stubble.

"Great. We can be friends, then."

Is she being sarcastic?

"I shouldn't have said that. It's cool if you play. But you said you don't, so I guess it doesn't matter, right? I was trying to be funny when I asked you if you played. It's become an inside joke between my sister and me. She loves guitar players, which is ironic, because even though we're alike in a lot of ways, I don't tend to like guys who play the guitar." Her eyes widen as if shocked by her own words. "That's not what I meant either. Guitars are fine. Guys are fine. But when the two are put together—" Her face turns as red as a bottle of Tabasco sauce. "Sorry, I ramble when I'm nervous. Not that *you* make me nervous." She winces at her confession, then brings her frantic little fingers to her heart-shaped lips.

My eyes flick to her mouth because . . . well, they just do. And lucky for me, she notices.

She drops her hand back to her desk. "Bad habit. I know. I'm trying to break it, but it's difficult—never mind. You don't want to hear about it. So, um . . . where'd you serve?"

And there it is. The million-dollar question they just can't help asking.

"I didn't."

"Oh. Are you a convert?"

"No," I say, honestly. "I'm not."

She blanches, and I feel slightly bad for making her uncomfortable—but my religious affiliation is as much her business as hers is mine. And, honestly, I'm sick of being treated differently. For once, I'd like someone to look at me as a person and not a potential missionary opportunity. If my lack of membership in her church becomes an issue in our partnership, *then* we can discuss my atheistic beliefs and come up with a solution.

"Of course not," she says. "That was a stupid question. I shouldn't have asked. I'm sorry. And, oh, my goodness, I'm rambling again—"

"Emmy." I cut her off. "Relax. It's not a big deal."

She looks down at her desk, and several strands of hair fall against her pink cheek, veiling her face. "Right. Sorry," she mumbles.

"Let's just get through this, okay?"

She nods, and I start to reach for my cell so we can exchange phone numbers but stop when her brand-new iPad mini catches my eye. I pull out my dollar notebook instead. I'd rather not spend ten minutes trying to tap her information into my ancient pay-by-the-month flip phone. I put my pen in my mouth and uncap it, jot my name and phone number on the edge of a piece of paper, then rip it off and hand it to her. "I have a busy schedule. Finding time to study together might be difficult." If not impossible.

"Yeah. For me too."

"Do you work?" Maybe I've misjudged her.

"No." She twists her hair off her face, then secures it in her bun. "Just busy." Or not.

She points to my notebook, and I slide it toward her. She writes her name in big loopy letters. *Emmy Jennings.* "I feel like I should warn you," she says, writing her phone number below her name. "You got stuck with the absolute worst-case scenario for a study partner."

I grunt in amusement. If she only knew. This would probably be a good time to disclose the fact that *she* got stuck with the worst-case scenario as a partner, not me, but again, not her business.

Emmy hesitates for a second, then pushes the notebook back. "I'm not the best student, but I promise to work hard, okay?"

Before I can reply, Brother Clark calls the class back to attention. I try to listen, but my focus is shot. I spend the rest of the class fighting my awareness of her. She moves her fingers ever so slightly in the air. Her foot bounces to a constant silent rhythm, only stilling when she pauses to tap a note into her iPad.

By the time class is over, I've missed most of the lecture. I knew BOM would be challenging, but with Emmy Jennings sitting next to me, it's going to be impossible.

Chapter Two

Emmy

Solo [soh-loh] n—A person who works, acts, or performs alone

THE WARM-UP ROUTINE AT THE barre is the same as it has been for the last thirteen years. Pliés first, then *tendus*, progressing all the way through *grand battements*.

Lengthening through my toes, my fingers, my spine and neck, I stretch every muscle until I'm limber and ready to dance. There are a thousand different ways I could mess this audition up. But I won't. I can do this. Even without Evie.

The energy in the studio is palpable—like we're all waiting backstage before the curtain rises on opening night at Lincoln Center and not in the ballet classroom in Provo. The lead in the fall workshop is the most coveted role of the semester, a fact that's hard to forget as Beethoven's Sonata no. 14 in C Minor fills the room. The dissonant chords are a mirror image of my mood—dark, brooding, but more than anything, determined.

Too soon the warm-up is over and Ballet Master Miller calls us to the center to show us the audition combination. Adrenaline courses through my veins. It's not that the combination is difficult; I've just never had to dance without my twin sister before. What if I can't do this without her? Thirteen years. Evie and I danced ballet together for thirteen years. And then she up and quit. I don't understand it. I didn't see it coming, but maybe I should have. She hadn't practiced all summer.

This morning when I left, she was still in bed. I wonder if she'll regret her decision to quit when she wakes up or if she'll be happy with her choice.

I try to put Evie out of my mind as Ballet Master Miller demonstrates the audition combination. I mark her movements, committing the sequence to

memory. Two eight-counts in, I make the mistake of looking at her in the mirror. Left, right. Upstage, downstage. Everything is reversed. My fingers start to
shake, and I drop my arm back to my side. At the end of her demonstration,
Ballet Master Miller motions for us to stand in the corner and then welcomes
in four judges.

The first group of dancers takes their place in the middle of the room,
and the audition formally begins. It's immediately obvious who's practiced
over the summer and who hasn't been *en pointe* since May.

The first group ends in fourth position, and the second group, my group,
is called to the center.

"Five, six, seven, eight," Ballet Master Miller counts.

I dance the first two eight-counts flawlessly. The third eight count, I stumble over a simple *pas de bourrée*. My pulse drums in my ears. I try to catch up
to the other dancers, but the choreography jumbles in my head and I reverse
the next arm position.

The double *fouetté* sequence at the end is challenging but doable. The first
turn is perfect, as is the second; I'm centered, and everything is tight. Everyone
around me hits their final mark, but with too much momentum, I turn twice
more.

A few giggles sound around me, behind me, everywhere in the room.

"Someone's showing off," a girl behind me whispers as we walk off the
floor.

Part of me wants to confess I was terrified and got lost, but that wouldn't
change the outcome of my audition or how my peers perceive me.

I'm relieved when the last group walks off the dance floor and the audition
ends. This is one reason I haven't gone to NYC yet. Auditions are the worst.
Well, that, and I promised Dad I would go to college before pursuing ballet professionally.

The judges inform us casting will be posted in thirty minutes on the
whiteboard inside the studio.

After changing out of our leotards into street clothes, we all sit quietly in
the hall. Voices come from inside, but they're so muffled I can't make out the
words. Time passes more slowly than ever, but true to her word, Ballet Master
Miller props open the doors exactly thirty minutes later.

My heart races as I walk inside the studio. My classmates take turns dragging their fingers down the casting sheet and stopping on their assigned role.
A few girls gasp, and my heart accelerates. By the time I get to the whiteboard,
my nerves are in knots.

I quickly scan the casting, and my stomach drops. The name next to the lead role, the solo, isn't mine. My finger continues down the page, almost to the bottom, searching for my name.

Emmy Jennings. Corps de Ballet. The lowest role a dancer can have in a ballet company.

My hand trembles as I pull it away from the paper. I'm halfway to the door when Ballet Master Miller's voice stops me. "Emmy, a word, please?"

I paint a stage smile on my face and walk back to the front of the room where she stands. The wrinkles next to her gray eyes deepen as she studies me. "I'm sure you're disappointed."

I concentrate on not letting my smile slip as I nod.

"You're a gifted dancer. Technically, near perfect," she says.

"Th-thank you," I stammer.

"Despite your stumble in the middle of the audition, your technique is flaw-less, and if I'd been a company casting the role, the solo would most likely have gone to you." She pauses. "But I'm not a casting director. I'm your teacher, and it's my job to train you to be the best ballet dancer you can be."

My throat thickens.

"The reason you weren't chosen as the principal dancer is because I believe some lessons are best learned in the corps. Allowing you to have every lead role would be a disservice to you. Do you understand?"

My eyes cloud with tears. I don't understand, but I push back my tears and force a nod. If she thought I wasn't willing to learn, it would hurt my chances to get the solo next semester.

"Good. I hope you'll accept the role in the corps?"

"Of course," I whisper.

She nods, pleased. "I'll see you in rehearsal, then."

As soon as I exit the Richards Building, the RB, I yank my phone out of my pocket to call Evie to tell her to meet me at home so I can complain about the audition. I'm halfway through dialing her number when I realize I can't call her. She'd blame herself for quitting ballet and me not getting the solo. I can't do that to her. I put my phone back in my pocket.

I have to learn to do this on my own now.

* * *

A gust of wind follows Evie inside as she walks into our living room, where I'm stretching on the floor. I hold up a finger to tell Evie to hold on so I can finish my phone conversation with Mom.

"Hey, Mom," I say. "Evie just got home. I should go."

"Okay, hon. Tell Evie to call me later. I want to hear about her first day too. And, Em?"

"Yeah?"

"Dancing will get easier without your sister; just be patient with yourself. Things will work out with your study partner too. Try not to stress over it. I love you."

"Thanks, Mom. I'll try. I love you too." I press End, set my cell on the floor next to me, and look up at Evie. "Mom says to call her."

"Will do. How was your first day?" Evie asks.

"Horrible." I readjust the bolster under my left calf and sink into a deeper stretch.

My identical twin looks at me with concern as she sets her books on the kitchen island. "That bad, huh?"

I groan. "The worst."

"What happened?"

I'm about to tell Evie about the audition disaster this morning but then decide to talk about a more neutral topic instead. "I, uh, sat next to this cute guy in my BOM class today."

Evie laughs. "And that's so tragic because . . . ?"

"Several reasons. Despite leaving thirty minutes early, I couldn't find a parking spot and was ten minutes late to class. And then our professor informed us we'd be partners for the rest of the semester."

"It stinks that you were late, but getting paired with a hottie? That's good, right?"

Compared to botching the audition this morning, being assigned to work with Rhys isn't bad. I just wish I could tell her that. But Evie hasn't asked about my audition, and I don't want to be the one to bring it up. She quit ballet, and I shouldn't drag her back into it. I let out a sigh. "He doesn't want to work with me. I could practically hear his disappointment when Brother Clark announced we'd be partners. So of course I got nervous and started rambling, and—it was bad, Eve," I say, using her nickname. "So bad."

Evie covers her mouth to stifle a giggle. "I'm sure it wasn't that bad."

"Trust me; it was. I was late on the first day of class. He probably thinks I'm a dumb blonde who doesn't care about school."

Evie sinks down next to me on our plush white carpet. "You'll have to prove him wrong, then."

I let my torso fall against my outstretched leg. If only I could talk to Evie about everything and convince her to come back to ballet. But it's too late. The audition was today, and she missed it. I'm on my own. In the corps.

Evie pats the back of my head. "Ice cream?"

"I better pass." It's hard to resist the creamy comfort, but I've already botched the solo, and ice cream isn't going to do me any favors.

"Hm. What about a greek yogurt?"

She knows me so well. "Now you're talking."

She hurries to the kitchen, and I shift into a straddle to balance my stretch. When she returns, she hands me a yogurt, then digs into a tub of salted caramel. I'm not going to lie. I'm jealous.

When we're both finished, we lean against the back of the couch.

"See? Nothing a little salted caramel—er, yogurt—can't fix," Evie says.

We used to do this all the time—eat ice cream and watch Ridge Dashly movies. And once upon a time, there was nothing the combination couldn't fix.

"Thanks, Eve, but it's going to take more than cream and sugar to repair this crazy-awful day." I set the empty container aside. "What would you say to a movie marathon? I would love some company and distraction while I stretch." Maybe if we spend a little more time together, I can work up the courage to ask her why she quit ballet.

"Well . . ."

I *chassé* to the DVD cupboard before she can say no and pull out our towering collection of Ridge Dashly movies. As soon as I take a step, the pile topples to the floor. We both laugh, and somehow my day doesn't feel quite so bad.

"We should limit our marathon to a two-movie mini because we have FHE," I say, sorting through the stack to search for our all-time favorites. "Are you in the mood for *Loving Grace* or *Sarah's Song*?" I wiggle the cases of our two favorite romance movies in front of her, waiting for Evie to pick one. I can't remember the last time we did this.

Evie glances at her cell. "I'm not sure—"

"We'll have to take an intermission to go to FHE, but that isn't for another two hours, so we can for sure squeeze one in now," I say.

Without warning, the front door swings open and Kennedy, a girl Evie met in one of her classes last semester, glides into our living room. Evie jumps to her feet and greets Kennedy with a hug. "How much time do we have?" Kennedy asks, flipping her chestnut curls off her shoulder.

"How much time do you have for what?" I ask, attempting to be part of their conversation.

Evie and Kennedy exchange smiles. "The most epic FHE ever," Kennedy says.

"Really? What's our ward doing tonight?"

"I don't know what *our* ward is doing tonight," Evie says. "But the Village is doing this massive welcome-back party."

"It's supposed to be epic!" Kennedy grins. "Live music and everything."

The DVDs fall to my side, forgotten, and two emotions overcome me. First, I feel horrible for monopolizing the entire five minutes I had with my sister to whine about my day. Second, I feel dread. Kennedy isn't the best influence, and I don't want Evie to make the same mistakes our older sister Lucy did. "I'm sure it'll be great, but shouldn't we go to our own? I think we get divided into families tonight."

"I forgot about that," Evie says.

Kennedy rolls her eyes. "You can get put into a family group next week. No one will care if you guys miss this one. Just pretend like you forgot it was starting back up this week."

"Or maybe we could stop by that other FHE after our own?" I suggest quickly.

"You *could* do that," Kennedy says to Evie, "but Q is supposed to be there, and guys like him get snatched up fast. You don't want to show up late and miss your chance with him, do you?"

I can't resist asking, "Q?"

"Quinton," Kennedy says. "Everybody calls him Q though."

Everybody except for me, apparently.

"He just got back from his mission in Europe," she adds. "I hear he has a touch of an accent now. Isn't that cool?"

"Yeah, cool," I mumble.

"So what do you say, Evie? Are you coming with me or hanging with your sister?"

Evie looks at me, torn. "I don't want to miss our FHE. But if I don't go with her to the Village's FHE, Kennedy's right—Q will for sure be off the market." Evie pauses. "Why don't you come with us, Em? It'll get your mind off your horrible day."

It's an empty invitation, but part of me wants to tag along if for no other reason than to get a few extra minutes with my twin. "No, thanks. You guys go ahead."

"At least get ready with us," Evie says.

I would, but after messing up the audition today, I should spend more time training for ballet and less time primping. "Thanks, but I need to finish stretching before I go."

Evie frowns. "There's more to life than ballet, Em." She turns to Kennedy. "This is why I quit. It takes over your entire life."

My heart sinks hearing Evie talk about ballet like this. We loved dancing together. It requires sacrifice, sure, but it's worth it. And it's not like ballet has taken over my *whole* life. I still date, occasionally. And go out with friends, sometimes. I'm here at BYU getting an education, for goodness' sake. That alone shows ballet hasn't taken over my whole life. Most dancers would never give up any of their dancing years, not considering how short ballet careers are. I'm giving up four.

One day I'll have more time. One day I'll get married and have a family. One day I'll have children and open my own ballet studio. But right now, my top priority is learning how to be the best dancer I can be.

Evie and Kennedy start up the stairs discussing what to wear to the party.

Desperate for more time with Evie, for a chance to remind her who she is and what she loves, I call up the stairs after them. "On second thought, I think I'll stop by with you guys for a bit." Maybe the party won't be quite as "epic" as they think it will be, and if I'm there, I can talk Evie into leaving and going with me to our ward's FHE.

Chapter Three

Rhys

BY—Zoo [bee / wī / zoo] n—A dating pool disguised as a university, where young Latter-day Saints come to meet their ~~soulmates~~ eternal companions

THE VILLAGE AT SOUTH CAMPUS is a multiblock megacomplex three blocks from BYU. With underground parking, fiber-optic Internet, and a heated pool, it's everything a guy could want. Too bad I live in the 110-year-old house across the street. No cable, no pool, no nothing. But it's cheap, and that's what matters.

My backpack hits the pressboard desk with a hollow thud, and the severely used books I purchased from the bookstore spill onto the dirt-stained carpet of my shared bedroom floor. I tried to find all ten textbooks online, but due to delayed delivery times—not to mention ridiculous shipping costs—the bookstore ended up being a bargain.

I scoop the books off the floor and set them on the shelf above my desk. The front door squeaks on its hinges, and a second later, Superman, aka Supe, my roommate, appears at our bedroom door.

"Yo-yo!" he says.

"Hey, man."

We meet in the middle of the room, clasp hands, and pat each other's back.

"It's been forever." Supe sets his bags on the bed across from mine and starts unpacking, or rather, flinging his clothes into the bottom of his half of the closet.

"How was your summer?" I ask.

"Amazing! Finally hiked Kilimanjaro. How was yours?"

I worked long hours hauling boxes for Smith's, took summer classes, and drove Mom to and from more doctor appointments than I'd like to count. "Same ol', same ol'."

His lips purse as if to say, "That stinks," then he continues unpacking.

"You signed up for classes yet?" I ask, changing the subject.

He grins. "Yep. Prayed about my schedule, and I'm pretty sure this is the year."

The year he meets Mrs. Supe. I laugh, and he gives me a dirty look—not that dirty though; mostly he looks constipated—and I laugh again.

"You should try it some time," he says.

"Praying?"

He rolls his eyes. "Dating." I hear the implied *duh* even though he doesn't verbalize it.

"Not going to happen." Not after Beth. Not after Kayla. Not after Lisa. And not after the brutal reminder they each gave me that no one at BYU will ever date a nonmember like me.

As if he didn't hear me, Supe steps onto his bed and flings open the threadbare curtain. "Do you see that, Rhys?"

I glance at the massive brick structure across the street. "The Village?"

He frowns. "No. Not the Village." Supe makes a show of squinting into the distance. "B.Y. Zoo, brother. Provo is the marriage capital of the world. The only reason people come here is to date and get married."

Pretty sure people come here to get an education from a well-respected private university also, but again, it's something I don't say out loud. He wouldn't listen anyway.

"It's been two and a half years since you transferred here and almost as many since you've been out with a girl. Don't you want to try the dating scene again?"

I snort. "We both know the dating scene doesn't want me, man."

Supe jumps down and sits on the edge of his bed. "I'm not suggesting you get married or anything. I'm just sayin' if you went on a date once in a while, you might not hate it here so much."

I pretend to chew over his suggestion. "Thanks, but I'll pass." Supe's a good guy. My lack of membership in his church doesn't bother him. As long as we avoid the subject of religion, we get along. Honestly, he's become one of my best friends over the last two years.

"So, Helaman on the wall or the ceiling?" Supe unfurls a life-sized poster of the Book of Mormon warrior and holds it up for me to see.

"Ceiling. Definitely." I can't wait to see him attempt to secure it upside down.

"My thoughts exactly." He grabs a box of pushpins out of his open bag. "Oh, hey, do you want to go with me to FHE tonight?" Supe asks. "It's just across the street at the Village."

Girls wearing too much makeup. Guys wearing too much cologne. All of them there for the same purpose: to find a soulmate. Scratch that—eternal companion. No way. "Nah. I've got to take care of some stuff. You?"

"Yeah, but I think I'm going to try to sell my parking spot in the drive-way before I head over."

He always has some plan up his sleeve. Supe struggles to pin the poster to the ceiling. I watch him for a second and then climb onto the bed and help him hold it up. "So what's your plan this year?" I ask.

He pushes a pin into the corner of the poster. "Glad you asked. It all starts tonight. I'm going to get some phone numbers and line up a few dates right away. You know, start the year off right."

"Numbers. Right." Sounds similar to last year's plan. Hopefully, his plot to get numbers doesn't involve a nursery rhyme this time.

"Shoot! I need to charge my cell. I forgot to plug it in last night." Poster forgotten, he jumps off the bed, scrambles to plug the charger into the wall, and connects his phone. "Phew." He wipes an imaginary bead of sweat from his forehead and climbs back onto the bed. "Close one."

We finish tacking up the poster.

"I met a girl," I say when we're finished. Why I feel the need to share this, I'm not sure.

"Oh yeah? Where?"

"Book of Mormon class. We're assigned study partners."

Supe laughs. "Well, that's . . . ironic."

I frown, and Supe laughs harder. "Oh, come on. Two nonmembers meeting in a Book of Mormon class. You don't see the humor in that?"

That would be funny. Awesome, actually, but . . . "She's a member."

Supe crosses his arms over his chest. "That does present a problem. Lucky for you, I've got two friends who would love to help you."

"Are both of their names Elder?"

"It's possible."

This is about as deep as our conversations on religion get anymore. Off-handed comments and lighthearted jokes. When I was new to Provo three years ago, Supe was the typical RM. He gave me a Book of Mormon. I read it. He invited me to church. I went. But when he asked me to take the missionary lessons, I made it clear my curiosity had more to do with wanting to blend in than a desire to investigate Mormon doctrine, and he backed off.

"Do you think I need to tell her I'm not LDS?" I can't help feeling bad for not having said anything today.

"Mmm." Supe bobbles his head side to side. "Are you planning to date her?"

I'd be lying if I say I'm not attracted to her, but for obvious reasons, I'm not entertaining the idea. "Nah. It would never work."

"Then as long as you do your homework, I think you're fine."

"Cool. That's what I thought." No big deal. I open my Book of Mormon and begin the first reading assignment.

* * *

My phone vibrates with a text in my back pocket, startling me awake. I must've fallen asleep studying after Supe went outside to sell his parking spot.

Mom: I know we already have dinner plans on Thursday, but would you mind picking up a few things for me tonight?

Cranberry Juice

Tofu

Vitamin D

Gingko

Ginseng

Mom's list of odd items comes in one text at a time, each filling me with more dread than the last. Her multiple sclerosis must be relapsing again. I curse as I slam my book shut and grab my keys. I'm about to walk out of the room when a buzzing sound stops me. I turn and see Supe's phone vibrating on his desk.

The last thing I want to do tonight is go to this party, even if it's only for a few minutes to drop off Supe's phone, but knowing how his plan relies on it, I can't leave it here either, no matter how much I wish I could.

Thing is, when I first transferred from UCAL to BYU at the beginning of my sophomore year, I had no clue about the unwritten dating code: members date members. Period. Problem is, for better but mostly for worse, I stand out here, and that attracts girls. Girls I can't have. It's not that I'm anything special. Anywhere else, I'm about as average as a person can get. Here though, I'm someone with a story, a question mark everyone wants answered. I look different. I act different. I *am* different.

It's easiest to avoid attachments and keep my nose down. Not hard to do when school, work, and my other responsibilities require most of my time. Stepping foot into that party is the opposite of sticking to myself.

As I lock the front door, my phone vibrates with a call. Cami. "What's up, little sister?"

"Trust me. You *don't* want to know."

Cami's always had a flare for the dramatic. Living in New York suits her perfectly.

"Wardrobe malfunction?" I ask.

"Don't tease me. How's purgatory—I mean, Provo?"

I look both ways and cross the street to the Village, catching the eye of a cute girl in a Beemer. "Purgatory pretty much sums it up." A sea of temptation with a big, fat, do-not-touch sign cemented into the sand.

"You've got to get out of there, Rhys."

"You know I can't." If I could move now, I would, but that isn't a possibility. Mom needs me.

A beat of silence passes. "How's . . . everything?" Cami asks quietly. We both know she's asking about Mom, although her guilt over not being in Provo to help and my insistence on her not feeling guilt for following her dreams to New York prevents us from discussing the situation much.

"Everything's great." I wind my way through the Village, trying to find the party.

"You still haven't cashed the check I sent."

"I don't need your money, Cam."

"I know *you* don't, but I want to help with Mom—"

"I have it under control. You don't have to worry. I've gotta go though. My roommate left his phone, and I've got to deliver it to him at a party."

"Party?" Her voice perks up. "That sounds promising."

"Two words: *Honor. Code.* They serve bottled water and root beer."

"You are at college, right? I mean, you're not secretly in jail or anything, are you?"

I laugh out loud. "Not in jail. No." Though sometimes it feels like it. Two more semesters and my time here is served.

"Explain to me again why you're at that Mormon college and not the normal university down the street?"

"Because BYU is cheaper than state schools. And its prestigious private-school name will land me higher-paying jobs after graduation." Plus, BYU has a football team worth rooting for, and I might as well enjoy something while I'm trapped in Utah.

Cami snorts. "Remember that when they try to convert you again."

I'll admit at first I was curious about the Mormon religion. It was interesting, and I'll give Mormons credit for enthusiasm, but forever families? Not my reality. I don't fit the Mormon mold, and I never will.

"Well, have fun at your party." Cami sighs when I don't respond. "And don't forget to text me an update once in a while."

"Will do," I say, although we both know I'll forget.

Chapter Four
Emmy

À la seconde [ah / la / se-cund] v—A movement into second position

To say the Village is big would be an understatement. It's like stepping into a cement corn maze with endless corridors. Altogether it takes us thirty minutes to find the correct room number.

Before we follow the loud din of voices inside, Evie stops to smooth her hair and then swings her Chloe bag off her shoulder and pulls out her favorite department store lip gloss. Color: Double Dare. Only Evie could make hot pink look classy and not eighties trashy. I'm partial to whatever brand the drug store sells with Daisy Duck on the tube. But to each her own, I guess.

Evie tries to hand me Double Dare, but I wave it away. "I'm good."

Her eyes crease at the corners as if to say, *You're really not.* When I ignore her, she loops her arm through Kennedy's, and they walk inside. I follow after them.

Vaulted ceilings, modern gray wallpaper, and several couches make for an inviting party area. A ping-pong ball bounces off a table at regular intervals, barely audible over the crowd.

We press through the mass to the back corner of the room where a group of twenty or so sits on a large sectional.

"We made it just in time." Kennedy points to a guy sitting on an otto-man, pulling a guitar out of a case. Messy-styled blond hair. Dimples. Broad shoulders. Cute, if not cliché. Evie takes one look at the guy, who I'm guessing must be Q, and does a squeal face at Kennedy. Sometimes it's hard to believe we share identical DNA. Evie and Kennedy crowd onto the end of the sofa, leaving me no room to join them. I scan the couch for a place to sit, but the only one open is right in front of Q. Great.

Careful not to bump his guitar, I slide past him and sit down. As he brushes his fingers down the guitar strings, the group quiets for the show. The song starts off slow and full of angst. Wait, I've heard this one before. Damian Rice. Good taste. And surprisingly, Q has a nice voice. Soft. Smooth. Sultry, even.

He scans his admirers, and our eyes catch. My face flames, and though I hate to admit it, I can understand what Evie sees in this guitar player. He's cute. But then a girl on my right sighs, and Q's gaze moves from me and settles on her with a wink. It surprises me so much I almost laugh at the hilarity of the situation. It's like witnessing the human version of an animal mating dance.

An intense urge to laugh or snort or do something else entirely inappropriate overwhelms me. Trying not to make a fool of myself, I press my lips together. Q must take my expression as flirting though, because the corner of his mouth quirks up and his eyes lock on me as he sings.

Mortified, I look down and study my peeling nail polish. As soon as he hits the last note, I stand from the couch to make my escape. "I'm going to get some water," I say as I scoot past Evie and Kennedy. They nod, and I pretend not to notice their disgruntled looks as I walk to the mini kitchen. Water bottles line the counter. I grab one and take a quick sip. Before I have time to set it down, someone taps me on the shoulder.

"Hey," Q says in a husky voice. But not real husky, like he's trying too hard husky.

"Hi."

He leans against the counter and crosses his feet. It's the kind of relaxed position only a guy who knows he's good-looking can pull off. Unfortunately, that kind of guy isn't *my* kind of guy. He's got the wrong twin.

"Did you like the song?" Q asks me the question, but he keeps scanning the room like he's at a buffet and wants to make sure someone else doesn't walk away with something better than what's already in front of him.

"Yeah. Sure. It was great."

"You don't sound too sure about that."

I'm sure I liked the song. I'm also sure I don't want to encourage him. He seems like the type of guy who requires a lot of attention, and I'm not interested in being the girl to give him that attention. It would be mean to lead him on, so I say, "It was a nice song."

"Pretty song for a pretty girl." Q reaches toward my face, and I rear back. "Easy there." He holds his hands up, then inches them toward me. "You have hair in your face."

I freeze, wanting to move away but physically unable. His fingers are rough against my cheek as he tucks loose strands of hair behind my ear. He leans against the counter again, watching me like he's waiting for me to react. Maybe I'm supposed to swoon or something.

"Thank you?"

His chest puffs like a strutting peacock. "Anytime." He grabs a bottle of water and takes a quick swig. As he sets it back down, he not so subtly checks me out. "So what are you? A dancer or something?"

I pull my draped pink cardigan tightly around me, trying to hide my black yoga pants from his appraising stare. Maybe this isn't the best outfit to wear to a party, but we're playing ultimate at FHE tonight, and I wanted to be ready so I could go straight there after the party. "Yeah. I, uh, dance ballet."

"Nice." Q smirks. "Want to show me a spin or something?" He swirls his hand in the air.

Do I want to show him a spin or something? That would be a negative.

"I mean it's only fair." He continues to flirt, oblivious to my disinterest. "I showed you my talent; you should show me yours."

I frown. "I'm not going to dance for you."

"Another time, maybe."

"Not likely."

Now Q frowns, but then a girl walks by, and his eyes light back up. *This* is why I'm not attracted to guitar players. They have less than a two-minute attention span.

My eyes wander over Q's shoulder to the door, searching for a valid excuse to walk away. While I don't find an acceptable reason to leave, I do find something worth staying for.

Rhys walks into the room with a determined stride that makes it obvious my study partner is here for a specific reason. I never knew the way someone walks could be attractive. A face, a personality, absolutely. But a walk? No clue. Rhys has serious swagger. I'll admit it. He's make-your-eyes-melt hot.

He holds up a phone to a guy sitting on a couch, and though I can't see his friend's expression because his back is to me, it's obvious from his body language he's very happy to see the phone.

Q follows my gaze to Rhys. "Someone you know?"

"What? Oh no. Well, sort of . . . We have a class together. Do you know him? Is he in your ward?"

Q appraises Rhys and shakes his head. "Nope. Never seen the guy before."

"Oh." I watch Rhys hand over the phone, slap his friend on the back, and then start toward the door. He is nearly outside when a guy in front of him collides with a girl, knocking a case of water bottles out of her arms and onto the floor. The guy doesn't stop, so Rhys stoops to help her instead. They pile the bottles back onto the flat, and then he rushes out the door. The girl he helped looks about as disappointed as I feel to see him go. Reluctantly, I turn back to Q.

"Em."

I sigh in relief when I hear Evie's voice behind me, but the feeling fades when I turn and find both Evie and Kennedy tucked under the arms of some way-too-muscled guy.

"You really are a twin!" Muscles says to Evie.

Q's eyes dart from me to Evie, and a Cheshire-cat grin grows across his face.

"If I hit on one of you, will you both go out with me?" Muscles asks.

Never heard that one before.

"We aren't conjoined twins, silly." Evie giggles, and Q can't take his eyes off her.

"I'm Q."

"Evie."

And that's my cue to go. There will be no sisterly bonding tonight. I check the time on my cell.

"You're not leaving already, are you?" Evie pouts.

I hate it when she acts like this to get a guy's attention. Maybe if I ask her to come to FHE in front of Q, she'll agree to impress him. "I should get to FHE. Why don't you come with—"

"I'll give you a ride home if you want to stay," Q says to Evie.

Evie beams. "I'd love that. Thank you." She turns back to me. "All settled, then. Have fun at FHE."

Well, that backfired. "You sure? I could stay a little longer . . ."

"I'm pahhhsitive." Evie's eyes flash to me like she's trying to convey a secret message. All that's missing is a conspiratorial wink.

"Right. Okay."

Evie turns a smile loose on Q, and I walk away. Nothing about this day has gone how I hoped it would.

Chapter Five

Rhys

Acronym [ak-ruh-nim] n—Shorthand for pretty much everything in the Church. Examples: CTR, FHE, YSA, BOM, EFY. It can also be applied to buildings on campus: HFAC=Harrison Fine Arts Center, WILK=Wilkinson Student Center

TUESDAYS ARE LIGHT ON SCHOOL, heavy on work. It's only 10:00 a.m., but after dropping off Supe's phone at the party and then buying and delivering all the items to Mom last night, I didn't finish studying until well after midnight. Not a good idea since I have to work a long closing shift at Hot Dog on a Stick at the mall.

I tighten the straps of my backpack and walk out of the HFAC—pretty much the farthest building on campus from my house. Driving my truck to school doesn't make sense because there aren't enough parking spots. I could wait for a bus, but I don't have the patience to sit for the next thirty minutes when walking home takes only twenty.

I pull out my cell to check my text messages. There are five. All of them from Cami, no doubt asking for an update.

I'm walking by the WILK, about to tap on the first text, when I see her. Long blonde hair, bright pink lips, and a figure that would distract even the most devout guys on campus. Of which there are several—guys, that is—currently surrounding her.

Emmy runs a hand through her hair, letting the golden strands fall through her fingers. She smiles at one of the guys standing across from her, and he grins like he's won a prize. She doesn't seem to notice the effect she has on him though.

Like she could sense me staring, her eyes flick up to meet mine. Without thinking, I wave like an idiot. Emmy's nose crinkles up at me, and then she turns back to her admirers. This is why I have no desire to date at BYU—I'm left feeling like a penny not worth picking up. To them, I'm worth *less*.

I grit my teeth as I shove my hand into my pocket and hurry home.

Two more semesters.

Twenty minutes later, I walk inside the house and flip on the bedroom light.

"Dude."

I jump at Supe's voice.

"What time is it?" he asks, rubbing the sleep out of his eyes.

"Almost ten thirty. Sorry. Thought you'd be in class already." I set my backpack on the edge of my bed, and the weight of the books presses into the mattress.

Grumbling, he rolls out of bed. "Thanks for bringing over my phone last night. I think I met a few good dating prospects." He yawns, walking over to his closet. I wait for him to elaborate, but he doesn't. I guess it's too early to hear about his search for the perfect bride. He picks up his stuff and stumbles to the bathroom.

I use the time to change into my red-and-yellow vertical-striped uniform T-shirt—maybe the most hideous article of clothing ever created. I tuck the shirt into my blue pleated shorts and pin my name tag over my chest. The next eight hours are going to be torture.

* * *

"I heard from the EQP that FHE in BYU's 150th Ward was better than anything he did all summer." Jen's red-rimmed glasses inch up her freckled nose as she smiles, obviously pleased with herself for cramming so many acronyms into one sentence.

I look her straight in the eye. "That's not what the AP said after he got back from working at the MTC. He said EFY was way better than any YSA or FHE he had been to since becoming an RM."

Jen groans as she dips a hot dog into the thick, creamy corn-bread batter and clips it into the fryer. "That was two sentences. And the game only works if the acronyms make sense in the sentence, Rhys."

"They did!" *I think.*

"Trust me; they didn't," Jen says as she walks through the swinging door into the supply room.

"Whatever," I call toward the door. "I still used more."

While Jen's gone, I restock the napkins and straws. It's a mindless task, so my thoughts start to wander back to the night of the party. As expected, I forgot to text Cam an update. I meant to do it today after class, but seeing Emmy side-tracked me. Luckily Mom is doing well, so there isn't anything to report anyway.

The timer on the fryer goes off, and Jen reappears. "How are your classes this semester?" she asks as she unclips the corn dogs.

"I'm taking the first half of the Book of Mormon. Need I say more?"

"Right." Jen hands the customer the corn dog and then pours herself a cup of water. "I remember how much you were looking forward to that."

I grunt. "My plan was to blend in with the walls. Glide through the semester. But that's not going to happen."

Jen raises an eyebrow.

"I got stuck with a partner."

"Eh. You'll have more fun in class now. Who knows, maybe you and your partner will become friends."

I shake my head. "Nah. I got stuck with—" How do I describe a hot girl to a quirky girl? No clue. "A girl."

Jen rolls her eyes. "You do know girls and boys can be friends, right? Case in point." She motions between us. "You act like girls are evil."

"Some are," I say, thinking about Emmy flat-out ignoring me this morning. "And I don't think a hot blonde is going to do anything for my concentration."

"Excuses. Excuses."

"Yeah. I guess."

"Yeah. I guess," Jen imitates me using a slow, deep voice and a thick tongue.

I smile. Jen is nothing like the other girls I've met in Provo. She's easy to be real with. Plus, she's leaving on a mission at the end of the school year, so there's none of that boy-girl relationship weirdness between us. She's a lot like Cami, only slightly less annoying.

"How's mission prep going?"

"Wonderful. Thanks for asking." She points a finger at me. "But don't think you're getting off the hook so easily. Tell me more about this study partner of yours."

"Not much to tell." I pull out a jug of ketchup and begin refilling the empty dispenser.

"Oh, so that's why she was the first thing you brought up when I asked you about your classes?"

One point: Jen.

"Just saying. You obviously wanted to talk about her."

"How many shots do you have to get if they send you to South America again?"

Jen glares. Vaccinations are the one thing about going on a mission Jen's not thrilled with. She grabs a rag off the counter and chucks it at me. "Clean some tables."

As a friend, Jen's awesome, but as a manager, she's ruthless.

Eight hours feels closer to twenty-four, but finally my shift ends.

When I pull into my driveway, my eyes are so heavy I have to fight to keep them open. Sleep isn't an option though. If I don't read the assigned chapters for Book of Mormon tonight, I won't have time until Sunday, and that's when I'm supposed to cram for statistics. I'm about to get out of the truck when my phone vibrates with a text. A shot of adrenaline pumps into my system. I never get texts this late unless it's an emergency. Not even from Cami. I hurry to flip open my phone, then sigh in relief when I see who the text is from.

Emmy: Are you free to study tomorrow night?

I stare at the phone for a second, trying to decide whether or not to text her back when another text appears on the screen. A smiley face. Emmy's real smile flashes in my mind, followed by the image of the guys drooling over her. I tap the phone against the steering wheel and then darken the screen. If she wanted to talk, she could have done it earlier.

Chapter Six
Emmy

Distraction [dih-strak-shuhn] n—Rhys

STUDENTS ARE SITTING IN SMALL groups when I walk into BOM Wednesday morning. I slide into my spot, *our* spot, pull out my iPad mini, and cue the voice recorder app.

Each time someone walks through the door, my heart jumps. I try to keep my eyes on anything but the door—the whiteboard, my desk, my phone—but that doesn't stop my thoughts from running wild. What if he doesn't show? What if he does? What if when he does he doesn't sit next to me?

Trying to distract myself, I review last week's notes. There isn't much there, only Rhys's name and phone number. Butterflies swarm in my stomach even thinking about sitting next to him for a whole hour. I'll be a nervous wreck the entire time, but I can't help being excited to see him again. I wonder if his eyes are as dark as I remember and if his voice is as smooth and deep.

The door pushes open, and even without looking, I know it's him by the way the energy in the room changes. It's kind of like the way the air feels when a principal ballerina walks onstage. My gaze flits to my notes, my shoes, the floor, trying and failing not to notice the dark jeans accenting his swinging step or the silver chain disappearing underneath his dark-gray V-neck shirt.

My fingers tap, tap, tap against the desk as his shoulders go slack and his backpack slides down his muscled back and onto the floor. A wave of his mild cologne floats past my nose. Spicy yet sweet. Completely intoxicating.

I wait for him to say something, maybe hey or hello, but he doesn't. Weird. I think. Or maybe it's not. Am I supposed to say hello first? No, he would've said hello if he wanted to talk. And obviously he doesn't.

I chance another look in his direction. He's sitting low in his chair with his legs kicked out long in front of him and his notebook already open on his desk.

Umm . . . "Hey."

He nods but doesn't look up.

Now what? I don't think I can stand another second of this, and we still have five minutes before class starts. "I, um, texted you this week."

"I saw."

"Oh." We've officially crossed the line from uncomfortable to full-blown awkward. "Oh-*kay*."

He pulls a pen out of his backpack and puts it between his ridiculously full, super-kissable lips and removes the cap. Well, at least I think they're kissable. They look like they'd be kissable, not that I'd know since I've never kissed anyone before.

"Why didn't you text me back?" The question falls from my mouth before I can censor it.

He looks up from his notebook. "I kinda got the impression the other day that you had no interest in me returning that text."

What did I say last class that made him think that? I replay everything that happened in fast-forward so I don't look like an idiot stuck on pause. "I'm sorry, but I have no idea what you're talking about."

"Outside the WILK? Last week?"

And there's my first clue this is a mix-up. "That wasn't me."

"If you say so."

"Was I wearing hot pink lipstick?"

His eyes flick to my mouth and then away. He's quiet for a moment, and I can't tell if he's trying to remember what I looked like last week or if he's trying to forget. "Yeah. Maybe."

"That was my sister Evie. I'm an identical twin."

He laughs humorlessly, then scrubs a hand down his face. "So that pretty much makes me a jerk." Rhys looks up, and it's hard not to squirm under his stare. His eyes are so deep it feels like he's searching my soul.

"Whatever Evie did, you have to promise not to hold it against me. Sometimes it's hard for people because we're identical, but we're very different. And—"

"Emmy," he cuts off my nervous ramble, and I nibble on my cuticle.

"Y-yeah."

"I should have texted you back. I'm sorry."

"It's okay," I say, trying to brush it off.

"Can we start over?"

I let out a relieved, "Please."

He opens his mouth to say something, but before he can, Brother Clark welcomes us to class. We say a quick prayer, and then the lecture begins.

Rhys leans forward as if hanging on Brother Clark's every word, and he jots down the most thorough set of notes ever created. I check to make sure my iPad is recording—it is—then note a few times at the top of my page so I can review the important parts later tonight.

Rhys looks at me and then nods down at his notebook. My shoulders tense as he slides the paper from his desk to mine. I can feel his eyes studying me as I study his words. His handwriting isn't messy, but it's small, and the words are smooshed together, making it difficult for me to translate. I squint at the paper, trying to keep his short, angular letters in their correct positions.

Emmy (not Emma)—What's your schedule like this week?

My heart races, and I have to remind myself that he's setting up a time to study. I write a note back. *Rhys (pronounced "rise," not "Reese")—Class every day until 2, and rehearsal from 3–7.*

My letters are big and loopy compared to his. I slide the notebook back.

His lips slant across his face as he reads my note. My cheeks warm, which is ridiculous since we aren't even talking. At least I can't ramble if my words are confined to paper. I try to concentrate on Brother Clark's lecture, but my ears refuse to hear anything but Rhys's pen scratching out another note. He touches my elbow with the edge of the paper when he's finished.

Four-hour rehearsal one week into school? You a football player?

I giggle, then write and push my response back to Rhys. *Clearly. Can't you tell by these guns?*

He reads my note with an amused smile, then writes, *Soccer player?*

My nose scrunches up, and I shake my head. *Ballet dancer*, I write back.

That explains the bun.

I self-consciously push a loose bobby-pin back into my hair and then point at his notebook. He slides it to me, and I write, *What's your schedule? You're not a football player, are you?* I write the note in jest, but truthfully, I hope he's not. We'd never find time to study between my rehearsals and his practices.

Sorry to disappoint, but I'm just a boring business major.

Not boring! What do you want to do with it?

Anything that pays the bills and provides health insurance. So . . . my work schedule changes every week, but what about tomorrow night at 7:30?

The butterflies take flight again at the thought of meeting Rhys anywhere but here. My contact with the opposite sex has been limited to my pas-de-deux partner in the studio, where every move is choreographed and each breath timed. I read his note again. It's just studying. Studying is easy. Okay, not for me. But after this first session, it will get eas*ier*.

Tomorrow's great, I respond.

Okay. Where?

Library?

He nods once, then refocuses his attention on Brother Clark. Unfortunately, my attention stays on Rhys. I'll have to listen to this lecture again before we study tomorrow night.

* * *

After a thirty-minute Pilates session, a knock sounds at the front door.

"Emmy, can you get that?" Evie calls from upstairs.

"Yep." I stand from the floor, and the joints in my feet pop as I walk to the door.

When I open it, Q is leaning against the doorframe. "Hey, baby. You ready?"

Baby? Umm, no.

"I'm Emmy. You're here for Evie. Hold on a sec." I don't invite him inside, but he struts in anyway.

Normally, I would shout up to Evie, but I'll take any excuse to get away from this guy, so I jog up the stairs and open Evie's door. "Prince Charming is here." Neither she nor Kennedy seem to notice the sarcasm in my voice.

"What do you think?" Evie turns to give me a better view of her outfit. Dark skinny jeans, V-neck top, chunky jewelry.

"You look great." I rest my hip against the doorframe. "Listen though. I don't know what it is about Q, but he's, um"—how do I put this nicely?—"a little too slick."

Evie's eyes move to Kennedy, then back to me. "I like him, Em. A lot. Be happy for me, okay?"

My mouth crowds to one side, but I manage a nod. Evie and Kennedy do this kiss-the-air-on-either-side-of-their-cheeks thing, then Evie straightens and walks out of the room like she's storming the runway at New York Fashion Week.

Q's voice floats up the stairs a moment later. "You look hot, baby."

Evie's giggle hushes only when the door closes behind them.

I hurry to watch Evie leave for her date. A big black truck with mean rims sits in our driveway. Q checks his reflection in the shiny paint as he walks to the driver's side, not bothering to open the door for my sister. Evie waves to me with a big grin on her face and then climbs, literally, into Q's raised truck before they drive away.

I turn to Kennedy. "Please tell me you don't see whatever it is Evie sees in him."

"I think you might be the only girl at BYU who doesn't see it."

I wish things could go back to the way they were when it was just Evie and me and life consisted of school and ballet.

Chapter Seven

Rhys

Scripture mastery [skrip-cher / mas-tuh-ree] n—A total of one hundred scriptures LDS seminary students memorize

PACING THE WALKWAY IN FRONT of the library, I shift my books from one hand to the other as I wait for Emmy to show for our study session. I'm standing in nearly the exact location where I saw her sister Evie last week. I chuckle to myself, thinking about the mix-up. I wonder how often it happens.

At exactly seven thirty, I see her walking toward me, and stand a little taller. Her tiny frame doubles in size every time she inhales. She must have run up the stairs from the RB and halfway across campus to get here on time. "Sorry . . . I'm . . . late," she says, out of breath.

"We could've said eight."

She shakes her head. "Didn't want to make you . . ." Another pause. "Wait."

"It wouldn't have been a big deal. We can meet later next time."

"No. Seven thirty is great. I've just been trying to squeeze in every second I can at the *barre*. And—" She sucks in another breath.

"You okay?"

She rests her fingers against her collarbone as if willing her body to calm. "Rehearsal was insane today. And those stairs." She laughs. "What is that? Like four or five flights? I always have to readjust to Utah elevation." She rolls her eyes. "We're practically at sea level in California, and all the smog makes it easier to breathe." She swirls her hand in the air between us, and I catch a hint of her sweet scent: coconut and something fruity. I breathe in deeply, trying to figure out what it is, but can't put my finger on it.

"Smog makes it easier to breathe, huh?"

The skin between her eyes crinkles. "No. Yes. I don't know. Maybe? It's like the smog gives my lungs something to grip. Or no . . . That's disgusting, and it doesn't even make sense," she mumbles. "I'm just going to—" She runs her fingers over her lips and then flicks them in the air, throwing away the key.

My mouth tugs up, and I bend to pick up the pretend key. I place it back in her hand and close her fingers around it. Her hand is so small in mine. And despite it being warm outside, too warm, her fingers are ice cold. "It makes sense," I say. Even though it doesn't, but I seriously do not want this girl to stop talking. This is the most enjoyable conversation I've had in a long time. "Should we . . . ?" I point my thumb toward the library.

Emmy nods, and we walk to the door. She reaches for the handle, but I step in front of her and open it first.

We pause in the lobby. "Downstairs okay?"

"Sure."

We walk into the annex and find a quiet place to sit. She sets her bag on the table and slides into a chair, and I sit across from her. Once situated, I pull out two copies of the Book of Mormon various missionaries have given me over the past three years and hand her one. Her head tilts to the side in question.

"I thought we could start fresh and mark them up together."

"Oh. Okay." She takes the book and then stares at the cover like she's scared of what she'll find inside.

I thought I'd try to level the playing field by having us both start with clean pages, but maybe this was a bad idea. She could be attached to her own set or something. "It's not a big deal if you'd rather use your own."

"No, this is a great idea," she says. "So I read the syllabus, and it's pretty straightforward. Each week there's an assigned passage and a set of questions to discuss. There isn't a formal assignment to turn in, so it should be pretty easy."

I don't tell her, but I've also read the syllabus as well as this week's Book of Mormon passage half a dozen times to prepare for today. "Sounds good," I say casually. "Why don't we take turns reading aloud, and then we can discuss afterward?"

The color drains from Emmy's face like I've asked her to recite the Declaration of Independence from memory. "Y-yeah, sure. Let's try that." She nods without looking up.

We open our scriptures, and I take the first verse, hoping the words won't stick on my tongue.

The next verse is hers. She straightens her book and then leans forward to read the first line of the passage. "Scripture Mastery." The relief in her voice is obvious but only heightens my anxiety. I am neither a scriptorian nor a master of scripture. Whatever that is. I try to smile back, but I'm sure it looks more like a grimace than a smile.

"I love this one. It reminds me of Primary." Her voice rises above a whisper, and she swings her arms like she's marching as she sings some song about going somewhere and doing something, though I have no clue where or what.

A few people from a neighboring table glance at us, and the color returns to Emmy's face.

I shake my head, chuckling. "You're so disruptive."

She slaps a hand over her mouth. "Sorry," she whispers.

I read my next set of verses, and then it's Emmy's turn again. She squints at the page like she can't see the words. She's quiet for a long moment before she attempts to read. "And it came to pass . . . that I Nephi." She touches the bun on her head, then blinks a few times and says the next chunk of words, or at least tries to. Maybe she needs glasses but is embarrassed to wear them.

"Would you excuse me for a second? I need to . . . I'll be right back." She jets away from the table, out the double doors, and disappears down a hallway.

What just happened? Did I do something wrong? I was joking with her about being disruptive, but maybe I offended her? My foot bounces under the table as I wait for her to come back. When she returns five minutes later, it's like she's had a shot of caffeine straight to the vein.

"I'm sorry if I—" I start to say.

"It's not you," she reassures me.

I've heard that line a few times since moving to Utah. Here it comes.

"I need to tell you something." She pauses to bite the side of her fingernail. "And I probably should have done it before now."

My knee bounces under the table with anxiety. "Okay. Shoot."

"I'm not stupid."

I lean forward. How did I give her the impression that I think she's stupid?

She looks down at the table where her Book of Mormon lies open, and she seems to shrink even smaller than she already is. "Sometimes people think I am, and I want you to know I'm not."

"I believe you." She had to have had a pretty high GPA to get here.

"I have trouble reading." She spits out the sentence so fast I mentally have to retrace her words to figure out what she's said. "It's a perception issue," she continues. "Or technically, it's a processing thing, but yeah, I'm not stupid." Her doe-eyed gaze lands on me full force. "I'm dyslexic."

My entire body deflates with relief. "I thought I'd done something to offend you."

"I can't believe I told a cute guy I'm dyslexic." She puts a hand to her forehead, hiding her eyes. "Oh gosh, I can't believe I admitted I think you're cute," she mutters. Emmy's elbows slide down the table until her arms rest flush against its surface and she buries her face in her arms.

"Emmy," I say.

She shakes her head.

"Emmy." I chuckle. "Look at me."

She groans but finally peeks up, her face red.

"I think you're cute too."

Chapter Eight
Emmy

Pas de deux [pah / duh / doo] n—A dance duet in which two dancers, typically a male and a female, perform ballet steps together

IT'S POSSIBLE I JUST HALLUCINATED. I pinch my thigh to be sure. Nope. Definitely awake. A second passes. And then another. I've shocked out. Did a hot guy really say he thinks *I'm* cute? I blink once, twice. He doesn't disappear.

The corners of Rhys's mouth inch up. "I've got an idea." He glances around at all the students giving us annoyed looks, then back to me. "Why don't we get out of here? We can pick this up again this weekend."

As much as I'd love to sit here and gawk at Rhys all night, I don't think staring at him all night will help my argument that I have a brain between my ears. Plus, he said he wants to meet again this weekend. Which, yeah, I'm definitely okay with. "Sure. That sounds good." I try to keep my voice casual, but it still comes out ten shades too enthusiastic and twenty decibels too loud.

As soon as we step into the lobby, he turns to me. "So." He slings his thumbs under his backpack straps. "When are you free this weekend?"

My stomach jumps into my throat. I know it's not a date, but I'd be lying if I say I don't want it to be. "I do have plans this weekend. Friday night and Saturday morning, I have rehearsal. Sunday is church." So that leaves Saturday night, but I am 100 percent not going to be the one to suggest we get together Saturday night because that's prime date night.

"I kind of assumed you'd be busy on weekends."

What did I say to make him think that? Church. Rehearsal. Plans. "Oh no! I didn't mean *plans*. I'm busy, but I don't have plans with a guy." I bite my lip. "That's not true either. I have rehearsal with David, but that doesn't count because he's my pas-de-deux partner." I look up and find that Rhys's lips have changed from a soft smile to a wide grin. I have no idea what I just said, but it must have been a pretty epic Emmy ramble because amusement is dancing like *Swan Lake* in his eyes. Kill me now. I turn toward the stairs, afraid if I stay I'll say something even more embarrassing than what's already slipped out of my mouth.

"Pas de deux?" he prompts as we start up the stairs.

Ballet. I can talk ballet. "It's French. Pas de deux means 'step of two.' It's a dance mostly found in classical ballet, like *Cinderella, Sleeping Beauty*, or my favorite, *Giselle*. Have you ever seen a ballet?"

He shakes his head.

"You should. It's life changing." I smile. "So pas de deux is usually a dance for a male *danseur* and a female ballerina, but there are some exceptions. Like in the '80s movie *White Nights*, where Mikhail Baryshnikov and Gregory Hines dance *pas de duex*."

"Have hot chocolate with me?" he says when we reach the top of the stairs.

"W-what?"

"Or ice cream." He shrugs. "Since it's still warm outside."

"Uh, s-sure. When?" Oh my gosh. Oh my gosh. Oh my gosh!

"Now. I thought we could figure out a study schedule or, you know, study."

Right, study. Because we're study partners, and at some point, we should actually study.

"Now's good." The words jump out of my mouth. "Or whenever."

"Great." Rhys nods toward the exit. "Let's go."

A slight breeze swirls around me as we walk outside. The stars are starting to show overhead. The evergreens lining the planters create a subtle symphony as the needles rustle in the wind around us.

"So, Emmy Jennings." He remembers my name. My whole name.

"Yes, Rhys Solario." I try to say his name like he did, rolling the *r*, but end up butchering it instead.

A smile inches across his profile. "Creamery on Ninth?"

"Sounds good."

We walk for a few moments, and even though I don't want to talk about it again, I need to know how he feels about my struggle with reading. "So I hate to bring this up twice in one night, but does it bother you? That I'm dyslexic?"

His eyebrows pull together. "Why would the way you see words bother me?"

"It bothers some people." I shrug.

"Does the way I see words bother you?"

"Why would it?" He can read just fine.

"Exactly."

"You know what I mean. This is part of who I am. No amount of therapy or practice will change the fact that I can't read like you do."

He stops and turns to face me, and I catch a wave of his fresh scent. It's like fresh laundry but with something spicier, more masculine mixed in. He places a hand on my shoulder, and a shockwave shoots down my spine. "Does the color of my skin bother you?"

Actually, yes. But not in the way he's asking. More like it makes me seriously attracted to him, but . . . "No."

"Good. Because it's part of who I am. It won't ever change."

I fight a smile but lose the battle.

"No one should have to hide who they are because they're afraid someone else won't like them, Emmy." His voice is laced with pain. He's speaking from experience. I wonder what he's had to hide. He looks like he's about to say something but then doesn't.

We continue on to the creamery, trying to find a regular time to study. "I know you work, but do you have anything else, like a busy calling, we'll need to work around?"

He laughs. "A calling won't be a problem for me."

"Me neither. I'm the visiting-teaching coordinator, so it doesn't require a specific time or anything. What's your schedule like?"

"I have school in the mornings, and most days of the week, I work the closing shift."

Hmm. "What time do you get out of church?"

His eyes narrow like I've made him uncomfortable. "Um . . ."

"If you don't study on Sundays, that's totally fine," I say quickly. "I just thought it might be the only day open we both have. When I was growing up, my parents were okay with us studying on Sundays. I think they thought of it as an appropriate quiet activity, but I know a lot of people aren't okay with it, so if you'd rather us avoid Sundays, I totally understa—"

"Studying on Sundays doesn't bother me." He grins, seemingly amused by my ramble. "I'm free after six."

He must have late church. Too bad. My ward meets early, but at least we have an option if the rest of the week doesn't work.

We round the corner to the creamery, and the automatic doors slide open. It's not as busy tonight as it is on the weekends, but it's still packed with freshmen escaping the confines of the dorms next door. We place our orders. Him: graham canyon. Me: low-fat lemon sherbet. Both in a cup with a spoon. I unzip my purse to pay, but Rhys hands the cashier his credit card first. "My treat."

"Thank you."

The booths are all taken, so we walk outside, and I kick off my flip-flops as we sit on the grass. We don't start talking right away, but the silence is comfortable. Easy. Like dancing used to be. I lick the sherbet off my spoon, enjoying the sweet citrus as it coats my tongue. I'll have to increase my time at the *barre* tomorrow to burn off the extra calories, but it's been a rough week, and as long as I don't make a habit out of it, I'll be fine. "This is show gewd," I say.

"Mine too. You have to try this." He offers me a spoonful.

Yes. A million times, yes. I take it, and he's right; it is good. But I can't focus on that because *I'm sharing a spoon with a boy*. We're practically kissing! Okay, we're not, but this is the closest I've ever come to kissing.

My heart kicks into overdrive, and I'm pretty sure the bulk of my blood supply migrates to my face because my cheeks are on fire. I wish I could bury my face in my bowl.

I hold out my spoon to him, praying he doesn't notice how much my hand is trembling. He takes it, and yum. In so, so many ways, *yum*.

Our fingers brush when he hands my spoon back. "Both are good, but they're better mixed together."

I try not to let my mouth hang open. "I think so too," I manage to say.

We settle back into silence, him because he's Rhys and comfortable clings to him like static and me because I'm afraid if I open my mouth again, I might do something super awkward, like ask him to kiss me. I wiggle my toes in the cool grass and lean back, letting the warm wind blow through my hair.

"Who did it bother?" he asks, snapping me out of the comfort of my daydream.

"Who what? Huh?" Because that's elegant.

"You said your dyslexia bothered some people. Who are some people?"

No one has ever asked me that before. People get uncomfortable, try to change the subject, and act like it doesn't bother them when it's obvious it does. But not Rhys.

Maybe it's the genuine tone of his voice when he asked me the question, or it could be the way he patiently waits for an answer. I'm not sure, but there's something about Rhys Solario that makes me feel more confident than

I am. I've never been eager to discuss my disability with anyone before, but right now, I want to tell him. "There have been many 'some people,'" I say, "but the person I was referring to was a boy in my first-grade class. One day we had a sub, and she didn't know about my dyslexia, so she had us popcorn read. You know, where you take turns reading out loud?"

Rhys nods.

"Well, when it was my turn, I tried my best, but I was nervous, and the words jumped off the page like a 3-D optical illusion."

He listens without interrupting.

"I didn't read well, obviously. The boy laughed, and so did all his friends. I've never been so humiliated in my life." Deep down, there's still a part of me that worries Rhys will think less of me because of my struggles. "It's stupid. It happened so long ago, but it's always stuck with me. That was the first time I realized I was different from other people and that I had something to be embarrassed about."

"He"—Rhys swirls his spoon around his bowl and then points it at me— "was an idiot."

"He was," I agree.

Rhys eats the last bite of his ice cream and then sets the bowl aside. "You asked me if your dyslexia bothered me. Does it bother you?"

It takes a second for my brain to process his question. "Well . . . I've always seen the world through dyslexic eyes, so I don't know anything different. Like you said, it's part of who I am." This is where I would normally stop talking because just because people ask how I am, it doesn't mean they actually want to know. But something about the way Rhys's steady, strong gaze holds mine tells me he's different.

"When I was a kid, I prayed and prayed to be normal. I craved to see everything the way everyone else did. If I'm being honest, sometimes I still think it would be nice to read easily. Listening to everything isn't exactly time-effective, you know?"

He chuckles.

"But dyslexia is also what makes me unique. It's probably silly, and it's certainly not scientific, but I'd like to believe that because my brain works differently than other people's, I'm more creative. Maybe even a better ballet dancer because of it. If I had to choose, I'd never trade the way I dance ballet to be able to read easier. So to answer your question, no, it doesn't bother me. Not anymore."

"Teach me. What can I do as your partner to make things easier for you?"

He's not running for the mountains or treating me like I'm stupid. He isn't even making jokes like he's trying not to be uncomfortable but really is. No, he sincerely wants to help. "Well, you can write bigger, for one thing. And it would also help if you would separate your words."

His laugh is full and deep. "Is my handwriting that bad?"

"The worst."

He awards me another smile. "I should have gone pre-med." He wipes off what's left of his smile with an open palm. "What else?"

"Don't make me read out loud."

He places a hand over his heart. "I promise."

"I want you to know I've learned to cope. I record all the lectures and relisten to them. And unless I'm nervous, like I was in the library tonight, reading isn't that big of an issue for me anymore. Especially with text I'm familiar with, like the Book of Mormon. I don't have a perfect GPA, but I did earn my spot here like everyone else. So please don't worry that I'll hold us back, okay? I promise to pull my own weight."

"I'm not worried," he says sincerely, and I believe him.

His phone chimes, so he pulls it out of his pocket, reads a message, and then hurries to his feet. "I'm sorry, but I've gotta go."

"No worries," I say, confused at his rapid change in demeanor.

He grabs his backpack and then offers me his hand. "I'm parked over there." He points to the lot in front of the John Taylor building across the street that houses the comprehensive clinic. There's student parking behind it. "Where are you parked?"

"Down by the RB."

"Can I drive you to your car?"

"Sure. Thanks."

Instead of talking like we did on the way to get ice cream, we walk in silence all the way to his truck.

"This is me." He indicates a light-yellow pickup. He quickly unlocks my door and opens it. I climb in, and he closes it behind me. Even though it's old, the inside is clean. It's simple. Manual windows, manual locks. So he doesn't have to unlock the door from the outside, I lean over the center console, pop the driver's side lock, and push open his door.

He seems surprised by the gesture as he sits down. "I don't think anyone has ever opened my door before. Thanks." He starts the ignition and drives to the RB parking lot.

"I'm there." As if he hadn't already figured it out, I point to the last car in the lot, my white Land Rover.

"Nice ride."

"Thanks," I say. "My dad insisted both Evie and I have the safest cars possible. He didn't love the idea of us driving, so he wanted it to be something big in case we crashed." I'm not sure why I feel the need to explain my car to Rhys, but now that I've started blabbering, I'm not sure how to stop. "I think he thought we'd be more protected. I don't like mine, but Evie loves hers."

"You *both* have one?"

"Yeah, but it's not—"

He reaches across me and opens my door. "I'll make sure you get in."

"Right. Sorry." I jet out of the car and then frantically search through my bag for my keys. As soon as I find them, I hit the key fob, and the locks jump. Once inside, I start the car and wave to Rhys that I'm okay.

He speeds away.

Chapter Nine
Rhys

Emergency [ih-mur-juhn-see] n—A sudden, urgent, usually unexpected occurrence requiring immediate action

I NEED YOU.

My heart pounds as I reread Mom's text. I dial her number and press Call. It rings and rings and rings. No answer.

"Pick up the phone!" I shout at the screen, then toss the phone onto the passenger seat. Rounding the corner into her neighborhood, I skid into the driveway and throw the transmission into park. I take the brick stairs up to the front door two at a time. When I open the front door, it smacks against the wall with so much force the picture frames rattle.

"Are you okay?" I ask, rushing into the kitchen. My head snaps side to side as I look for a problem, an intruder, something to justify the emergency text she sent. But all I see is Mom calmly picking up a bowl of overturned fruit.

"I'm fine, but your dinner has seen better days."

I glance at the rabbit fodder Mom calls food heating in a cast-iron skillet on the stove and then back to her, confused. "What?"

"It's Thursday."

I wipe the sweat off my brow. Thursday. Thursday. Thursday. Judging by the squinty-eyed stare she's giving me, Thursday should probably mean something, though due to the adrenaline still coursing through my veins, my brain is fuzzy and I'm coming up blank.

"We had a dinner date, remember? You're an hour late."

Thursday . . . dinner. Right.

"Figured a text would light a fire under ya."

I glare at her. "*I need you?* Ever hear of the boy who cried wolf?"

Mom laughs and turns back to the stove, wafting the scent of charred . . . something . . . into my nose. "What *is* that?"

"Blackened tofu mushroom burgers. Smells delicious, huh?"

Vegetables pretending to be meat. That is not okay. "You're joking, right?"

"It's healing food, Rhys. We should eat to live, not live to eat."

After working in the food court all day, I can't say I disagree, but healthy or not, I'd give anything right now for a pot of *menudo* simmering on the stove or fresh tortillas frying on the *comal*.

I'm about to sit at the table when Mom turns from the stove and hooks a finger on my shirt, stopping me. She eyes the collar of my white under-shirt and gives me a knowing look. Luckily, instead of launching into an-other lecture about being my true self, she only sniffs the material. Her nose scrunches up, no doubt smelling the rancid remains of too-sweet corn-bread batter and the burnt grease we cook it in. "I hope you don't eat that junk you sell. It'll kill you."

Frowning, I sink into a chair at the table. "We have more threatening prob-lems than mall food, don't you think?"

She ruffles her fingers through my hair, ignoring me, then readjusts the magnetic bracelet on her wrist as she walks back to the stove. "You're sweet, but you worry too much."

"You don't worry enough, so I have to make up for it."

She clucks her tongue and starts dressing the "burgers." "I'm taking care of myself. That's why I had you get those things from the store Monday night."

My jaw clenches, and I turn away to hide my reaction. Getting upset will only increase her stress levels, and that's the last thing we need. I open the cupboard to get a glass for water, and that's when I see the meds I picked up for her last month sitting on the top shelf, unopened. "You haven't touched them." I'm disappointed but not surprised.

She places organic tomatoes, organic lettuce, and a healthy but repulsive amount of bean sprouts on top of each tofu patty, then replaces the top half of the whole-wheat bun. "Because I haven't needed them. The alternative therapies are working."

"You need them even if you feel like you don't." If she only understood how important these meds are to maintaining her health, maybe we could stop having this argument.

"Why are you so pessimistic?"

"Realistic," I correct.

"Hmm. Help me get these on the table." She motions to the counter, and that's when I notice there are three plates, not the usual two.

"Someone joining us?"

"Didn't I tell you? Claire is coming over to try a new treatment on me."

Anyone but Claire. "What kind of treatment?"

"Bee sting."

Mom's tried some weird stuff over the years, but intentional stinging? She's got to be pulling one over on me. "Funny."

"Not kidding. I've studied several articles about it relieving symptoms and triggering the body to heal itself."

Magnetic bracelets, a vegan diet, now bee stings? Enough is enough. She's going to kill herself if I don't make her understand the gravity of the situation. I push away from the table, stalk over to the cupboard, and yank down the unopened bottle of medicine I worked a month to pay for. "If you want to feel better, you have to take your medication." My palm slams against the top of the bottle, and I shake out one oblong yellow-and-white pill. "Here." I thrust my hand out at her.

She stares at the pill for a moment but doesn't move to take it. "Why are you so against me using natural methods to heal myself?"

"Because what you have cannot be healed by all this stuff you try."

"Maybe not, but pumping unnatural lab-made substances into my body won't heal me either."

"You're right. Nothing will cure your MS, but this medication *will* relieve most of your symptoms."

"And give me a hundred other ones." Mom breathes slowly in through her nose and then just as slowly out her mouth. "I appreciate your concern. But this is my life and my body, and I choose to manage my symptoms through alternative modalities."

"Like being stung by magical bees." How does she not realize that every single one of her choices directly affects me? Every phone call, every text sends me into panic. She may be my mother, but I'm the man of the family. I can't stand around and watch her disease get worse.

Mom's chapped lips curl into a smile. "They aren't magical. That would be crazy. Just regular old honeybees."

"Even better."

The doorbell rings like a bell signaling the end of a boxing match, and I slink back into my seat, defeated.

Mom pats my cheek as she walks by me into the living room to answer the door. "Be nice to Claire, okay? She's trying to help me."

Why can't Mom see that *I'm* trying to help her? "I make no promises," I mutter.

Mom returns with Claire, who's carrying a small jar of very angry bees. "Oh my, Rhys. You have so much bad energy surrounding you. Have you thought about doing a cleanse? You might be constipated."

"And I'm out." My chair scrapes across the yellowing linoleum floor as I push away from the table.

"You can't go yet." Mom waves me back into my chair as I rise to my feet. "You haven't even touched your dinner."

I kiss her cheek. "I'll eat that cardboard you call food if you take your medication."

Mom narrows her eyes. "Drive home safely. Love you."

I'm almost out the door when I hear Claire ask Mom where she's having the most trouble. I pause in the doorframe to listen to her answer.

"Numbness in my hands and feet." That explains the knocked-over fruit bowl when I walked in and why she asked me to help her put everything on the table. I close my eyes, letting the knowledge sink in. She'll probably need a wheelchair again soon. Possibly even daily care.

"Hands and feet it is, then. Come here, little guy."

"Ouch!" Mom yelps. "That hurt more than I thought it would. Must be a good sign."

My shoulders slump as I let the door fall closed behind me and walk to my truck. If I could just get Mom to accept her condition the way Emmy's accepted her dyslexia.

I pick up my phone in the passenger seat and find Emmy's name. I tap out a vague apology for leaving so quickly and let her know I won't be able to meet up this weekend. But something stops me from sending it.

Emmy was so open and honest tonight. It doesn't seem right to blow her off with an ambiguous text. She deserves an honest explanation face-to-face.

My hands sweat at the thought of seeing her again. Telling Emmy about Mom will take time. Time that I look forward to way more than I should.

I erase the text and then stare at the blank screen. I feel bad about dodging her questions about church stuff. Supe said I don't need to tell her, but it seems like her honesty requires my own. I type another text telling Emmy what a great time I had getting ice cream with her tonight and that I'd love to meet up this weekend to study but then stop myself when I realize my wanting to meet up with her has very little to do with wanting to study.

I erase the text.

As good a time as I had with Emmy tonight, any sort of relationship with her besides study partners doesn't have a happy ending. I know this. Every time

I've tried to date at BYU, it ends the same way—with me getting rejected. I don't want to go through that again. Emmy's a great girl; she's honest, funny, and sweet, but that doesn't mean she's different. When it comes to a real relationship, girls here are all the same. They want to date returned missionaries. They want to get married. The sooner I get that through my head, the better.

The screen dims, and I set the phone on the passenger seat.

A relationship would never work, but maybe if I can get my head on straight, we could be friends, like Jen and me.

Friends. That's perfect. I'll take the weekend to clear my head, and Monday morning before BOM, I'll apologize. We can figure out a study schedule and start a friendship.

Easy.

Chapter Ten

Emmy

En l'air [ahn / lahr] a—In the air

"It comes down to two possibilities, and unfortunately, neither is good for you," Evie says, analyzing why Rhys hasn't returned any of my texts this past weekend.

"I was afraid of that."

We continue our walk down the second-floor catwalk in the RB early Monday morning.

"The first possibility is that he has a girlfriend," she says. "And given the fact that he got a text and beelined the heck away from you, that makes the most sense." She stops in front of a large viewing window and stares at Q, where he's playing basketball below.

Ugh. I hoped Evie would've lost interest by now.

"Possibility two," Evie continues. "He doesn't have a girlfriend, but he had some kind of emergency—family, work, school? Doesn't matter what the emergency was since he was kind of cold after seeing your fantabulous car."

Hmm. "There is that, but he freaked out before he saw my car."

"Do you think it's the dyslexia thing? Fake text to give him a valid excuse to leave?"

I chew the question over. "No. He wouldn't have been relieved in the library when I told him I have dyslexia."

"You're right. And didn't he say some philosophical quote about not feeling sorry for yourself?"

I nod. "He said I shouldn't have to hide who I am."

"Yeah, that." She pauses for a moment. "It's definitely the text, then. Did he look guilty or worried after reading it?"

"Is it bad if I say I'd rather he looked worried than guilty?"

"It's bad for whoever he was hypothetically worried about, I guess," Evie says and then turns her attention back to Q. "Yes! Go, baby!"

Q looks up after shooting a three-pointer, his fingers shaped like a gun that he fires at Evie in celebration.

"How are things going with Q?" I ask, hating the fact that I have to be so aware of how I divide our conversation time now that it's been reduced to sporadic five-minute increments.

"So good, Em. He's different from other guys I've dated. He has goals. Like real goals. He's studying to be a lawyer like Dad—but not a corporate one who files papers for famous clients all day. No. A real courtroom, put-the-bad-guys-in-jail kind of lawyer. And he's so valiant. He's always talking about how important it is for us to follow the rules."

I look down at Q swaggering across the court and try to see what Evie sees in him. Goals are a good thing, and I'm glad he's apparently so valiant. But how much does he really know about Evie? Does he know how smart she is? That she was accepted into every school she applied to, including Ivy Leagues, but chose to come to BYU because we didn't want to be apart? Does he know how far behind she is in school? That she's changed her major so many times because she loves learning and wants to study everything? Or how much she used to love ballet? Somehow, I don't think so.

"He asked me to be his girlfriend last night," Evie says, whiplashing me out of my thoughts.

"It's only been a week. You're exclusive? Already?"

Evie's eyes stay glued on Q. "Yep."

"Are you sure that's a good idea?" I ask, thinking about our sister Lucy.

"Relax, Em. We're taking it slow. I mean, it's not like he asked me to marry him."

"I know, but isn't that where dating leads?"

"I could only hope." She smiles down at Q with a dreamy, far-off look in her eyes. "Well, it looks like he's done. I should get going." She gives me a quick hug and jogs to the stairwell in the middle of the long hall.

"Want to get dinner tonight?" I call after her.

"Actually, Q doesn't have class the rest of the day, so I'm cutting, and we're heading up to Salt Lake. Next week, okay?" She kisses the air between us in good-bye.

I turn back to the viewing window and look down at the basketball courts. My eyes lock with Q's. His lazy gaze skims over me, and then he winks. The gesture catches me so off guard I stumble away from the window, then speed walk down the hall to the ballet studio to get away.

When I reach the end of the hallway, hushed voices whisper in the stairwell to my right. I look over and see David, my *pas-de-deux* partner, with his long-term girlfriend, Hailey. A glint on her left hand catches my eye, and I hurry into the rehearsal studio to give them privacy.

A few girls sit on the Marley, the gray dance floor, preparing their feet and shoes for class. I sit next to them and take out my pointe shoes and kit. I tape the hot spots on my toes, then wrap my feet with strips of cotton and slip on my ballet shoes. The pink ribbon is soft against my skin as I wrap the silk around my ankles. David walks in with a goofball smile.

"I see you popped the question—only took you, what? Seven semesters?" I say jokingly.

He chuckles as he sits next to me. "Actually, no. She asked me."

That is so like David. He's an amazing dance partner, but as a boyfriend, he would drive me nuts. "I knew I liked Hailey."

David tugs on his ballet slippers, and then we walk to the *barre* against the far wall, our usual spot close to the windows. Other dancers file in around us until the *barre* is nearly full.

"I probably should have said this earlier, but I'm sorry about the solo," David says.

"It's okay." I did want the solo, but part of me is relieved I didn't get it. I've never had to dance without Evie before. "Being in the corps will give me a chance to settle back into ballet without Evie and really work on my technique."

David frowns. "That solo should have been yours, and you know it. You're by far the best dancer here."

I look around, hoping no one heard that. "It's not about that," I whisper. "I'm not sure I'll be as good a dancer without Evie. You know I struggle to learn new choreography. What if now that she's gone, I can't do it? What then? Ballet isn't only my career goal; it's my life." It's the first thing I think about when I wake up and the last thing on my mind before I go to bed. I've worked too hard for my life to fall apart as quickly as a pair of pointe shoes.

David arches an eyebrow, unimpressed. "You have a little trouble learning choreography. Who cares? Lots of dancers do. You don't need Evie. I'll help you. We've got this." David is quiet as he rolls out each of his ankles, but I can tell by the way his eyebrows pinch together that he's still chewing something over. "Why'd she quit anyway?" he finally asks. "You two were the unstoppable ballet twins."

"The unstoppable ballet twins?" I repeat with a laugh, but he doesn't seem to hear me.

"She's always been a little impulsive, but walking away from ballet after so many years is extreme even for her."

I nod. Evie has joined and quit so many activities over the years I can't even remember them all. But somehow, after thirteen years of dancing together, I thought ballet was the one thing she wouldn't abandon. Clearly, I was wrong. "I guess she decided she couldn't do it anymore."

"That makes no sense." David balks. "She loves ballet."

"Yeah, I thought so too," I whisper.

David's eyebrows rise and then fall in one smooth motion. "I love your sister, but . . ." He shakes his head. "She's going to get herself into trouble one of these days."

"Tell me about it," I mumble.

Ballet Master Miller walks into the studio, cutting off our conversation, and we begin the formal warm-up as a class. Twenty minutes later, we move on to center work.

Rehearsal goes by in an unending blur, and by the time class is over, my head is spinning, but David stays after to help me drill the new choreography. I'm lucky to have him as a partner. He's the best male dancer at BYU, and working with him has made me better.

David's fiancée pops in to watch us rehearse a little after 9:30 a.m. By ten, the next class starts to trickle into the studio, and we're forced out.

When I peel my point shoes off my swollen feet, I find several of the hotspots on my toes have turned into full-blown blisters.

"You okay?" Hailey grimaces.

I follow her gaze to my feet. "You should have seen my feet after a month of rehearsing for my first *Nutcracker*. This is nothing." I take out a pair of scissors and moleskin from my dance bag and cut several pieces to patch up my feet. The skin underneath my big toenail is already black and blue. To anyone else, my feet are ugly. But to me, they're my most cherished part of my body. Evidence of a life well spent.

I say good-bye to David and Hailey and head to the locker room. After changing out of my leotard and tights into a breezy sundress, I look in the full-length mirror and find that my snow-white legs are dotted with angry bruises. Normally I wouldn't care about hiding them, but BOM class is next, and I don't want to look like an albino dalmatian in front of Rhys. I shouldn't care what he thinks since he didn't bother to answer any of my texts about getting together to study again last weekend, but I do. As I wiggle back into my pink tights, I can't help feeling silly—liking a guy who doesn't like me back is beyond dumb. This has got to end.

I pull out my phone and send Rhys a text, asking him to meet me before class, where I'll suggest we "meet" via e-mail to study.

There. Problem solved.

Chapter Eleven

Rhys

The Drought [thuh / drout] n—A phenomenon caused by the change in missionary age for women from twenty-one to nineteen, resulting in less women on campus to date

THE STORM DOOR SLAMS AGAINST the kitchen wall, startling me, and I hit my head against the underside of the kitchen sink.

"I've met the girl I want to marry," Supe announces Monday morning.

I rub my forehead and feel something wet. I look at my fingers and see blood. Great. "What's her name?"

"No clue. But she has the sweetest spirit, *and* she's beautiful, so I'm going to ask her out," he says, settling into a kitchen chair. "This drought is killing every RM on campus. It's sucked the dating scene dry, but this girl is like a fresh drink of water."

A fresh drink of water? "You are one strange man, my friend."

"Maybe, but she could be the one."

"If I had a nickel for every time you've said that."

He snorts. "I know, I know. You'd be a rich man."

Focusing on the clogged sink, I wiggle the wrench, trying to loosen the connector. After several attempts, it still won't budge. I shimmy out of the cupboard and try forcing the connector from a seated position, where I have more leverage. Pressing my body weight into the wrench, the piece finally yields. A thick, greasy sludge drains out of the pipe onto the floor.

"Can you hand me the snake?"

Supe jerks his feet up, his eyes wildly searching for a rogue reptile.

I laugh. "That wiry contraption over there"—I point to a tool on the table behind him—"is a snake, and I need it to make sure the drain is clear before I put everything back together."

He slowly lowers his feet to the ground and leans back in his seat, trying to play off his exaggerated freak-out. "Right." He hands me the snake and watches me thread it into the pipe. "Why don't you call management? Isn't this part of their job description?"

This is part of management's job. I'm sure the owners are paying them a nice sum each month to keep this place running. They don't have to do much, but if they did, I'm sure they'd be all too happy to pass along the extra cost to the owners, who would then hand down the expense to us. I sigh. "Because I'm quicker than they would be, and I can't afford to have my rent raised."

Supe nods. "I fully support you as resident maintenance man."

"Knew you would." While Supe is probably in a better place than I am financially, he's living in this hole for the same reason I am: money is money, and neither of us has any to spare. I pull the snake out of the drain, and my cell chimes with a text.

Supe picks up the phone to hand it to me, but then, seeing my hands dirty with sink gunk, asks, "Want me to read it to you?"

"Yeah. Thanks." I begin reconnecting the pipes.

"It's Emmy. She wants to know if you'll meet her before class." He looks up from the screen with a raised eyebrow. "Things going okay?"

I shrug. "Fine. I guess."

"You guess?"

"She's a nice girl. I just feel awkward around her."

"Why? You're just studying."

After standing, I set the wrench down on the sink and wash my hands.

"You like her," he guesses. "That's why you're uncomfortable around her."

I keep washing my hands.

Supe laughs. "Rhys, that's awesome."

"It would be."

"But . . . ?" Supe frowns.

I turn off the faucet and dry my hands on the back of my pants. "I'm not a member, and she is."

"You're the only person defining yourself by member versus nonmember labels. And I think you've built it up to be bigger than it is."

"Maybe you're right." I've had too many bad experiences with member girls not to be cautious.

"I understand why you're gun-shy. All I'm saying is maybe you've let that ruin your time at BYU. If you like this girl, she's got to be pretty great. So have a little faith in her and let her get to know Rhys, not Rhys-the-Nonmember. You can tell her about not being Mormon when the time is right."

"When's that?"

"You'll know when you need to say something, but you're definitely not there yet, so enjoy BYU, get to know this girl, and chillax, man."

"Chillax?"

"You heard me." Supe hands me my phone as he walks out of the room.

I lean against the counter. Maybe he's right. Maybe I have built up my past experiences to be worse than they actually are. Just because a few girls were closed-minded doesn't mean all the girls at BYU are. Emmy seems cool, and I enjoy talking to her, so what's the harm in getting to know her? In letting *her* get to know *me*?

I send her a quick text that I'll meet her before class today.

* * *

I get to the JSB ten minutes before class starts, ready to apologize for not texting her back this past weekend—again. Emmy is standing next to a bench, and her back is to me. I tap her shoulder, and she spins to face me, nearly dropping her phone. She pulls out her earbuds and slowly winds the white cords, not looking at me.

"Hey," I say.

"Hey," she mumbles. She digs through her oversized purse, and I get the impression it's more to avoid eye contact than to find anything.

This apology might be harder than I'd hoped. "I'm sorry I couldn't get together this weekend. I—"

"It's fine. We knew scheduling would be difficult." She shrugs, but I can tell by the way she still hasn't looked up that not calling was a mistake.

I run my apology in my head one last time to make sure I don't mess it up, and it hits me. Emmy told me personal things about herself, about her dyslexia, and admitted she was attracted to me. Emmy doesn't care about my not calling. She thinks I've rejected her. I'm a jerk.

"E-mail might be better for you than meeting in person anyway." Her voice doesn't waver.

"Better for me?"

She nods, gaze still down. "Because of your busy schedule."

I shift my feet side to side, then settle into a wide stance. E-mail would solve our time issues but would make her have to read more. I wonder if that would be more difficult for her. Though, not having to read in front of me might be more comfortable for her. "If you think it's best, I guess that's okay."

"Great." She turns toward the JSB.

I stand in the middle of the sidewalk for a moment, watching her walk away. "Actually, no. It isn't great." I jog to catch up and stop short in front of her, causing her to almost run into me. "I think we'd both get more out of this class if we meet each week and discuss the material face-to-face."

She rubs her sparkle-glossed lips together, but she doesn't say anything.

"You're acting funny," I say.

"I'm not acting funny." Her chin inches up, but her eyes stay on the ground. Proof that she is in fact acting funny.

"You are, actually."

Her perfect posture straightens even more. "S-sorry?"

And now she's apologizing to me. Great. I've messed this up. "Emmy, no. I don't want you to be sorry." I want her to give me a chance to say *I'm* sorry. To clear up what I should have cleared up the first day of class, to start on the road to becoming friends. "I had a great time with you last Thursday. I'm sorry I had to run off so quickly. It had nothing to do with you."

"It's fine," she says, but what she means is *It's anything but fine.*

"I'm sorry about everything. I'd like for us to be friends."

"Friends. Sure." Her voice is carefully casual, like she's trying hard to be cool with how I treated her. "Listen." She traces a line on the sidewalk with a pointed toe. "If you want to change partners, I won't be offended."

"Why would I want to change partners?"

"I can think of a few reasons." She widens her eyes but keeps them cast to the ground.

"Name some."

She pales. "Name some what? Reasons?"

"Yes."

"Well, uh. My dyslexia, for one."

"We've already talked about that. Not a reason. What else?"

She hesitates. "Y-your girlfriend?"

"My what?" My voice raises an octave. How on earth did I give her the impression that I have a girlfriend? I told her I thought she was cute too. She must *really* think I'm a jerk.

"Your girlfriend," she says again, this time without stuttering.

"I don't have a girlfriend."

She glances over her shoulder at the JSB like she's planning to make a run for it but then shakes her head and addresses me instead. "Of course not. I'm sorry. I figured that since you were so eager to leave Thursday, and then you didn't text me about getting together to study—I thought it may have had something to do with your having a significant other." Her face turns red, and then she brushes past me into the building. I hurry to open the door for her. She mumbles a quick thank-you, her eyes flashing to me almost as if by accident, and then she does a double-take. "You're bleeding!"

I touch my fingers to my forehead. Sure enough, blood. Stupid sink.

Emmy fumbles to open her massive bag, then slides it off her shoulder and props it against the wall. "Give me your hand."

I hold out my hand to her, and she flips it palm up, then sets a first-aid kit in it. No wonder girls carry big bags.

"What happened?" she asks.

My lips tug into a grin. "The bottom of my kitchen sink attacked me."

She looks up in question.

"It was clogged. I wanted to fix it. It put up a fight."

She pulls out a strip of gauze from the kit, dabs a little hydrogen peroxide on it, and mouths, "Sorry." She touches the medicine to my cut, and I try not to wince. "Did you win?" she asks.

"That's debatable."

She blows cool air on my wound. Coconut. But there's still something else. She leans closer to study my forehead, and I breathe her in. What is it? Before I can answer my own question, I stop myself. This is not something a friend would do. My chest tightens, and I level my head, pulling away from her. Her cheeks flush, and she pushes off my chest. She takes longer than needed to dig through her kit but finally pulls out a small Band-Aid.

I hold up a hand. "No Band-Aid."

She narrows her eyes at my cut. "You sure?"

"Can't let the sink know it won this round." I lift her bag off the ground and hand it to her. She slings it over her shoulder, and we start down the hall again. We don't take more than a step before awkwardness creeps in like a slow-moving fog. I can't let that happen. Not if I want to pass this class. Not if we're going to be study partners. Not if we're going to be friends. "So what are you doing walking around with a first-aid kit?" I ask. "You pre-med or something?"

"Dance major, remember?"

"You always carry one of these around?"

Emmy looks up. "On ballet days, I do. For my feet."

I'm not sure why girls in satin slippers would ever need a first-aid kit to prance around the stage, but whatever. Brother Clark walks into the classroom right behind us and starts booting up his computer.

"Before I forget," I say as we take our seats. "You free Thursday to study?"

Her fingers tap double-time against the desk. "Uh-huh. I mean, yes. Thursday is okay. Where?"

"I would suggest my place, but it's not exactly hospitable to studying." I laugh. "I have a ridiculously small living room and a loud roommate."

"No worries. Evie should be home, so you can come to my place. I have rehearsal until seven though. Is eight too late?"

"Nah. That'll work. You sure though?"

"Absolutely."

* * *

I look at Emmy's address in my notebook. Her house isn't far. Nothing in Provo is far. But it is up the hill in the tree-streets neighborhood near Kiwanis Park. Makes sense. She drives a Land Rover. Where else would she live?

White house, black shutters, pink-and-purple flowers overflowing from the front planters onto the brick walkway. Two white rocking chairs sit on the porch. It's exactly where I'd picture a girl like her living only it's nestled at the base of the mountains instead of on a cliff next to the ocean.

I pull my keys out of my ancient truck, noticing the discrepancy between her house and my ride. Study partners or not, I should have found a neutral place to meet.

At her front door, I tuck my keys into my back pocket and then tap my knuckles on the door. I readjust my backpack while I wait.

The door swings open. "Hello." The girl's hot-pink lips curl into a practiced smile. "Come in."

The dark wood floor gives slightly under my weight as I step inside. "Emmy here?"

"I'm impressed. You can tell us apart already." Emmy's twin smiles. "You must be Rhys. I'm Evie. It's nice to meet you."

"You too."

"Sorry, Emmy isn't home yet. When were you supposed to meet?"

"Eight." It's fifteen after; I got held up replacing the oil in the deep fryer at work.

Evie pulls out her phone like she has to double-check the time herself. "She wouldn't be late. Not for this." She looks up. "That means she's in flow."

"Flow?"

"Yep. When Emmy dances, she has zero sense of time. I think it's a dyslexia thing because it never happened to me. I can't prove it, but I'd bet it's what makes her so good at ballet. It's like the laws of time and gravity don't apply to her."

"Right. I'll call her, then."

Evie shakes her head. "Don't bother. She'll never hear it over the sound system. Do you know where the RB is?"

"Yeah."

She grins. "Great. Emmy'll be there. Upstairs, at the end of the hall, in the ballet studio."

"Thanks, but if you could just tell her I stopped—"

"Uh. No."

My eyebrows furrow. "No?"

"Sorry, but no. She'll be mad at herself when she realizes she missed you."

Feeling that I'm getting nowhere fast, I decide to cut my losses and take a step toward my truck.

"Rhys," she says, stopping me. "She waited all weekend for you to text, and you didn't. Go to the studio."

Evie shuts the door in my face. Apparently she likes to have the last say. And unlike her sister, she doesn't mince words.

Even though I doubt it's a good idea, I drive to the RB. Partly because I feel bad about everything, but also because Evie scares me to death and I don't want to cross her.

After parking, I jog up the front stairs and then up another flight to the second floor. The hallway is long. At least the length of a football field, and it gives me plenty of time to ponder the lunacy of being here.

Amplified piano music pours into the hallway. The closer I get to the sound, the slower my steps become. When the music suddenly stops, so do my feet. I don't dare get any closer without music to hide the sound of my footfalls—I might still decide to bail. But then the music begins again, and sane or not, my feet move as if pulled by some unseen magnetic force. When I get to the door, I stop, paralyzed because she's balanced on her toes and I don't want to startle her. And because I have never seen anything so beautiful in my life.

She's in tights and a black bathing suit thing with a sheer skirt over the top. A few strands of hair have escaped her bun and are stuck to her flushed face.

She has this far-off look in her eyes as she dances. Swaying, swirling, soaring, she tangles my insides into a knot.

This is not the same timid girl I met in BOM. This girl is confident, self-assured. Every move she makes is exact. She's good. Better than good. She's incredible.

Emmy glides across the floor and leaps into the air. She appears weightless, suspended in time. Her sister was right; gravity doesn't apply to Emmy.

Her strength, her confidence, everything about her is larger than life.

I should leave. But I can't. I'm mesmerized.

Chapter Twelve
Emmy

Flow [floh] n—Complete absorption in what one does, aka "the zone"

IT DOESN'T FEEL RIGHT.

I'm balanced, the steps are correct, but something is off. I'm ending half a count too soon. I come off pointe, roll my neck, and circle my arms, but it doesn't loosen the tension. Evie would know what I'm doing wrong if she were here. I push the thought away and walk back to my starting position to try yet again.

"When you said you danced . . . I had no idea."

I jump at the sound of Rhys's voice behind me. My eyes dart up to the clock in the front of the room. Eight thirty. "Oh my goodness. I'm so sorry. I lost track of time." I hurry over to the stereo and turn it off. "How long have you been here?"

He drops his gaze to the floor and rubs the back of his neck. "That was incredible. I've never seen anyone move like that."

"Thanks, but I'm having an off day."

He points to the middle of the room. "You call that an *off day*?"

"Yeah. No matter how hard I try, I can't get the combination right."

"Maybe you're trying too hard?"

I shake my head. "There's no such thing as trying too hard. Not in ballet." I reach down to untie the pink ribbons from my ankles but then pause, not wanting Rhys to see my feet. Calluses, raw skin, bruised and discolored toenails—not exactly attractive. I retuck the ribbons against my ankle.

"It doesn't look like you're trying too hard. I only meant maybe you need to relax and enjoy it."

"Easier said than done." When Evie was here, I could enjoy everything about dancing because whenever I got lost in the music, she was always there to find me. Things are different now.

Rhys walks a few steps closer. "You think?"

"I know." Dancing on my toes and making it look effortless isn't easy.

"Do you love it?" he asks. "Dancing?"

"More than anything."

He's quiet as I pick my things up off the floor.

"I can tell you love ballet," he says. "What I meant to ask was if you still enjoy it."

"Of course I enjoy it." Dancing is who I am before anything else. Emmy equals ballet dancer.

"Huh."

"What do you mean, *huh*?" I hoist my ballet bag onto my shoulder.

"Nothing. It looked like you were fighting against it."

As much as I hate to admit it, dance has become work. Rhys misses nothing. "Ballet is harder without my twin," I admit out loud for the first time. "Learning new combinations isn't my forte. It was easier to hide my struggles when my sister was dancing with me. We had a system."

He listens intently, and I continue. "We both wore different-colored leg warmers. Pink on the right, purple on the left. She stood in front of me, and I watched her instead of the mirror. That made it easier for my brain to process new combinations." That makes it sound like I can't physically dance without Evie. "It's not just about learning the steps though. It's like there's this gaping hole inside of me without her." I catch my rambling stream of consciousness before it becomes a treatise. "So I guess you're right; dancing is a fight now. It's ridiculous for me to still need my sister, isn't it?"

"Not at all. But I am sorry about your sister."

I shrug. "It is what it is."

"For what it's worth, I think you're an incredible dancer without her."

My face heats at his compliment. It's one thing to have someone watch a performance. It's something completely different to have a front-row, exclusive ticket to seeing me stumble through new choreography. "Thanks."

"Do you still want to . . . ?" Rhys points to the door, reminding me of the reason he's here. To study.

I turn off the lights as we walk out of the studio.

"I didn't mean to offend you," he says as we walk down the hall.

"You didn't."

"You're quiet though."

I sigh, and we start down the stairs to the first-floor locker room. "I hadn't realized ballet had become work."

"What about it is the most work?"

"All of it." I laugh. "It requires everything I have every day. I love it, but it's demanding."

"Sometimes the things we love the most are the most demanding," Rhys says in agreement.

"Sounds like you have experience."

"You could say that," he replies but doesn't say more on the subject. "When did your sister quit?"

We reach the bottom of the stairs and turn toward the locker room. "The night we were supposed to drive back to school at the end of summer." I snort. How ladylike.

"Seriously?"

"I was shocked too. But I shouldn't have been. Evie has a track record of quitting. Cheerleading. Swim team. Art. Piano. Anything that caught her attention, she jumped into without thinking about the consequences. It should be more shocking that she stuck with ballet for thirteen years." Our feet slow to a shuffle, and we stop outside the locker-room door.

"Thirteen years. Wow. She danced a long time. Why'd she quit now?"

"No clue. Bored, maybe?" I point my thumb over my shoulder at the locker room. "I'll only be a few minutes." I hurry inside and call Evie. "I can't believe you told him where I was," I say before she can say hello.

"Yes, you can," she says without a trace of remorse.

"Evie!"

She chuckles. "I'm glad he found you. Unfortunately, Q called, and we're meeting up, so . . ."

"Eve, you promised you'd be home."

"I know, but I wasn't sure if you were coming back."

She has a point. If I had kept better track of time, this wouldn't have been an issue. "Yeah. You're right. Have fun, and I'll see you later."

After hanging up, I change into my favorite V-neck black dress that flares out at my knees. It's a little dressier than what I normally wear to school, but it's the end of September and I won't have too many more chances to wear it before the weather turns. Soon I'll be wearing my favorite carnation-pink coat, the one with a soft white lining and black polka dots. I guess there are a *few* good things about winter.

I frown at my reflection. My hair more closely resembles a rat's nest than it does a bun, so I pull the bobby pins out one by one and let my hair tumble down my back. My face is flushed and shiny from rehearsal, but it's nothing a little powder can't fix—I hope. I swipe a coat of mascara over my eyelashes, then dab a bit of gloss onto my lips.

There. That'll have to do.

When I walk out of the locker room, Rhys is leaning against the wall, feet crossed in front of him like he doesn't have a care in the world. He looks up from his phone, and his eyebrows shoot up. "Wow. I mean . . . Your hair is so long."

"Oh yeah." I forget how shocking it is to people when they first see my hair out of a bun. I comb my fingers through a few strands. "You ready?" I start to walk down the hall and then pause when I don't hear his footsteps behind me. I turn back and see he hasn't moved. "Rhys?"

"Yeah. Sorry." He hurries to catch up. "Back to your place?"

"Actually, Evie had to go. So . . ."

"Can't go there," Rhys finishes.

"And the library didn't work well last time."

He chuckles. "My house is too crammed."

"Hmm."

We reach the double glass doors and walk outside toward the parking lot, still without a final destination. He pulls his phone out of his back pocket and looks at the time. "Do you need to be home at a certain time?"

"Not really. Why?"

"I've got an idea of someplace we can go, if you're up for it."

My heart pounds in my chest, and I remind myself this is only a study thing.

"I think we'd have fun," he continues. "And it's a long enough drive that we could study on the way there and on the way back. What do you think?"

Even though I would like to get to know Rhys better, my initial reaction is to say no. I have ballet tomorrow, and I need to be well rested. I open my mouth, but then I hear Evie's voice in my head saying, *There's more to life than ballet, Em,* and I see this handsome, smart, intriguing guy standing in front of me, and I start to wonder if maybe she's right. Maybe taking a break from ballet for one night isn't a bad idea. It's not like extra sleep is going to solve my issues on the dance floor. And we do need to study. "As long as your idea has nothing to do with dancing any more impossible ballet choreography, I'm in."

A grin slants his jaw. "Do I look like a ballet dancer?"

My eyes graze over the dark jeans riding low on his hips and his wide stance that, while hot, is anything but graceful. By the time my eyes make it to his, I'm as equally sure of the fact that he's not a ballet dancer as I am that I'm attracted to him. Not trusting my voice, I shake my head.

"Okay, then. Let's go."

"How far are we going?" I ask.

"Salt Lake." He glances at me as we walk down the steps to the parking lot. "Is that too far?"

No. But it's been so long since I've been on a date—even though this isn't a date—I'm not sure if I can hold it together that long. At least not without rambling myself into an even deeper pit of embarrassment.

"Emmy?"

"Oh, sorry. No, it's not too far. But I have rehearsal tomorrow, so I should be home by twelve."

"Not a second later than twelve." He draws an *x* across his chest. "I guarantee it."

When we get to the edge of the parking lot, it dawns on me that I'll either be reading or, rather, stuttering, for the next hour from the Book of Mormon in a dark car, or I'll be driving. And if I drive, we'll be taking my car—something he didn't seem to like last time. Neither is a good option, so I pick the lesser of two evils. "As I mentioned last time, I'm not the best reader. Do you care if I drive and you read?"

"Fine by me."

I exhale in relief as I press the key fob, illuminating my SUV's cabin lights, and get in. I fasten my seat belt, and the steering wheel moves to its preset position.

"Fancy," he says.

"Overly."

He looks at me in question, and I try to wave it off. The last time we talked about my car, it didn't end well.

"You don't like it?" he asks, not letting the conversation drop.

"No, it's great. I'm very blessed."

"But . . . ?"

"I'd rather drive a Civic or a Prius or something."

"You're serious?"

I nod. "This car is too big. Don't get me wrong. I love that I don't have to worry about my safety. But if you haven't noticed, I'm short, and this car has about a million blind spots. Small cars are easier to see in."

"That makes sense."

"What's your dream car?"

He doesn't hesitate. "Truck. Ford F-150 SVT Raptor. Four door. Super crew. Black."

"Not that you've thought about it or anything."

"Not at all." He grins, then falls silent and looks out the window. "I was one paycheck away from buying it, but then things changed and . . ." A heavy sigh replaces the end of his sentence.

"You didn't get your truck," I finish.

"Like you said earlier, it is what it is, right?"

I offer him a sad smile. I almost ask what changed and why he didn't get his truck, but his drooped posture and distant stare tell me that isn't a conversation he wants to have right now.

"All right, navigator. Navigate," I say.

"Are you talking to me or this contraption?" His eyes flash to the navigation system on my dashboard.

"Definitely you," I say to Rhys, then glare at the in-dash screen. "That thing never works right." I roll my eyes thinking of all the unintended detours it's taken me on. "Once, Evie and I decided to go to San Diego. It was right after we got our licenses, and we thought we'd put our new driving skills to good use. We didn't realize we had long passed the exit until we were almost to Mexico. We could literally see the red, green, and white Mexican flag flowing on the Tijuana hillside."

"That's awesome." Rhys chuckles.

"Our dad didn't think so. He drove two hours from LA to find us and caravan home." I look at Rhys, eager to see his face light up again with laughter, but I find that his expression has changed to somber as he squints at the BOM in his lap. I reach up and turn on his reading light.

"Thanks."

"No problem." I drive to the freeway, and once I've merged onto I-15 North toward Salt Lake, Rhys pulls out our weekly BOM assignment.

His voice is soft and soothing as he reads, so unlike the sterile voice on the scripture recordings. Each whispered word floods my body with heat, and although his voice is deep and masculine, his tongue caresses each word like a prayer. I'm so lost in the sound of his voice that it feels like hardly any time passes before he tells me to exit the freeway. We turn down several streets and finally pull into the parking lot of our destination.

My mind has come up with a thousand different ideas of where he could be taking me: Temple Square, dessert, maybe the mall. But nothing could have prepared me for this.

Chapter Thirteen

Rhys

Semantics [si-man-tiks] n—The meaning of words and phrases in a particular context

"You said no dancing."

"No. I asked you if I looked like a ballet dancer," I remind her.

Emmy eyes the neon signs illuminating the darkened windows of Joe's Dance Club. "Semantics."

"I know it looks a little shady, but I promise it's completely respectable. At least tonight. I swear this will be fun. If it isn't, we'll leave."

She studies the dance club like it's a snake about to bite her. Her eyes stop on the twenty-one-and-over sign posted on the door. "I'm not—"

"It's all ages on Thursday nights."

She gives me a "Gee, lucky us" expression, and I second-guess bringing her here. Emmy doesn't belong in a place like this. She belongs in a studio or on a stage or I don't know . . . in church or something.

After seeing her in her element in the ballet studio earlier tonight, I couldn't help thinking about what Supe said about letting her get to know the real me. Not that Joe's is exactly "me," but the music, the people, everything here feels comfortable, like I don't have to put up a front or pretend to be something I'm not. But now, seeing the shock on her face . . . I scratch the back of my head. "Maybe we should go."

"Oh, no. We're staying." She opens her car door before I have a chance to do it for her and hops out. I hurry to meet her at the front of the SUV. Gravel crunches beneath our feet as we walk to the entrance. Heart pounding, I glance sideways to gauge her reaction better, and my breath catches. The contrast between her long blonde hair and that black dress is—I force my eyes forward.

I push open the paint-chipped door for her, and we walk inside. It's packed tonight. It's always packed on Thursdays. Joe's is the best all-ages Latin dance

club in Salt Lake, drawing everyone from senior citizens to students like
Emmy and me.

"Okay?" I ask.

Emmy nods, looking around the dance floor like she's never seen anything so fascinating in her life. I follow her gaze to a gray-haired man leading
his gray-haired wife around the dance floor. I hope I'm like that when I get
older. Maybe not exactly like that—less pasty white, more milk chocolate.
Definitely less wrinkles.

I look back at Emmy. "Can I buy you something to drink?" I point to
the bar on the far wall and then realize it sounds like I offered to buy her a
drink. "Maybe water or a soda? Milk?" I add and then wince. *Milk?*

She glances at the bar. "I'm good."

They aren't serving alcohol tonight, but still, what kind of guy brings an
angel to a bar? This was a bad idea. I glance at the door.

"Want to dance?" Emmy cuts into my thoughts.

I swallow a lump in my throat and nod. Her already wide smile grows
even wider. I follow her to the dance floor, but before we step into the flow of
bodies, she stops.

I look down at her in question. She rises onto her tiptoes and cups her
hand around her mouth next to my ear. "I don't know how to dance like that."
She points to a couple who looks like they're trying to win a professional dance
competition.

"Trust me?"

"Should I?"

"No." I snake my arm around her waist. "But dance with me anyway."
I wait for a downbeat in the pulsating music and then step backward, moving her with me. Another quick step forward and we're dancing. My knees
bend, bringing our faces closer together. The moves flow as easily as the music
between us. She doesn't fight against me or overthink the steps. She relaxes in
my arms, allowing me to lead her.

"You can dance," she says.

"I can," I admit, "but not because I've trained like you. Because it's in my
Latino blood."

The music picks up, and a man on the other side of the room shouts a shrill
"Ey-yi-yi!" Lights circle around the dance floor in bold beams of color—red,
green, purple, and blue—like a dream, one I know I will soon wake up from,
but tonight, right now, I'm content to keep dreaming.

I try a faster step, turning her body in quick movements side to side to see if she can follow. She can. I release my hold around her waist and lead her into a spin. With each rotation, her hair catches the wind and flies against my face.

The music hits a crescendo, signaling the end of the song. I tug her close, then dip her back, her hair sweeping across the floor. The last note lingers in the air, and when it finally dissolves, I pull her back in one fast motion.

Instead of letting go like I should, I cradle her close for an extra moment. Her blue eyes hold mine. Completely alive, high on adrenaline. Reluctantly, I release my grasp around her waist but not my hold on her hand.

She stands on her toes and pulls my head close so I can hear her voice. "Again."

Chapter Fourteen

Emmy

Latin dancing [lat-n / dans-ing] n—NOT ballet

Trumpets pierce the air in flowing harmony with the singer's voice. The time signature of this song is free and unrestricted, nothing like the straight lines that comprise classical music. Its red-hot, curved lines blur together. It pumps my blood and moves my feet. I can't understand a word of it, but it's beautiful and awakens something deep inside me. Something I didn't know existed.

Rhys is an amazing dancer. It's obvious he's not trained, but the way he moves tells me he believes what he said in the RB: that dancing should be fun. Every line of his body, every flex of his muscles says he believes it. The way our bodies move together causes my heart to stutter. He must notice because his lips inch up into a knowing smile. Those lips. This music. These moves. They're in his blood, like classical music and ballet are in mine.

I've never felt this way dancing with a man before. Pas de deux is beautiful, but it's choreographed—a staged act, rehearsed and perfected over weeks of training. But this . . . this is something completely different. I don't have to think about the moves or what comes next or if I'm on count or where to put my hands. It makes me feel free. This is real. *This* is dancing.

Rhys spins me around so my back is flush against his chest, and his arms circle around me. I explore the lines of his muscles with my fingers and the rich color of his skin with my eyes. Our feet never miss a beat.

His cheek touches mine, and when I meet his gaze, it's like looking into his soul, like seeing a piece of Rhys he keeps hidden. There's more to him than he lets on, and I want to know more. With a key change in the music, he turns me to face him.

He looks deep into my eyes. There's something about him, about the way I feel when he holds me in his arms. The safety, the passion. This moment feels significant, like he's asking a question and I'm answering.

And that's when I realize I want this to be something. I want him to feel what I'm feeling. But does he? Or is this dance to him as much an act as *Swan Lake* is to me? I look down, trip over my feet, bounce off his chest, and lose time with the music.

His hand leaves my waist even though the song is still in full swing, and he lifts my chin until I'm looking into his eyes again. "Stay with me, Emmy." He pulls me closer, forcing my body to follow his.

The music winds down, signaling its end. The singer's voice repeats a phrase over and over. It has so much emotion. So much feeling. I like how the words sound, even if I don't understand what they mean.

"What does *bésame* mean?" I ask.

Rhys's movements continue, but they become muted, like he's less aware of the steps and more aware of me. He doesn't release his hold around my waist; if anything, his grip tightens. "Kiss me." His voice is difficult to hear over the music, but the words are unmistakable. His forwardness takes me by surprise, but I want to. I want to so badly I lean against his chest and tilt my chin up to him. My heart pounds so hard against my ribs I'm sure he can feel it.

Rhys looks down as if he's just now become aware of my hands on his chest. His eyes widen. "No, Emmy." He shakes his head. "*Bésame means* 'Kiss me.'"

* * *

"Tell me you didn't kiss him." Evie winces.

"No. But I leaned in." I close my laptop screen and swivel in my chair to face her.

She rests her head against my bedroom wall and presses her eyes shut like it pains her to hear about my near first kiss with Rhys last night. "What are you going to do?" she asks.

"There's nothing I can do except drop BOM and hope I never, ever, *ever* run into him again."

"You can't do that."

"Actually, I can." I stand up from my desk chair and plop onto my bed. "The withdraw date isn't until the end of next week. I checked as soon as I got home last night."

"I thought you liked him?"

"I do like him. But he didn't exactly kiss me when I leaned in . . ." My eyes close, and I relive the horrific drive home. "He read the scriptures for next week's assignment the entire way home, Eves. The entire way."

"Oh, Em. How do you get yourself into these messes?"

I grab my pillow and smother my face. "Why?" I groan. "Why did you have to tell him to come to the RB last night?"

"I thought—"

My glare holds her words hostage, and she lifts her hands in surrender. "I need to die in peace. Can you shut the door on your way out?"

She frowns like there's more she wants to say but then backs away from the door and shuts it quietly behind her.

Chapter Fifteen

Rhys

For the Strength of Youth [fohr / thuh / strengkth / uhv / yooth] n—A pamphlet of guidelines LDS youth live by; no French-kissing, no one-on-one dating (until you're courting—whatever that is), modest clothes, etc.

I'VE WRITTEN AND ERASED AT least a dozen text messages to Emmy since we parted last night, but nothing feels right. When I told her I wanted to be friends, I meant it.

But that black dress.

I cannot stop thinking about it.

I shake away the image.

I write another text, trying to explain why I backed away when she leaned in for a kiss, but I can't word it right. It sounds like I didn't want to kiss her, and that's not true. I did want to kiss her. I just didn't want to mess things up. I deserve a medal for my self-control. Frustrated, I toss my phone aside and drag my hands through my hair.

Supe walks into our bedroom and falls face-first onto his mattress.

"You okay, man?" I ask.

"She's engaged." He groans into his pillow.

"Who's engaged?"

"The girl I wanted to marry."

I almost point out he didn't even know her first name last week or that by this time next week, he won't remember this girl, but that would be cruel, so I don't. "How'd you find out?"

"By asking her on a date."

I hold my fist to my mouth to suppress a laugh. "Brutal."

"You're telling me." He looks up at the ceiling. "Helaman, my man, what would you do?"

I glance at the life-sized poster. "Are you asking a piece of paper for girl advice?"

He turns to face me, propping his hand under his head. "Got a better idea?"

My phone burns a hole in the mattress beside me—I can't even text a girl. "Not really. No."

"Didn't think so." Supe kicks his shoes off, and they hit the floor with a thud. "So how'd things go with your study partner yesterday?"

"Great, actually. I took your advice and chillaxed."

"Oh yeah?"

"Yeah. I took her dancing at Joe's—" I pause to gauge Supe's reaction, but his expression is blank, so I add, "Bad idea, I know."

But he says, "That's awesome!"

At the same time, I say, "It was stup—Wait. What?"

"A few dates are exactly what you need." Supe pushes up to a sitting position.

"Really? I wasn't sure it was a good idea."

"Why not? You just want to get to know the girl, right?"

I shrug, unwilling to admit how much I like Emmy.

"I'll take that as a yes," he says smugly. "Is she interested in you?"

A smile pulls at the corner of my mouth, exposing the truth. She leaned in to kiss me. Unless I'm reading the signs wrong, she likes me.

"Yes again." Supe laughs. "So what's the problem?"

"You know what the problem is."

"Rhys, for the last two and half years, you've hated living here. You go to class, take care of your mom, and work . . . and then this girl comes along, and bam! Totally new Rhys. You go out, you smile . . . I respect you for thinking this through, but you're *over*thinking things at this point. She doesn't need to know everything about you."

I disagree. If I take her out, I risk rejection, likely humiliation, and possibly even my grade in BOM. I feel like I crossed a line even dancing with her last night, but at the same time, I'm trying to figure out a way to cross it again. I frown. "Even if I did ask her out, I wouldn't know what the rules are."

Supe walks over to his desk, unzips his scripture case, and pulls something out. A second later, he slaps a pamphlet against my chest.

"*For the Strength of Youth*?" I read the title.

"Consider that"—Supe points to the pamphlet—"your guide book."

"What am I supposed to do with this?"

"Read it."

I thumb through the pages of a pamphlet designed for Mormon teens. "Group dating?" I snort when I read that heading. "Sounds like the lamer parts of middle school."

"You're acting like a middle schooler, so it's perfect."

I roll my eyes.

"We'll double." Supe continues, undeterred by my lack of enthusiasm. "That'll pull me out of my dating slump and keep things casual for you."

Casual. Casual is good. I like casual. Casual I can do. A group date might help with the awkward one-on-one thing Emmy and I have mastered too. For once, Supe's right. This is perfect. I can take Emmy out like I want to but in a way that doesn't say I'm searching for an eternal commitment.

"Next Friday?" he asks.

"It's a date." If she says yes.

* * *

I called Emmy twice yesterday after talking to Supe. Spaced the calls a few hours apart to make it look like I wasn't desperate, but she didn't pick up either time, and she hasn't called back. Not a good sign.

I'm pretty sure the more time that passes will only make things that much worse when we finally do talk. As much as she rambles, I think more goes on in her head. And if she gets too much in her head, I don't think we'll recover. I glance at my phone: 10:00 a.m. I have to be to work at eleven. While Emmy's house isn't on the way, it's close enough.

I grab my uniform and chuck it into my truck. There's no way I'm going to her house dressed like a clown.

I park in front and walk up her brick sidewalk. My pulse races as I knock on Emmy's front door. Forever passes before the lock turns and the door creaks on its hinges as it opens.

"Rhys." She wraps her big sweater around her tiny body. "W-what are you doing here?"

"Next Friday, I'd like to take you out. On a date. A double date, if that's okay."

She stares at me. Blinks twice. Several seconds pass.

"Emmy?"

"Yeah. I heard you. It's just . . ."

I screwed this up. Supe's idea stinks.

Emmy traces an invisible crack on the ground with her toe. "When I'm around you, I get all jittery and forget how to talk."

"I think it's cute."

"I ramble—"

"I like that too." I never have to wonder what she's thinking.

"I end up saying anything that crosses my mind."

"One of the best things about you."

"But last night, when I . . . when we . . . well, you know, that was a new low for me. I guess what I'm saying is . . ."

Her sister Evie picks the perfect time to come down the stairs. She looks at Emmy and me. "Give the poor guy a break, Em. Say yes to the date." Evie winks at Emmy and then shimmies between us and dashes out the door.

Emmy's head falls against the doorframe. "This is not my life."

A few loose strands of hair fall against her cheek. She bats them away, but they fall right back. She takes a deep breath, the kind of breath that says she's about to tell me something I don't want to hear.

"Emmy," I say quickly, cutting her off. "I'd really like to get to know you better. Will you please come out with me Friday night?" I sweat for a second as she considers it.

"Okay," she finally says, and I'm more than a little relieved. "But on one condition."

"Name it."

"If I start to say or do something embarrassing, you have to stop me."

I smile. "It's a date."

Chapter Sixteen

Emmy

Allegro [ah-lay-groh] a—Fast. Way too fast

I'VE ANALYZED THIS DATE FROM every angle imaginable, and while I'm super nervous I'll mess everything up, I can't not go.

"Blot." Evie hands me a tissue, and I remove the excess lipstick.

"Good?" I ask.

Evie nods her approval. "Good."

"Great," Kennedy says without looking at me, then turns a page in her magazine.

I look in the mirror. My hair is down, like I had it the night Rhys took me dancing, because I know he likes it that way—I can tell by the way he looks at me when it's loose. I'm wearing a pair of dark jeans that feel funny after living in sundresses and tights all summer. They're casual, but paired with a flowy white shirt and a chunky necklace, I think they work. I bite my lip and scrutinize my reflection.

Evie waves her hand as if to protect her paint job. "Are you excited?"

I lift one shoulder. "A little nervous." Okay, a lot nervous. Enough-that-I-might-throw-up nervous.

"Don't be," Evie says. "It'll be fun."

"Ready to go now, Evie?" Kennedy asks.

"Actually, I want to see my sister off first." Evie winks at me, and I can't help smiling. "When is he supposed to pick you up, Em?"

"Seven." I pull my phone out of my pocket and check the time. "That's still thirty minutes away." I groan. I'm never going to last thirty minutes.

"Perfect!" Evie claps her hands. "I have so much to catch you guys up on." Evie launches into a detailed description of her latest date with Q. I try to concentrate on what she's saying, but my thoughts keep slipping to Rhys. I forgot to ask him what we're doing on our date and who we're doubling with. What if I'm underdressed?

"Em?" Evie cocks an eyebrow.

The magazine in front of Kennedy's face falls to the mattress. Obviously I've missed something. "He actually asked you?" Kennedy says.

My eyebrows draw together. "Who asked who what?"

"Now I've got your attention." Evie grins. "Q didn't ask me to marry him; he asked me how I would feel *if* he asked me to marry him . . . one day."

Oh.

Kennedy bounces on the bed like a kid waiting for a bedtime story. "I'm just hearing about this now because why?"

"*Beecaauuuse* . . ." Evie draws the word out as if to prolong our antici-pation. "I wanted to tell my best friend and my sister at the same time."

It wasn't that long ago that I was both her sister and her best friend. So much has changed in the last few months. Evie's changed. As if to prove my point, she pulls her lip gloss out of her pocket, applies a shiny coat, and then smacks her lips together. She's always been self-aware, but the incessant atten-tion to what she looks like, acts like, talks like has been over the top lately.

"Details! Details!" Kennedy claps her hands with excitement.

"Wait. Marriage? I thought you were taking it slow?"

"We were, but like I said a second ago—when you were oh-so-attentively listening—when you know, you know. And . . ." she grins excitedly, "he asked what type of ring I like, so . . ."

"Eek!" Kennedy squeals. "I can't wait to go wedding-dress shopping with you!"

I frown. "It's been less than a month. You hardly know each other."

"The anticipation is killlllling me," Kennedy says. "What did you tell him?"

Ignoring Kennedy, Evie faces me. "Q says people should take dating seriously and think more about marriage."

"Sure, but Q didn't just ask your feelings about marriage; he asked you what type of ring you want." I'm not naive. I get that relationships can prog-ress quickly in Provo, being that there are thirty thousand celibate adults liv-ing here, but we both watched our older sister Lucy fall too fast, too soon, and neither of us wants to walk that path.

"Why are you making a big deal out of this?" Evie scrunches her nose.

"*I'm* making a big deal out of this?" She was the one who wanted to an-nounce all this like the Royal Ballet was coming to town.

"Yeah." Kennedy laughs. "We're in college. Looking at rings isn't a big deal."

I stare blankly at Kennedy instead of glaring at her like I want to. Her eyes widen and then roll like I'm overreacting as she turns back to her magazine. "Marriage is a huge deal," I say.

"Look, I know you don't want to give up ballet to get married, but can't you support my decision?"

I shake my head. "I don't think he's right for you."

"You don't even know him. But maybe if you'd step out of your frilly little pink world once in a while, you'd see that there's more to life than ballet. Maybe you'd even see how happy Q makes me." Evie walks out of my room, and Kennedy follows her.

The doorbell rings a few minutes later, and it's obvious I'll be answering it myself. I grab my purse, take a deep breath, and walk to the door. There's no way I'm going to let Evie ruin my date with Rhys. Not a chance.

Chapter Seventeen

Rhys

*BYU dating scene [B-Y-U / dey-ting / seen] n—Planned ahead, paid for,
paired off; bonus points for creativity*

"So, GOOD NEWS AND BAD news and then more good news."

"Bad news first," Emmy says, shutting the front door behind her. She stows her keys in her purse as we walk down the brick walkway to my sorry excuse for a truck.

"The bad news is my roommate has the flu and can't make it."

"And the good news?" she asks.

"My roommate has the flu and can't make it."

She laughs.

"It's good news because now you won't have to put up with Supe for an entire evening. But bad news because the date I planned requires at least one other couple."

Disappointment shadows Emmy's face as I open the passenger door. She says a quick thank-you as I shut it behind her, and then I hurry to the driver's side, not wanting to waste a single second of our date. "The actual good news is that my friend Jen from work and her date agreed to take Supe's place."

"Perfect! Where do you work, by the way?"

"At the mall." I purposefully neglect to tell her where in the mall. I'm not ashamed—it's an honest living, and I've worked there long enough to make more than minimum wage—but telling Emmy would be humbling, to say the least.

We make a U-turn at the end of the street, then start down the road to Orem to meet up with Jen and her date. Emmy stares out the window at the mountains. Her eyes trace the switchback trail that leads to the Y. She's quiet but not a fidgety-nervous quiet like she normally is. Just quiet-quiet, like she's lost in her thoughts.

"They're beautiful, aren't they?" I say.

"What?" She looks at me, and I nod toward Y Mount.

"The mountains."

"Oh. Yeah." She shakes her head as if to clear away her cluttered thoughts. "I love them. It's strange. I grew up in the California hills, but the mountains feel like home." She smiles, but it doesn't touch her eyes. Something is up.

"Hey, are you okay?"

"Sorry. Yeah, I'm great. It's not you . . ."

It's me, I want to finish the line but give her a playful look instead.

She smiles. "It's Evie."

"Evie?"

"Yeah. She's dating a guy that's no good for her."

"Is he not a member or something?" I jokingly ask, but a pit forms in my stomach as I wait for her answer.

"No, he is, but his membership in the Church isn't what counts. Just because he's a member doesn't mean he's a good guy."

Whatever I was expecting her to say, it was not this. I nod dumbly, wishing I could form a more coherent response but too stunned to come up with one on the fly. Emmy's different. Maybe it's because she's dyslexic and she's probably had to combat labels her whole life, but she seems more open-minded than anyone I've met here.

"From what I can tell," Emmy says, "he's kind of egotistical." She cringes. "Or I don't know him that well, so that's not fair, but whenever I'm around him, I don't get a good feeling. He gives me these flirty looks when Evie isn't looking, like winks at me and looks a little too long. Evie claims he's strict about following the rules, but he seems to find a lot of gray area. I'm not even sure he can tell us apart." She slaps her forehead. "I'm not explaining it right. That sounds petty, doesn't it?" A line appears between her furrowed eyebrows.

"It doesn't sound petty. Promise."

Emmy frowns. "Let me try to explain it again." She shifts in her seat. "My older sister, Lucy, married her husband, Jeff, right after they both graduated high school. By the time they turned twenty, Jeff was no longer active at church, and they had a baby on the way. The problem is Lucy and Jeff had different ideas about what their lives would be after they got married. Jeff wasn't ready to be married for a lot of different reasons, and I don't think Lucy was either.

"Evie's relationship with Q is a lot like Lucy's relationship with Jeff. It's like Evie sees what she wants to see in Q: RM, temple worthy, good calling, goals. I don't think she realizes that marrying a member is not a guarantee that the marriage will be a happy one. And getting married in the temple doesn't mean the marriage will last forever. Right person. Right place. Right time. You know? I think the stars in Evie's eyes are blinding her to the reality of who he really is."

My heart slams against my chest, and I have to consciously force my jaw not to hang open. She may not realize it, but for the first time in three years, she's made me feel like who I am as a person is more important than what my beliefs are.

I've been walking alone on an alien planet for the last three years, and finally I've found someone who makes me feel human again. I know she's talking about her sisters, but that pit in my stomach disappears, and I can't help thinking we might be able to have more than just a friendship.

She glances up, and her cheeks are pink. "Darn it, Rhys. You were supposed to stop me when I started to say something embarrassing."

"Sharing your concerns about your sister is not embarrassing. Have you told her how you feel?"

"I've tried."

"Maybe you need to try harder." I wink, and she laughs.

"I think you've said that before."

My mouth tugs up. "I think maybe I have."

As I pull into the parking lot, Emmy reads the big blue-and-yellow sign. "Walmart?"

"Yep." I came up with the idea after Supe convinced me that a first date is important. Personally, I would prefer dinner and a movie. Maybe it's cliché, but there's no disputing that it's an easy way to get to know another person without pressure.

"Consider me intrigued."

I grab a bag from behind my seat and then help Emmy out of the car.

Jen is standing on the sidewalk in front of the automatic double glass doors with her date. He's tall and lanky and every bit the fumbling newly returned missionary Jen explained him to be.

She waves, appraises Emmy, and then gives me an impressed nod. Her nonverbal way of saying what we're both thinking: Emmy's out of my league.

"You must be the Emmy I've heard so much about," Jen says as we walk up.

"*The* Emmy?" Emmy asks, laughing.

Jen's eyes flick over to me, and I glare at her. "The way Rhys talks about you, yes—*the* Emmy."

"And you must be Jen," Emmy says.

"That's me." Jen extends her hand like she's already a missionary. They shake hands, something everyone does here regardless of age, and then Jen backs away. "And this is Tanner." She motions to her date. "He's from Washington. The state, not D.C."

"Nice to meet you, man. I'm Rhys."

He gives me a firm handshake. "You too."

We stop inside the entrance, and they all turn to me for an explanation of what could be the most horrifically awful first date ever recorded in history. "Supe would've explained this better, but he's not here. So tonight"—I hand them each a sheet of paper with a list on it—"we're having a scavenger hunt." It sounds worse than I thought it would. Like I'm some preteen chick at a slumber party. I'm surprised to find all three of them studying the list.

"We'll split into teams: Jen and Tanner, Emmy and me. The list is divided into two parts: dares and shopping list. Do all the dares on your list, and take a picture as proof with one of these." I hand Jen a Polaroid camera and keep one for myself. "Emmy and I will do the dares first and then the shopping, and Jen and Tanner will do the reverse so we don't bump into each other all night."

"Where on earth did you get these?" Jen inspects the camera like it's an ancient artifact.

"Supe."

Jen laughs. "Enough said."

I hand Jen a ten-dollar bill to cover the cost of the items. "Once you've completed all the dares, buy everything listed and meet back at the camping-gear section. Winning team picks the movie; losing team buys dessert. Time begins . . . now."

Jen threads her arm through Tanner's and pulls him away. Emmy and I jog to the housewares department to complete dare number one: fill the empty picture frames on the shelf with Polaroids of ourselves.

"Do you want to take the pictures, or should I?" She holds up the Polaroid and wiggles it.

"I've got a better idea." I walk over to her and bend my knees until I'm standing right beside her. "Make a funny face." Pressing my cheek against hers, I hold the camera so it's facing us and take enough pictures to fill several frames. I slide my favorite one of us into my back pocket when Emmy isn't looking.

After completing all the dares—riding a bike in the sports section, pretending to sleep in a chair in the home furnishings department, and dancing to music in the electronics department—we search for all the items we need to purchase.

"Vienna sausages? Marshmallows?" Emmy's nose crinkles up. "What kind of list is this?"

"You'll see."

"This isn't some crazy trust-building exercise, is it?"

"No." I chuckle. "This is not some crazy trust-building exercise."

"Okay, then," she says. "Final item on the list: pick a movie from the five-dollar bin."

We get to the bin as Jen and Tanner are walking away to start the dares. Emmy digs through the pile and holds up a DVD.

"*Center Stage*?" I ask.

She nods enthusiastically.

"I think my sister watched that at least a dozen times." I laugh.

"That's it? I've seen this movie triple that." Emmy sets the DVD back in the bin. "And wait—you have a sister?"

"I do. Cami. She lives in New York City." Mom and I both wish Cami lived here, but we're proud of her for following her dreams. I show Emmy an action flick, and she shakes her head.

"I've always dreamed of living in NYC. She's a lucky girl."

"She loves it." I hold up another movie, and this time Emmy's face lights up. I hand it to her, and she flips it over to study the back. Her face falls. "Too bad. It looks good too." She tosses the DVD back into the bin, and I look at her, perplexed.

"It's R," she explains.

Ratings. Right. Not something I've ever had to worry about before now. *Nice going, Rhys.*

She fishes for another movie. "I have five siblings," she says, continuing our conversation.

"Five, huh?" Evie I've met. She mentioned Lucy earlier, and her famous quarterback brother I know of, but somehow five still takes me by surprise.

"Yep. Two older sisters: Charlotte and Lucy, Jason, Evie, and the baby of the family, Drew."

"That must have been fun growing up with so many brothers and sisters. I wish I had more siblings." It would be nice to have more people to help shoulder the load.

"Are you and Cami close?"

"We are. But the distance is hard. We both work a lot, and the time difference makes talking difficult."

"I'm sorry. That must be hard. I'd be lost without Evie." She shuffles the DVDs. "It's strange how time changes things, isn't it? Like with my brothers, Jason and Drew. They used to be close, but then a few years ago, something happened and they've been at war ever since. They can hardly stand to be in the same room anymore. It's sad, and, wow, I'm oversharing again, aren't I? Feel free to stop me anytime."

"No way. I like learning about you."

I wish I could get her to keep talking, but Jen and Tanner should be done shopping for all the items on their list soon. "Find anything?" I ask her.

"Actually, I think I've got the perfect one." She holds up a DVD. "Everybody loves *Shrek*, right?"

"Haven't seen it."

Emmy's mouth falls open. "You haven't seen *Shrek*? Who hasn't seen *Shrek*?"

"Uh, me?"

"How have you not seen this movie? It's a classic!"

I stare at the lime-green ogre on the front cover, unsure how anyone could consider this movie a classic—especially a girl who's made classic art her life—and chuckle. "Long story, and I promise to share it with you later, but we better buy this and get back to camping gear, or we are going to be treating Jen and Tanner to dessert tonight."

"Oh! You're right." We run for the cash registers, and when we get to the front, Jen and Tanner are standing in line in the next row over. It's a toss-up to see who will win.

We end up winning, but only because the woman in front of Jen insisted on using an enormous stack of coupons. Emmy and I jog back to the camping section to wait for the losing team. The bright-green Astro Turf crunches beneath us as we sit in front of a six-man display tent.

"That was so much fun!" Emmy grins at the pretend campfire, then smiles up at me.

Honestly, I had my doubts about this, but it's turned out way better than dinner and a movie ever would have. "You're right; it was fun."

When Jen and Tanner arrive, we unload all the bags. Toothpicks, a candle, miniature marshmallows, graham crackers, and vienna sausages. The girls laugh when they realize we've bought a convenience-store campground dinner in miniature.

"This is awesome." Jen pops a mini marshmallow into her mouth. "Clever, Rhys."

"Wait." I hold up a finger. "It gets better." I pick up *Shrek*, then jog over to the electronics department—conveniently located right next to the camping section. I hand the movie to a worker, and he pops it into the DVD player. By the time I sit back down, *Shrek* is playing on every TV screen.

"This is by far the best date I've ever been on," Emmy whispers.

"Yeah?" I'm skeptical about that. I mean, look at her. She has to have been on some pretty stellar dates with guys trying to impress her. Running around Walmart and eating hotdogs out of a can couldn't possibly rank in the top twenty, let alone be the best date she's ever been on.

"Yeah," she says. "Best date ever."

Despite my lingering reservations about getting to know her better, I can't resist putting my arm around her and pulling her to my side. And maybe I'm imagining it, but she seems to like being near me as much as I like being near her.

Chapter Eighteen

Emmy

Assemblé (ah-sahm-blay') v—To put together

"CAN'T SAY I'M NOT HAPPY about winning tonight." Rhys settles into the driver's seat beside me with a big grin. I love the contrast of his bright white smile against his delicious dark skin.

"Me too!" I say. "And Jen's great."

"Yeah. She makes work almost bearable."

Jen pulls up beside us after we've backed up, and Rhys points to the street, indicating for her to lead the way to the restaurant for dessert. We reach the driveway, and he's about to merge onto the main road when his phone buzzes. When he not only pulls out his cell but reads the text, I'm taken aback. We're stopped, so it's not like I'm worried we'll get into a car accident or anything, but using a cell phone during a date, a *first* date, no less, is rude.

"Is everything, okay?" A hint of irritation colors my question.

He drags a hand through his hair, his fingers disappearing into the thick, dark strands.

"Not really, no." Rhys taps his phone against the steering wheel.

"Rhys?" I ask, suddenly worried.

He hands me his phone. "Will you please text Jen and let her know we won't be able to do dessert tonight?"

My eyebrows furrow as I take the phone from his hand. "Yeah, sure." I slide my thumb across the screen and see a list of names. Mine and a few other girls. Not what I hoped to see. I click on Jen's name, and the conversation thread appears. I don't mean to read it, but my eyes land on the words before I can stop them.

Jen: I thought she was a spoiled princess?

Rhys: Long story, but that wasn't her.
Jen: So . . . you like her, then?
Rhys: More than I should.

There's something about seeing a text not meant for me but that's about me that makes whatever this thing is between Rhys and me real. I quickly text Jen and hand the phone back to Rhys. He stuffs it in his pocket, and we zip back to Provo.

Rhys pulls down a street in south Provo. Redbrick homes line either side, and the yards are one of two extremes, impeccably maintained or on the verge of death. It's quiet here. A normal city street, not the bustling college town I know Provo to be.

Rhys turns into a driveway, shuts off his truck, and jumps out of his seat. Do I follow him? Wait in the car? He didn't exactly invite me inside, but it's not like he told me to stay put either. My hand is on the latch and pushing the truck door open before I can talk myself out of it.

At the front door, Rhys fumbles with his keys. There's enough light that I can see his forehead crease with worry. I have a feeling that whatever, or rather whoever, is on the other side of that door, is the reason Rhys keeps cutting our time short and turning hot and cold with me.

I start to follow, but he turns suddenly, and I almost pummel into his chest.

"I'm sorry. I—" He tugs on the ends of his hair, then wipes the back of his hand across his brow. "This isn't how I planned to tell you." Rhys steps inside the house, and I follow him in. He disappears down a darkened hallway, and I gently shut the door. When I turn around, the first thing I notice is that what I *see* does not match what I *smell.*

What I see is a brightly decorated, clean home. Blue walls, a red couch, and a rug that somehow ties the two together.

What I smell is feces.

Down the hall, a woman's soprano voice mingles with Rhys's deep baritone. A door closes between us, and the sound of rushing water filling a tub cuts off their conversation.

I sit on the couch to wait for Rhys, and the smell begins to dissipate. An eternity passes before the door creaks open again. Sitting straight, I wipe my hands along my pants and then realize my posture might make me look too rigid, so I force my shoulders to relax.

In the TV's reflection, Rhys's broad shoulders fill the hallway, and he wheels a woman who looks far too young to be in a wheelchair toward me.

Her curly brown hair is nearly as long as mine. And the way she's slumped makes her appear smaller than she probably is.

Rhys's voice, although hushed, reaches my ears as he talks. I can't make out his words, but his tone is gentle, almost pleading, as he speaks to her. The woman listens but turns away.

The floorboards creak as Rhys pushes her wheelchair down the hall. Right before he enters the living room, he drops to his knees and puts a pair of slippers on her feet. His back is to me, but I can still see him reach out to the woman and her bat him away. Despite her obvious displeasure, Rhys buttons her sweater anyway. He takes his position behind her again and wheels her the rest of the way into the living room.

"Emmy," Rhys says, his voice almost a whisper. "I'd like you to meet Mary Solario. My mother."

Chapter Nineteen

Rhys

Diagnosis [die-uhg-noh-sis] n—The process of determining the nature and circumstances of a diseased condition

EMMY AND I HAVEN'T SPOKEN since we left Mom's house. And as I pull up in front of Emmy's, I can't help thinking I've ruined any chance of a relationship. I turn off the ignition and move to open my door, but Emmy puts her hand on my arm, stopping me. "Is she why you're here?"

One of the things I like best about Emmy is that she isn't afraid to ask questions. I love her innocence and her wide-eyed curiosity. She also gets when I don't want to talk any further about a subject. Like right now, instead of pressing for answers, she waits for me to take the lead. "Yes. She's why I'm here."

Nodding, she looks around the truck's interior, then back at me. "You had to move here and take care of her. She's why you didn't get your truck."

I let out a quick breath and nod. "Any hope I had of buying that truck went up in flames when I decided to move here." I laugh humorlessly. "I was upset at the time. It seems stupid now, but I had worked hard to afford that truck, and not only did I have to leave UCAL, I also had to cash in my savings."

"It's not stupid. If I had worked so hard for something and my dream had died, I would have been disappointed too."

That's true, but . . . "Mom's dreams died too."

"Do you live with her? Is that why we can't study at your place?"

"No. Mom wants to maintain as much of her independence as she can for as long as she can. I tried to convince her to let me move in, but she said no."

"Oh. What made her choose Provo?"

"When she wasn't able to work full-time anymore, she got really into network marketing. Provo is a mecca for that kind of thing."

She nods, smiling, and I study the angel sitting next to me. My eyes follow the curve of her lips, and her bright-blonde hair glows in the moonlight. She's told me so much about herself over the past few weeks, and I've shared so little. It's unfair to dump anymore on her tonight, but she deserves to know more.

"When I was in second grade, my dad moved our family from Arizona to Denver." I pull at my collar. "That's where Mom's left hand first went numb." The truth doesn't exactly roll off my tongue. This is the first time in years I've volunteered any significant piece of information about myself to anyone. "The numbness didn't last long, and because it was her left hand, it didn't affect her life much. She was able to keep working, and she was still able to cook and clean, so nothing much changed. We all thought it was a fluke, something brought on from stress. Nothing to be concerned about, you know? But then a few months later, she was so dizzy she had trouble standing, and she got so weak she couldn't zip her jeans.

"At first Mom and Dad made it work. Dad picked up the slack while we waited for her to get back to normal. But after a few years, he couldn't take Mom being tired or grumpy or sick anymore"—I crack my knuckles against the steering wheel—"so he left."

Emmy blanches. "Your mom got sick, and your dad *left*?"

School of hard knocks. "Yeah."

Emmy exhales, shaking her head.

"After he left, Mom, Cami, and I limped along. Mom took temp jobs when the vertigo and fatigue lessened, and I found small jobs fixing things around the neighborhood to help out when she couldn't. But when her legs went numb, we knew it was more than a coincidence. Cami and I talked Mom into going to see a doctor, and after several visits and scans that cost more than we could afford, we finally got a diagnosis."

Emmy leans forward as if scared to hear the results, much like I remember feeling when I was sitting in the doctor's office the day my life came crashing down.

"Multiple sclerosis," I say. "MS."

"Oh, Rhys." Emmy's eyes squeeze shut for a moment. "I'm so sorry."

I shrug. "It's nothing."

She shakes her head. "It's not nothing."

"It's been my life for so long it's hard to remember anything else." And it will be my life for one more semester, until I have my diploma and I can work a real job. After that, things will change. Life will get easier.

I clear the emotion out of my voice. "Things haven't always been bad. After Mom was diagnosed, she took medication for a while, and her health improved. She even held down a full-time job while Cami and I were in high school. I think that's why we both felt confident moving away from home for college."

"Where did you guys go?"

"All three of us moved from Denver, actually. Cami graduated a semester early and moved to New York to pursue her dream of working in fashion. Mom moved to Provo to start her own network-marketing business. And I moved to Los Angeles to go to school at UCAL."

My senior year of high school, when I got the acceptance letter to UCAL, I felt invincible, like for the first time in my life I was finally creating my own destiny. Dad had left, and Mom had been sick, but that was all in the past. Los Angeles, UCAL, was my future, and no one could stop me. But now, sitting next to Emmy, admitting my escape to LA, I'm ashamed. I should have been caring for Mom.

"What happened? How did you end up in Provo?" she asks, confused.

"Mom's disease relapsed." The perfect kink in my plan. The one thing I will never be able to control.

"But you were in school. Why didn't Cami come?"

"She had just been hired as an intern at her dream job. Mom and I agreed we couldn't ask her to come home."

"Don't you have extended family?"

"Nah. Mom's an only child, and both her parents are gone."

Emmy nibbles her fingernail. Without thinking, I reach out and pull her hand away from her mouth. I move to let go, but her grip tightens, so I rest our hands on the center console instead. My eyes trace the woven pattern of our fingers. Hers are a pale white, mine a deep brown. Everything about us is different. Our families, how we grew up, and probably how we see our futures. But right now, holding her hand feels right.

"Will your mom be okay?" Emmy asks quietly.

"Mom's symptoms come and go, but when she's on medication, she does much better." I massage the back of my neck with my free hand. "You remember the night we got ice cream?"

A smile touches her lips, and she nods.

"I had to leave because Mom sent me a 911 text."

Emmy's thumb rubs the back of my hand, and I loosen my grip, realizing how tightly I'm holding on to her—like she's my lifeline. But as soon as my hold lightens, Emmy's grip strengthens like she's not willing to let me drift away without a fight.

"There is no cure," I continue. "Her medications help alleviate her symptoms, but because they can't cure her, she refuses to take them. All she wants to do is change her diet or try some weird new potion. I'm constantly battling with her to take her disease seriously. I wish she would accept that she has MS and take her medication. If she had been on her meds, maybe she wouldn't be in a wheelchair right now."

"Is it possible that her way of fighting her disease is just different from yours?"

"Yes. But it doesn't make it any less frustrating. All the pamphlets and support groups say to get mad at the MS, not the person who has MS, but every time she tries some new-age therapy instead of taking her FDA-approved medication, I want to scream."

Emmy is silent for several moments, as if processing all the information. Some first date. I look at my cell for the time. We've been sitting here for over an hour. It's nearly midnight. "I should walk you in," I say, even though that's the last thing I want to do.

As we head up the brick steps to her front porch, Emmy reaches for my hand. The simple gesture reassures me that she's as reluctant to say good night as I am.

She unlocks the front door but doesn't open it. "Thank you for trusting me."

She squeezes my hand, and a warm chill races up my arm. Everything inside of me wants to kiss her, but I can't remember what the rules are, and I don't want to rush things, so I stuff my hands in my pockets.

"What are you doing tomorrow?" she asks.

"It's my day off, and Mom needs help around the house."

Emmy doesn't miss a beat. "Let me come with you. After rehearsal. Two hands are better than one, right? Or no, four hands are better than two . . ."

I try to disguise a smile as the words flow out of her mouth. I love it when she does this. This night turned to trash, but I'd live through it all again to listen to Emmy ramble.

Chapter Twenty
Emmy

Grand jeté (grahN / zhə'tay) n—A big leap

IT'S STILL DARK OUTSIDE WHEN my alarm goes off Saturday morning, but even at 5:00 a.m., I'm wide awake. The mountains are shadowed in darkness, only their jagged peaks visible against the moonlit sky as I drive to campus. The closer I get, the harder my heart pounds. The air is frigid as I hurry up the front steps to the RB.

I've only come to the ballet studio once by myself since the beginning of the semester because it feels like accepting the fact that Evie won't ever dance with me again. I've wanted to but haven't had the courage to face the *barre* alone until last night when Rhys told me about his mother. She's courageous and is facing her problems head-on. I can do that too. I can be courageous. I may stumble. I may fail, but I can try.

I hurry down the hall to the studio. The room is hollow without music or dancers to fill it. The *barre* looms in front of me like a challenge.

After putting on my pointe shoes with shaky hands, I turn on some music, do a quick warm-up at the *barre*, and then move to the center of the room to face my fear.

Feel the notes, Rhys's voice echoes in my mind, reminding me dancing is meant to be fun. I slide into fourth position to wait for the song to begin. If I let go, I can do this.

Piano music swirls around the room, reverberating deep inside me. Instead of concentrating on choreography or the technical aspects of each eight-count, I let the music move through me like the night Rhys took me Latin dancing. The chords and the steps are different, but the feeling is the same. I'm carried away in the moment, floating across the floor.

The melody dips and then swells into a dramatic crescendo. My arms, my legs, my whole body rises with it. I pull my muscles in tight and center my weight. Each breath is connected to every movement, and I'm completely in sync with the music.

Without fighting each step, peace settles into my soul. Dancing feels better than before. Before Evie quit. Before I didn't get the solo. Before dancing required so much effort. There's more emotion, and I trust my technique enough not to overthink the steps. I let the thousands of hours I've spent on my toes drilling positions and turns and jumps into my bones guide me across the floor. But instead of just relying on my skills, I allow myself to do what Rhys taught me: relax into the swaying, flowing, feeling of the music and finally enjoy dancing again.

Each song blurs into the next. Breathless, I take a reluctant break. I can't wait to tell Rhys about my breakthrough. When I check my phone, I find several hours have passed. I'll have to hurry home to get ready so I can make it to Rhys's mom's house on time.

The sun is rising over the mountains when I exit the RB, majestic rays of light highlighting the snow-dusted peaks. I pull into the driveway and then hurry inside and up the stairs. Evie is just walking out of her bedroom, yawning.

"You were out late last night," she says and follows me into my bedroom, plopping onto my bed. She does this after we fight sometimes—pretends like nothing happened.

"I got home pretty early, but we talked in his truck for a while," I say curtly and drop my ballet bag to the floor. It's not that I don't want to talk. I do. I just don't know how anymore. We either end up fighting, or she ditches me for Q or Kennedy.

"Good night?" she asks.

"Sure."

Evie huffs at my one-word answer. "Come on, Em. Don't be like this. Can't we forget our argument and talk?"

I shrug.

"Fine." She breathes. "I'll talk; you listen." She pulls her feet up and sits crisscross on the mattress. "I waited all day to talk you and Kennedy at the same time, and then you made me feel bad. Why aren't you happy for me?"

"I'm worried that you're taking the same road Lucy did."

"Because Q brought up rings?"

"Yes. No. Maybe partly, but it's more than that. He doesn't seem to bring out the best in you. You've started ditching school and staying out late . . ."

"How does that make me like Lucy?"

"Lucy forgot who she was and what she really wanted because of a boy, and I'm worried you're doing the same."

"Wow, Em. That's a pretty big accusation, don't you think?"

"I don't mean for it to be, but you've changed a lot since you've started dating Q, and it worries me."

Evie squints like she's trying to read between the lines and decipher what I'm trying to say. Rhys is right. I need to tell Evie exactly how I feel. I take a deep breath, trying to summon my courage. "I . . . I feel uncomfortable around him."

Evie smiles a little. "You've never been comfortable around guys."

"That's true," I say, "but this is different. The way he looks at me." I shake my head.

"How does he look at you?"

My face heats. "A couple seconds too long, flirty."

"We're identical. That has to be confusing for him."

She's not taking me seriously. "He makes me *uncomfortable*, Evie."

Her shoulders droop. "I'm in love with him, Em. He might be the one. Can't you try to get to know him?"

My mouth goes dry. "You love him?"

She nods.

The last thing I want to do is get to know him, but telling Evie that will only make things worse between us. As frustrated as I am that she's ignoring my concerns, I don't know what else I can say. She's my sister, and I love her. "Don't get caught up in the excitement of the relationship because your friends think he's cool."

"Because my friends think he's cool," she repeats. "Are you jealous of Kennedy? Is that what this is about?"

"I'm not jealous of Kennedy."

"Says the jealous sister."

"That's not what this is about," I say, and a lump forms in my throat. "But I do miss you."

"I miss you, too," she says softly. "Things have been different since I quit ballet, huh?"

I nod. "Yeah."

"I didn't want my quitting ballet to affect us. I'm sorry it has." She's quiet for a moment. "I think that means we need to make a better effort to connect. What about we do that movie marathon we talked about at the beginning of the semester?"

I smile. "I'd like that. Tonight? Maybe after I'm done helping at Rhys's mom's house?"

"Sure . . ." Evie smiles, and the tightness in my throat loosens a bit. "His mom's house, huh? Things must be going well."

"Yeah." I tell her about my date last night and about his mom and her MS, and by the end of my story, although our situation hasn't changed—she hasn't decided to rejoin ballet, and she isn't about to break up with Q—I do feel a little better about our relationship.

Evie stands to leave, and I catch her hand. "I'll try," I say. "To get to know Q. I can tell he means a lot to—" Before I can finish my sentence Evie wraps me in a tight hug.

"Thank you. Thank you. Thank you!" she says. "You're going to love him. I know it!"

* * *

"What can I help with?" I ask Rhys.

Rhys scrubs his hand over his head, ruffling his hair. "Are you sure you don't mind?"

"Positive. I'm here to help, remember?"

Rhys's gaze drifts down the hall to his mother's closed bedroom door. "She probably won't be up for a few more hours. Last night was pretty rough on her."

"Even if she does wake up, it'll be fine. I'd love to get to know her better." We didn't get to talk much last night. His mom was tired and, I suspect, embarrassed, so she said a quick hello, and then Rhys helped her into bed.

"If she wakes up, come and get me, okay?"

"Okay," I reply. "So what can I do?"

Rhys lets out a breath. "Now that Mom's in a wheelchair, she won't be able to reach anything in the cupboards above the counter. It'd be great if you would help me move a few things down so she can reach them when I'm not here."

"Of course."

Rhys leads me into the kitchen and shows me what to pull down, and then he goes outside to start the yardwork.

One by one, I take out the things Rhys's mother will need: glasses, plates, bowls. Once everything is out, I stand a few feet back and look into the cupboards to make sure I haven't missed anything. Sure enough, on the top shelf is a pill bottle. I pull over a chair from the kitchen table and hop up on the counter so I can reach it.

"What are you doing up there?"

I almost fall off the counter at the sound of her voice. "Mrs. Solario." I swipe the pill bottle and hurry down from the counter. "I was trying to be quiet. I'm sorry if I woke you."

Her eyes roam over everything on the counter. "Pretty hard to wake someone who can't fall to sleep."

That's when I notice her droopy eyelids and the dark shadows underneath them. "You didn't sleep last night?"

"Difficulty sleeping. One of the many gifts MS gives me." She situates her wheelchair at the kitchen table where I've pulled away the chair and then rests her head on the table.

I glance out the kitchen window at Rhys mowing the lawn. His muscles flex beneath his thin cotton T-shirt as he maneuvers the lawnmower in straight lines. As if he can feel the weight of my eyes, he looks up and catches me staring. His lips kick up into a delicious grin, making my insides squirm, and then he turns the mower away to start on the next section of grass.

"Can I make you something to eat?" I ask Mrs. Solario.

"I'm not hungry, but a glass of chamomile tea would be wonderful. Thank you."

I pick a mug up off the counter, and she points to a long cupboard against the far wall. "The packets are over there."

After heating the water, I dip in the tea bag and then set the mug in front of her. "Do you mind if I sit with you?"

She lifts her head from the table and pushes her tousled hair out of her eyes. "I may not be good company this morning, but no, I don't mind." She wraps her hand around the mug, and I notice her skin is littered with tiny red welts.

"Are you okay?"

She looks down. "Oh yeah, I'm fine. Just another failed therapy."

"I'm so sorry."

"Don't be. Bee-sting therapy was worth a try."

I wince, thinking about how painful one sting is, let alone several. "I remember getting stung as a kid. I don't think I could do it on purpose."

"You'd be surprised what you're willing to endure to cure an ailment. Medical science can't cure me, so I might as well try everything else. At least then I'm being proactive."

I nod. "When I was diagnosed with dyslexia, my parents and I tried everything to fix me. I know it's not the same, but I can understand wanting to explore every solution."

"Rhys didn't tell me you were dyslexic."

"Until last night, he didn't tell me you have MS."

We both laugh. "That's my son. With a mother like me, I have no idea how he grew up to be an introvert." She takes a sip of her tea. "He thinks I'm crazy for trying all the things I do."

"He's only worried about you."

"I know he is. But what's the harm in letting me try everything I possibly can?"

I bite my lip to keep from saying anything about how much stress that unopened bottle of medication causes Rhys. His mom follows my gaze to the counter where the medication sits. "You think I should take medication too, don't you?"

Knowing this isn't any of my business, I scramble to think of an appropriate response. "I—uh . . ." I pause to recompose myself. "If there were a pill that could help me read better, I would probably try it."

She ponders my response for a moment. "I've tried medication before, but my symptoms always came back. It felt like I was sitting in the middle of the road waiting for whatever Mack truck came along next to hit me. Fatigue. Numbness. Vertigo. But with alternative therapies, I'm at least standing in the street waving the middle finger at the semi. It doesn't mean it won't still hit me, but at least I'll go down fighting." A forlorn expression crosses her face. "Rhys thinks medication is the only option." She looks out the window at Rhys working. "This relapse has been hard on him. I can live with this disease, but I wish he didn't have to." She taps her pointer finger against the side of the mug. "Being the reason your children can't live their dreams will make you do anything to try to solve it. Even kill innocent bees." She chuckles but quickly turns somber.

"He just loves you and wants you to be okay," I offer.

"Maybe it's time to try meds again."

I continue listening, knowing advice isn't what she wants.

"I won't give up alternative methods of controlling my disease, of course, but if taking the pills will give Rhys peace of mind, I think he's earned it." She pauses and then says, "Will you please hand me the pills?"

I give her the bottle.

She opens it and swallows a pill with a gulp of water. "So tell me, how did you meet my son?"

Stunned by the fact that she took her meds, I somehow manage to squeak out, "Book of Mormon class."

Her brow furrows. "That's . . . interesting. I didn't know he was taking that class."

"It's required."

"Hmm."

Outside, the lawnmower rattles to a stop, and a moment later, Rhys appears in the kitchen, sweat dripping from his brow. "You're up," he says to his mom.

"I'm up. Emmy was just telling me about how you met in Book of Mormon class."

Rhys's eyes slide to me and then back to his mom. "It's required."

"So she said."

They stare at each other for a long moment. Long enough I begin to feel uncomfortable. Rhys glances away first, his gaze falling on the open pill bottle in the middle of the table. "Please don't tell me you dumped those down the drain."

"Nope." His mother wheels away from the kitchen table. "Decided to try them again."

"You're serious?"

"As a bee sting." She winks at Rhys. "I'm still going to try other therapies, but I'll take the meds again too." She turns the wheelchair toward the hall. "It was nice talking with you, Emmy. I'm going to go lie down and see if a meditation CD can't help me find some of that sleep I lost last night." She wheels away, and Rhys stands there as if in shock.

"I've been trying for years to get her to take her meds. How did you convince her?"

"I didn't. She decided on her own."

He sits in the chair across from me. "Whatever you did to help her make the decision, thank you."

I shake my head. "Really. It wasn't me."

October

Chapter Twenty-One
Rhys

Agency [ay-juhn-see] n—The ability to choose right from wrong

EMMY: WHAT ARE YOU UP *to on this beautiful Saturday morning?*
Rhys: I'd like to see you . . .
Emmy: But?
Rhys: I need to change my oil first.
Emmy: I need to do that too! Maybe we can go together.
Rhys: Actually, I do mine myself.
Emmy: Teach me?
Rhys: Of course. 12:30?
Emmy: It's a date.

I try not to smile as I text her back to meet at my place in an hour, but it's nearly impossible. I never would've thought she'd be interested in learning how to do a chore like this.

"Judging by the look on your face after reading that text"—Supe points at me—"I'm guessing things went well on your date with that girl."

"Emmy," I say more sharply than I mean to.

He raises an eyebrow. "Right. Emmy."

"Things are going good."

"Oh yeah?"

"Yeah. She's actually coming over in a bit."

Supe pauses, then bends to unzip his backpack. He stows a few books inside, then rezips it before turning to me, his expression wary. "Two weekends in a row, huh?"

Maybe I'm reading more into his question than I should, but it seems loaded. "Yep."

"So . . . you like her, then?"

"Of course I like her."

"I think I may have underestimated how *much* you like this girl. Have you told her?"

"Not yet." I was going to tell her two weeks ago, right after I told her about Mom, but I had already dumped so much information on her that night, it didn't feel right."

"Sooner may be better than later."

"What's that supposed to mean?"

"Nothing."

"Weren't you the one who convinced me it wasn't a big deal to take her out on a date?"

"A date, yes. But—"

"Chillax, Supe," I say, tossing his own words back at him. "I'm just waiting until we get to that point where she needs to know, like you said. Trust me though; it won't be an issue."

He scratches at his nose. "You've lived here for two and a half years, man. Tell me you aren't that dense. A group date is one thing, but *dating* is a big deal to us."

Us as in *Mormons*. *Us* as in *him*. *Us* as in *not me*.

"Emmy's different." I wouldn't have asked her out otherwise. She likes me for me, not for what religion I practice. She cares more about what type of person she dates than what religion they belong to. She said it herself: just because two people are both Mormon doesn't mean the relationship will last.

"I'm sure you're right. It's just, you're finally liking it here, and I don't want things to end badly, you know?"

I shrug, not wanting to continue the argument, and I look at the picture I took at Walmart with Emmy. Supe may not believe me, but she *is* different. Our date proved that. The date Supe convinced me to go on. The date he made me believe was okay. I love this picture of our faces pressed together. Only half of each of us is in the frame, and it's super blurry, but even here you can tell she's different from other girls. I hold it up for him to see. He leans forward, squints at it, and then blinks up at me.

"Emmy isn't judgmental. She likes me for who I am and not for what I believe," I explain.

Supe winces at my insult. "I didn't mean to upset you, man. I'm just trying to help."

Leaning forward, I rest my elbows on my knees and mutter a curse under my breath. Supe needs to mind his own business. He doesn't know Emmy like I do.

"So when's this mystery girl of yours coming over today? I'd like to meet her before I head to the library for a study date."

Before last night, I was excited to introduce Supe to Emmy. But now? "Not sure I want you to meet her. You might try to steal her."

He laughs. "I don't think we have the same taste in women, brother."

* * *

"That's it?"

"Yep."

Emmy leans against the grill of her SUV. "Changing my oil wasn't what I was expecting." She frowns at her hands. "I barely even got my hands dirty."

Laughing, I stand in front of her. I thought she'd like using the vacuum method to change her oil, but obviously I was wrong. "Are you upset?"

"No." She looks up at me. "I appreciate you teaching me. I just thought—"

"We were going under the car?"

She nods sheepishly.

"Well, we could do my truck that way . . ."

Her eyes light up. "I can't believe I forgot you needed to change your oil. I was so excited to do something on my own. Well, okay, not actually me doing it—you did most of the work—but still."

Her enthusiasm is contagious. "It won't be as clean as your car."

"Let's do it!"

I've never loved changing oil, but when she smiles at me like that, there's nothing I wouldn't do for her, including climb under my truck like a grease monkey. I walk over to the side of my truck and hold out a hand. "After you."

We shimmy underneath, positioning ourselves so our heads are close enough together that I can show her what to do but keeping enough space between us for a catch pan.

"Last chance to back out," I say.

"No way."

I hand her a wrench, and she gets a determined look on her face. A small crease forms between her eyes as she concentrates on following my instructions. "Am I doing it right?" she asks as she unscrews the drain plug.

"Looking good."

She turns to smile at me, and, of course, that's the exact moment the oil starts to flow. Oil catches the edge of the plug and splatters all over her face.

"Oh my goodness." She squeals. "I didn't get it on you, did I?" She turns to face me.

"No. But you do have a little right here." I reach out and drag my thumb across her cheek. Her breath hitches, and her gaze flicks to my lips so fast I almost miss it. I start to lean in . . .

"Yo, Rhys!"

My hand darts away from Emmy's face, and she jerks up, hitting her head on the bottom of the car. Hard. She yelps, then rolls to her side, away from me.

"You guys okay under there?" Supe asks, completely oblivious to the moment he's massacred.

I stick my head out from under the truck and shake my head. "Not now."

Supe's brow furrows, and then he shrugs and walks down the driveway to his car to leave for his study session.

By the time I turn back to Emmy, she's already scooted out from under the truck and is standing up.

"How bad is it?" she asks, then stoops to look in the side mirror of her SUV.

I look at the bump already forming on her head, then grab her hand and walk straight inside to the freezer to look for something to lessen the swelling. I find a leftover Spongebob popsicle from Supe's cartoon-themed luau last year, and Emmy looks at me in question.

"Don't ask." I brush the hair off her forehead.

"Is it bad?"

"Nah." I press the bright-yellow popsicle to her forehead, and she recoils.

"It has to be pretty bad if you're pressing a popsicle to my forehead."

"Correction. I'm *trying* to press a popsicle against your forehead, but you're making it very difficult."

"It's cold."

"Kinda the point. Now come here."

She leans her head toward me and closes her eyes. I touch the popsicle to her skin, and she sucks in a sharp breath. Slowly, she inches away.

I chuckle. "You've got to hold still, angel."

She smiles up at me. "Angel?"

"Yeah. I, uh . . ."

"I like it."

I hold her gaze with mine. "I like you."

"Do you?" she asks.

I nod. "I do."

"Me too."

My hand falls from her face, and I set the popsicle on the counter. "I mean it, Emmy. I like you. A lot. I know you could be with any guy you want, but for some reason, you're here with me." I shake my head. "I don't deserve a girl like you."

"Don't say that."

"It's true. I mean look at us." I glance down at my cheap clothes and scuffed shoes. "I'm not like you. I don't have a penny to my name, and I have obligations a mile long. And even besides all that, I'm not—"

"Rhys." Emmy touches my cheek, and my brain stalls.

I look into her big blue eyes, and I'm transported back to last weekend when we were sitting outside her house in my truck. When I felt safe. Like I wasn't alone anymore. Wanting to feel that way again, I take a step closer. I want to believe so bad that I am enough for her, but am I? I'm not so sure. "I can't give you what you want," I admit. And I know And I know Supe's probably right, I should say more . . . but I don't. I'm selfish, and I want to enjoy this one moment with her.

"You are what I want." She rises to her tiptoes and presses her lips to mine, cutting off my argument. Her sweet scent caresses my nose. Coconut and . . . blueberry. Like blueberry pancakes smothered in coconut syrup. Heaven.

My hands move from her face to her silky hair, the soft strands tangling around my fingers. Her arms tighten around my neck, and I struggle not to deepen the kiss. She sighs softly, and I almost lose my willpower. I pull back. This is . . . "Whoa."

Her uneven breaths tickle my lips, and she tips her head down as if to hide from me. "Did I do it wrong?"

I urge her chin back up with my own. "Do what wrong?"

"Kiss. Obviously you're an incredible kisser. Of course you are. I knew you would be, but . . . I'm not. I mean, I've never—"

"You've never . . . ?" Wait. Not possible. "I'm your first kiss?"

Her cheeks turn scarlet.

I kiss her softly, partly to reassure her, but mostly because I already crave her again. "That was the best kiss I've ever had," I whisper. "Emmy. There's so much you don't know about me, but if you give me time, I promise we'll get there."

"W-what are you saying?"

"I'm asking you"—I kiss her cheek and then her mouth—"to be my girl."

Her lips bloom into a full smile, and she tugs me back to her. "Yes."

She's sweet and soft and pure and exactly everything I've always wanted but never realized until this second. Kissing her is like finding a piece of myself I didn't know I was missing. Crazy. This whole thing is crazy. I'm falling in love with a girl I barely know. A girl who barely knows me.

"Can I see you tonight?" I ask.

"You have no idea how much I want that, but after dance, Evie and I are going to spend time together."

"I should probably pick up an extra shift anyway. What about Sunday night? We should probably sneak in a little study time."

"Perfect. What time do you get home from church again?"

I have to tell her. Tomorrow.

"I'm available anytime."

Chapter Twenty-Two

Emmy

De côté [duh / koh-tay] v—To sidestep

"ARE YOU SURE YOU DON'T mind?" Evie asks.

"It's fine."

"Because I know it was just supposed to be you and me tonight, but Kennedy got into a fight with her roommates, and I felt bad for her, so I invited her to hang out with us, and then she suggested we shop for Halloween costumes because we're going to a party in Salt Lake with Q next weekend. But if you'd rather it just be us . . ." Evie bites her lip.

"It's not what I had in mind, but it'll still be fun."

Evie smiles. "Thanks, Em. You're the best."

Thirty minutes later, I'm sitting in a dressing room at the mall, watching my sister and her friend try on costumes.

"What do you think?" Evie presses an unidentifiable frilly pink costume against her shoulders and inspects her reflection in the dressing room mirror.

"It's very . . . short." I grimace.

"It's not *that* short," Kennedy says when she walks out of dressing room.

"If you were a toddler," I say, and Kennedy frowns. "Keep searching. You'll find something."

Evie tosses the dress into the growing mountain of rejected costumes in the corner of the dressing room. "I give up."

"Why don't you ask Mom to send one of your old dance costumes?"

"It'd take too long," Evie says. "This is so stressful."

I sit on a faux-leather lounge chair next to the dressing room. "It's just a costume. What's so stressful?"

Evie trudges across the graying carpet and plops down next to me. "I don't know. Things have been different between Q and me lately. He's been distant the last week, and whenever I try to talk about it, he shuts down. I guess I just thought if I found the perfect costume, it would wow him or something." She rolls her eyes. "Stupid. I know."

"I get it, but I'm sure he's just overwhelmed. Prelaw is rigorous, and midterms are coming up."

Evie slings her arm around me and squeezes. "You're probably right," she says, adding a smile for my benefit. "Enough about me. How are things with Rhys?"

My cheeks heat. "He sort of asked me to be his girlfriend yesterday."

Evie pushes back so she can look at me. "*What*? Are you serious?"

I nod. "He kissed me."

Any sadness lingering on Evie's face disappears. "Aw, Em! I'm so happy for you! I knew he was gaga for you."

"Gaga?" I giggle.

"Yep. Completely."

I tell Evie all about yesterday, from changing our oil to him kissing me and everything in between. When I'm finished talking, she gives me a tight squeeze and then walks back to the rack in search of a costume.

Kennedy emerges from the dressing room with an armful of rejected costumes, grabs another dozen off the rack, and then disappears back inside.

Evie pulls a fuchsia dress off the rack and holds it up. I think it's supposed to be a butterfly. It's worse than the frilly pink one. "Not it," I say.

Evie shoves it back on the rack.

Kennedy comes out of the dressing room with a big grin. "This is it," she says, twirling so we can take in her costume. It's red and formfitting. And so short I hope she's wearing something underneath.

"Oh. My. Goodness!" Evie says. "I'm so jealous you found it first."

Wait. What?

Kennedy claps her hands in victory. "Best part? There are two!" She pulls an identical dress out from behind her back. "Thing One and Thing Two." She grins. "We can be twins!"

Evie takes it from Kennedy and hurries to a dressing room to try it on. She emerges a minute later and scurries to a mirror.

"Q will love that!" Kennedy points at the dress, though I can't really call it a dress. It's more of a swath of material strategically draped.

"Uh . . . I'm not sure," I say. "It's a little short."

Evie bites her lip as she appraises her reflection. "Maybe I can wear a pair of tights under it or something."

"Don't be a prude," Kennedy says. "If you want Q's attention, this will definitely get it."

Evie looks in the mirror again. "It *is* Halloween. And it's not like I didn't wear less when I danced."

"A leotard on stage is different from a skintight dress meant to attract attention."

"Says who?" Kennedy sneers, and I back down, not wanting to get into another argument.

"Well . . ." Evie says. "I'll keep looking, but I think I'd better buy this today in case I don't find something else. Besides, it's lunchtime. Food court?"

"Yes, please! I'm famished," Kennedy says.

Thing One and Thing Two pay for their dresses, and I try not to think about the fact that Mom and Dad used to call Evie and me by the same nicknames when we were little. Receipts in hand, we start toward the food court.

"What are you going to eat, Em?" Evie asks.

"Umm." I scan my options. "Actually, I'm not that hungry. I'm just going to get a cherry limeade from Hot Dog on a Stick."

"Hot Dog on a Stick. That sounds good, but I'm craving Chinese," Evie says.

Blah. Our brother Jason made us eat Chinese takeout after every single one of his football games growing up. Just thinking about the oil-drenched noodles makes me queasy.

"I'm going to have a salad," Kennedy says. "Dressing on the side. I want to look good in this baby." She wiggles the bag containing her costume.

"Good point," Evie says. "Salad it is."

Evie hates salad. Hates it. "I'm sticking with Hot Dog on a Stick," I say. "You sure you don't want to join me?"

"No, thanks." Evie links her arm with Kennedy's, then looks at me. "We'll meet you back here?"

"Sure." As much as I love hanging with my sister, I need a break from Kennedy.

I walk to the Hot Dog on a Stick, set my purse on the counter, and search for my wallet.

"Emmy?"

My gaze snaps to the girl waiting to take my order. "Jen? How are you?"

"You here to see Rhys?"

I glance around, confused. And then it dawns on me: he works at the mall with Jen. He works *here*. Oh my goodness. He's going to think I'm stalking him. I'm not. I only wanted a cherry limeade.

"You didn't know he works here, did you?" Jen asks, taking in what must be my stunned expression.

I shake my head.

"Oh, he is going to love this."

As if on cue, the storeroom door swings open and Rhys walks in carrying an overflowing bucket of fresh-cut lemons. The sweet citrus scent wafts by, and I breathe in deeply.

Rhys's muscles bulge beneath his red-and-yellow striped, too-tight shirt, and he's looking down at the bucket as if to make sure he doesn't drop any. "I chose to CTR and come to BYU, but I didn't think I'd be surrounded by RMs who were once APs and future SPs," he says to Jen.

"You've used all of those before, and I have no clue what an SP even is, so yet again, you lose. And BTW, your GF is here."

Rhys stops short, and several lemons fall to the floor. He quickly turns toward the back wall and sets the bucket of lemons on a counter and then wipes his hands down his royal-blue pleated shorts as he turns to face me. "Hey, Emmy."

Mexicans blush. I had no idea. And, dang, if it isn't the cutest thing I've ever seen. Rhys is already crazy attractive, with his high cheekbones and strong jaw that always has a hint of a shadow growing, but man, oh, man, the way his cheeks redden makes my heart kick into overdrive.

"Hey, Rhys," I say, trying to sound unaffected.

He drags the back of his hand across his brow. "So how does it feel to be dating a clown?"

"A clown?"

He takes a step back and sweeps a hand down his torso. It is . . . festive, but no one would ever mistake Rhys for a circus performer.

"Don't talk about my boyfriend like that," I say.

He straightens his ridiculously tall, short-brimmed hat. "This isn't a deal breaker?"

"No way. Are you crazy?"

The edge of his mouth kicks up. "Crazy about you."

A choking sound distracts us both, and Rhys whips around to where Jen is sitting on the counter watching us. She grips her neck, pretending to gasp for air. "Please. Stop. Too much cheese."

Rhys smiles. "What are you doing here? I thought you were hanging out with your sister tonight."

"I am. Sort of. The night hasn't turned out like I expected. We're here with Evie's friend, shopping for Halloween costumes."

"That's . . . cool."

Jen walks up and leans against the counter next to Rhys. She points at Evie sitting at a table a few feet away picking at her salad. "I get that they're identical, but I have no clue how you confused her for Emmy."

Rhys and I laugh.

"My twin and I are very different," I say.

"Ya think? You're like this graceful little ballerina Barbie, and she's, I don't know, a Bratz doll goes to prom or something," Jen says.

I cringe at her description of Evie. She's so much more than the way she looks or the way she's currently acting. I laugh, trying to play off my discomfort.

"Men are so unobservant." Jen playfully shakes Rhys.

Rhys chuckles as she walks away and then turns back to me. "So you're either here because you're stalking me or because you're hungry. Should I be worried or take your order?"

"Take my order. Although, now that I know where you work—"

"The truth comes out," he says. "So what will it be?"

"One cherry limeade, please."

"Coming right up." He prepares the drink and then hands it to me. Another customer moves into line behind me. "Still on for tomorrow?" he asks.

"Can't wait."

"Me neither."

Chapter Twenty-Three

Rhys

Stereotype [ster-ee-oh-tipe] n—Standardized image held in common by a group

"WHAT HAPPENED TO KEEPING THINGS casual?" Jen says as Emmy walks away.

"Things changed."

"Oh, I totally get it now," Jen says sarcastically. "Seriously. What's up?"

I measure out the sugar and ice and then dump them both into the bucket of fresh-cut lemons. "I like her," I admit.

"Like her how? As a study partner? A friend?"

My lips twitch. "No, I like her, like her."

"As in you love her like her?"

"As in I-asked-her-to-be-my-girlfriend-and-she-said-yes like her."

Jen's head rears back. "Oh-kay, wow, not to be rude or anything, but isn't that like the biggest cliché ever? Go to BYU, find a pretty girl, date a few weeks, and then propose?"

I raise an eyebrow at Jen. "For the record, you were the one who brought up marriage, not me, and I hardly fit the BYU stereotype." I hold my arms out to the side so she can get a good look at my obviously nontraditional BYU student-ness.

Jen's eyes scan me from my thick Hispanic hair to my beat-up work shoes. "You fit in here more than you'd like to think, Rhys Solario."

"I don't, and you know it."

"We're going to have to table this discussion because I can see you're not going to budge on this right now, and I want more info about you and Emmy." Jen's stare settles on me, waiting for an answer.

"I feel different when I'm around her. Like I'm still me but a better version of me."

"If you say she completes you, I am literally going to throw up in that bucket of lemons you're about to stomp."

I chuckle. "You asked."

"My mistake. I'm actually still wondering how you confused the 'Olsen Twins.'"

I follow her gaze to the table where Emmy sits sipping limeade. Wow, she's beautiful.

Jen waves a hand in front of my face. "Earth to Rhys."

I struggle to shift my attention back to Jen.

"Dude, you've got it bad."

"Shut up." I pick up a rag and toss it at her.

She catches it and waves it like a white flag in surrender. "Just sayin'."

I set the metal plunger in the bucket of lemons and begin stomping lemonade. I feel ridiculous. The stupid hat, the stupid shorts, the stupid stomping motion that makes me feel like a stupid monkey pumping an old-fashioned push car. But then I look up and find Emmy watching me with smile on her face. Not an amused smile. Or an embarrassed-by-what-I-do-to-make-a-living smile . . . just a happy smile. Supe can't be right about her. "Can I ask you a question?"

"Sure." Jen tosses the rag into a bucket of bleach water in the corner.

"Supe said something the other day about my dating Emmy, and it's made me think."

"Okay . . ."

"Is it that big of a deal that I'm not a member?"

The skin around Jen's eyes crinkles. "Truth?" She releases a lungful of air as she leans against the counter across from me. "It is a big deal. But I think you already know that. Why haven't you told her?"

I cross my arms over my chest. "In the beginning, I didn't say anything because it wasn't her business. We were only study partners, and I was keeping up with the work. And then when we started to become friends, I wanted her to get to know me for me and not just as that nonmember guy. I tried to keep things casual by only meeting to study and taking her out on one group date, but then she met my mom, and things got real, and . . . I fell for her." I pause. "Now we're dating, and Supe said some stuff that makes me think not being a member is going to be some huge deal."

"You need to talk to her, Rhys."

I scrub a hand down my face. "I've screwed everything up, haven't I?"

Jen bumps her foot into mine. "It's not over till it's over."

"That's exactly what I'm afraid of."

Jen winces. "That didn't come out right."

Whether it came out right or not doesn't make it any less true. What if I'm wrong about Emmy? What if when I tell her she walks away? I spend the rest of my shift at war with myself about when and how to tell her. While not telling her isn't something I did with malice, it's become a thing. A thing I don't know how to deal with. The only thing I do know is that the longer I don't tell her, the harder it is to do. The next time we're together, I have to confess.

Chapter Twenty-Four

Emmy

Pas de chat [pah / duh / shah] v—Like a cat stepping

"YOU NEVER TAKE OFF YOUR shoes." Rhys pulls out the last of my bobby pins, and my hair cascades down my back. I meant to change into comfy clothes after church, but Rhys was already here when I got home, so I'm still in my black dress and ballet flats.

"Of course I do!" I shut the blue Book of Mormon in my lap and set it aside. It's clear neither of us is focused on studying for our BOM midterm anymore.

"Let me clarify." He runs his hands through my hair and watches the strands fall through his fingers. "You never take off your shoes around *me*."

He's right. I don't. And if I can help it, I never will. I stare at him with a blank expression, hoping he'll let the subject drop.

"No response?" he asks, amused.

Of course he doesn't let it drop. He never lets anything drop. I shrug, and his hand falls from my hair. He leans toward me, and I back away. "What are you doing?"

"Getting rid of your mental block." He lunges at my feet.

I stand up and run into the kitchen, half giggling, half terrified he's going to pry my shoes off and see my abused feet.

He runs after me.

"Don't even think about it!" I stand on one side of the kitchen island, and Rhys stands on the other.

"Let me get this straight." He takes a slow step toward me. "You'll hold my hand, you'll kiss me, but you refuse to take off your shoes in front of me?"

I give him a definitive nod. "Pretty much, yep."

He chuckles. "I can't tell you how weird that is." He prowls around the island like a cat stalking its prey. I fake left, and he goes right, jetting around the island so fast I barely get away.

Squealing, I run back to the couch and sit on my feet. He all but pounces on me.

"Rhys! No, don't. Please!" I scream between fits of laughter.

Heavy footfalls pound down the stairs, distracting Rhys.

"Get off of her!" Evie shouts, a curling iron clenched between her white knuckles.

"Whoa!" Rhys jumps to his feet and holds his hands up in the air. "It's not what it looks like."

Evie raises the curling iron higher.

I scramble off the couch and stand protectively in front of Rhys. "We're playing. I'm okay."

"You were screaming!" Evie glares at Rhys.

"He was trying to take off my shoes."

Her eyes sink to my shoes, then move to Rhys before finally landing on me. "Your shoes?"

"Yeah. I, uh, don't want him to see my mangled dancer feet."

Evie lowers the curling iron to her side.

Rhys clears his throat behind me. "You won't take off your shoes because you think I won't like your feet?"

"Umm, maybe?"

Evie rolls her eyes and trudges back up the stairs shaking her head.

Rhys steps closer. His fingers brush the hair off my shoulders, and his breath tickles my cheek. "You think your *mangled dancer feet* are going to scare me away?"

"Yes!"

He lets out a little puff of air, not quite a laugh but not a grunt either, just an amused, breathy chuckle. "It's going to take a lot more than your feet to break us up," he whispers.

As I turn to face him, his grip on my waist tightens and my stomach free-falls—the same way it does when I take center stage for a performance and the spotlight is about to turn on. His lips touch mine so gently I barely feel it. I close my eyes, expecting to feel the pressure of his kiss, but it doesn't come again. When I open my eyes, he's watching me with a grin.

Did Evie turn up the heater? "It's hot in here. Like insanely hot, right?" I fan myself with one hand, and his grin grows. "I think we should take a walk."

He looks out the front window into the pitch-black night and raises an eyebrow. "It's freezing outside. Literally. I think it's supposed to snow tonight."

"Snow is good. I like snow. Don't you like snow? Everybody likes snow, right?"

He sucks his bottom lip into his mouth as if to stop himself from laughing at my discomfort. "Sure, angel. Let's take a walk. But you should change your shoes in case it snows." His eyes move down to my feet. "I can help if you want." He winks.

"Yeah, I think I'll pass." I inch around him, then dash up the stairs. I slip off my church shoes and pull on a warm pair of ankle booties.

Before I go back downstairs, I walk to Evie's room to let her know Rhys and I are leaving.

Evie's door is closed, but I can still hear her heated phone conversation. It's probably Q. Things have still been strained between them. She hasn't gone out with him every night, and his phone calls have become less frequent. I don't know what's going on, but she deserves someone who will treat her better. Instead of interrupting her conversation completely, I call "Be back later" through the door and then jog down the stairs.

Rhys is sitting on the couch lacing his boots. A stair squeaks under my foot, and he glances up. "All set?"

"Almost." I grab my carnation-pink coat off a hook by the door. I've always loved the black-and-white polka-dot lining, and I'm excited it's finally cold enough to wear it.

Rhys stands from the couch and walks over to help me into it.

"Thank you," I say.

"My pleasure."

As soon as we open the door, a gust of wind bursts into the room. I jump back, and Rhys slams the door. "You sure you want to go for a walk?" he asks.

My eyes are drawn to his kissable lips. "Walk. Yes. We should walk."

Rhys lets out a deep breath. "Mexicans aren't built for cold weather." He opens the door, and we step outside. "I must really like you," he mumbles.

"I. H-have an. Idea," I say between shivers.

"Does it have anything to do with a heater? The indoors, maybe? Because I want you to know I'd be okay with that idea."

I nudge him with my elbow, and he catches it and tucks me into his side. He smells like something masculine and clean. Like Rhys. I take another deep breath.

"No," I say. "I was thinking we could go tunnel singing."

"At the risk of sounding redundant, I fully support going back inside."

"Have you ever been?" I ask him.

"Inside? Yes, I have. It's wonderful. Warm. Toasty. Very hospitable."

I tilt my head back until I'm staring into his dark-chocolate eyes. "I meant tunnel singing."

He schools a playful grin. "I can't say that I have."

"We have to go, then. But we'll have to drive."

"Oh, thank heaven. Is this tunnel heated?"

"No. It's outside in front of the Marriott Center." I thought everyone went freshman year. It's like a rite of passage. "You've really never been?"

"Do I look like a singer?"

My eyes narrow. "Is this a trick question? Because I vaguely remember you asking me a similar question the night you took me dancing, and it turns out you can seriously dance."

"I feel like we keep having this conversation," he says. "For the record, I asked you if I looked like a *ballet* dancer. You said no. I never said I couldn't dance."

"And I repeat: se-man-tics."

His laugh is deep. "I don't sing."

"Not even in the shower? At church?"

"Not even in the shower."

I shake my head. "You're impossible."

"You love me though." He freezes, and I suck in a breath.

I like him. I like him a lot. But to love someone, you have to know more about them. You can't fall in love with someone in one month. Can you? I didn't think so, but Lucy did, and so has Evie . . . Maybe I've always just been too focused on ballet to fall so quickly. Maybe being in the corps has been a good thing after all.

"That's not . . . I mean I *do* like you." His eyes dart from me to the ground to his truck.

I try not to laugh at his discomfort. There's only room for so much awkward in one relationship, so I give him a free pass. "Which is why we're going to get in your truck and drive to the tunnel by the Marriott Center and sing."

He exercises his jaw like he wants to say something, and I giggle.

"You can't let things drop when you didn't even want to pick them up in the first place. I like you, and I'm pretty sure you like me too. Let's just . . . be."

He studies me for a long moment. "Be. Right. I can *be*."

"Good. Me too. Let's go *be* at tunnel singing." I nod toward his truck, and he leaps into action, opening the passenger-side door for me. As soon as we're both inside, he turns on the heat. Unfortunately, the truck is cold and icy air blows out of the vents. He shuts off the air, and we drive toward the tunnel, shivering. I rub my hands together, but it doesn't help.

Rhys reaches for my hand, brings it to his mouth, and blows. His warm breath starts a fire in my hands that ignites my entire body. I have a feeling *being* isn't going to last long.

Chapter Twenty-Five

Rhys

Peculiar people [pi-kyool-yer / pee-pl] n—One stereotype Mormons live up to; tunnel singing. Enough said

WE PULL INTO THE MARRIOTT Center parking lot, and the clouds look like they're going to burst overhead.

I pull into a space and think of the night Emmy and I shared ice cream at the Creamery. I nod in the direction of where we were through the windshield. "Remember when we—"

"I'll never forget," she finishes, seemingly reading my mind.

"Promise me."

Her brow momentarily flexes with tension, but a smile relaxes it away. "Rhys, I promise you I will never, ever forget that night." A playful glint darkens her eyes. "That was the night you dropped me off and growled about my car."

I shake my head. "I'm serious, Emmy."

"Me too. You were pretty grumpy that night."

My gaze lingers on her face, taking in the way her blue eyes shine in the moonlight and how her hands move as if driven by some silent music only her ears can hear. Her cheeks tinge with pink when she catches me staring.

I have to tell her.

"You okay?" she asks.

How do I explain myself?

"Rhys?" Emmy tugs my hand, yanking me out of my thoughts.

"I'm fine." I reassure her with a smile as I cut the engine, then hurry around the front of the truck. When I open the door, she's smiling up at me. My breath hitches. "Wow, you're beautiful."

Emmy grins at my compliment, then smooths her dress. It's black. And hugs her curves and is without doubt the sexiest thing I've ever seen. She stands, and I offer her my arm—not that I have much practice with that sort of thing, but it seems like something Emmy would like. The frosty air nips at our exposed skin, and she tucks her hand into the crook of my elbow as we hurry to the tunnel.

"Are you cold?" I ask.

Her dangly earrings swing back and forth as she shakes her head.

There's no snow on the ground now, but by the time I drop her off tonight, I'm sure everything will be covered with a white blanket.

We arrive at the tunnel, and Emmy picks up a hunter-green hymnal from a stack at the entrance and holds it out to me. I wasn't lying when I said I can't sing. I really can't. Reluctantly, I take it. BYU Tunnel Singers is embossed in gold across the bottom.

A group of students sway side to side in a circle in front of us, their arms clasped behind each other's backs. Several guys are dressed in suits and ties and shiny shoes, and most of the girls are wearing long skirts. I shuffle my beat-up boots, aware of how out of place I am here.

Emmy guides me to the front of a large circle, then stands inches in front of me. I wrap my arms around her waist, and she weaves her fingers with mine.

A song is announced, and Emmy flips to the page. With her back to my chest, I can feel her tiny frame inflate as she takes a deep breath and then slowly exhales the most beautiful sound I've ever heard as she sings the first word of the hymn.

Voices blend into one smooth melody and echo off the arched ceiling. Chills cover my arms, and warmth spreads out from my core. The song concludes, and the director calls out another. Emmy's nose crinkles. "I don't know this one."

That makes two of us. She starts to sing but almost immediately stops. The words are so small, and this darkened tunnel must make it difficult for her to even see the words, let alone read them. On the second line, she mixes up the lyrics by switching the word order, and she deflates in my arms.

The tunnel singers keep singing what should be a beautiful melody, but it's awkward, and the timing is off. If Emmy weren't so uncomfortable, it would be funny.

I rub my hands up and down her arms, hoping my touch will calm her so she can regain her confidence and start singing again. But it doesn't work, so I loosen my hold around her and place my hand under hers on the spine of the hymnal and begin tracing the line.

My voice comes out scratchy and rough as I start to sing. The warm feeling inside me intensifies into a fire. At the fourth line, Emmy begins to sing again.

My throat constricts, and it's difficult to push the words out without choking on them. Despite my emotion, I continue singing. For her.

At the end of the first verse, Emmy looks over her shoulder and mouths, "Thank you."

I kiss her cheek. "No thank-you necessary."

A few students start the second verse, because I guess verse one wasn't painful enough, and the director waves off the song. The next song is called out, and I can tell by the way Emmy's shoulders relax that she has the words of this one memorized.

After several more hymns, it's late. The director says it's mission-call time, and several people walk into the center of the circle. A scrawny guy whose suit is at least two sizes too big announces his mission call to Mexico. He pumps a fist above his head, and a chuckle escapes my lips. Emmy elbows me in the ribs.

More mission calls: Africa, Germany, Canada. All over the world. After the last call, the group launches into a song I've heard around campus before. Everyone gets really into it. Even my heart starts to pump a little faster. Fast enough that I start to feel warm again. When the song ends, the hymnbooks close, and gradually the warmth in the tunnel extinguishes. Students stack their books and then hurry into the dark night. When we get to the mouth of the tunnel, Emmy's eyes grow wide. "Rhys, look! It's snowing."

My focus moves from Emmy to the night sky. White flurries circle in the air around us. She drops my hand and takes a few steps away. She lifts her face to the sky, then twirls in a circle. Her hair catches the air and fans out like a flamenco dancer's skirt.

"This is my favorite day." Her eyes sparkle in the moonlight when she stops spinning.

I have a love-hate relationship with the first snowfall—I love how it looks, hate how long the season it ushers in lasts. She reaches her arms out to me, and I hurry over and scoop her into my arms. Her head tilts up to the sky again, but my eyes stay on her. "This is your favorite day of the year, huh?"

She nods her head. "Ever."

I wipe a delirious grin off my mouth. Her favorite day ever. "Me too, angel. Me too."

I've felt alone for so long, but in this moment, with Emmy holding on to me, I feel like this problem, like my life, isn't so bad. Every curve ball life has thrown at me, every setback and restart and fail isn't without a silver lining. Because it's led me to her.

My heart speeds up, heating my body all the way to my core, and something shifts between us. I search Emmy's eyes to see if she can feel it too. But it's too dark, and I can't tell if she does or not.

I know she'd rather let things *be*, but this intense feeling bubbling inside my chest is like nothing I've ever experienced before, and I need to know if she feels it too. I kiss her softly. Once, twice, and then I rest my forehead against hers. "Please tell me you feel that," I whisper.

Her eyes glisten in the pale moonlight. "I feel it," she says, her voice shaking.

Our lips meet again, and I never want to stop kissing her.

The thought paralyzes me.

When I don't move, she pulls back and smiles up at me.

My heart starts to pound so hard in my chest it feels like I'm going to explode. This is the moment Supe talked about. The moment when everything changes. We're more than just friends. She's my girlfriend. I feel more, and no matter how much I want to, I can't just let things be.

I have to tell her.

The tips of her fingers tickle the back of my neck, sending warm shivers down my spine. "Rhys?"

"I'll never forget the way you look tonight. You're so beautiful."

She studies me for so many seconds I think she must see right through me.

"I need to talk to you about something. Can we sit?" I look for a bench and find one farther down the walkway, nestled under a tree.

Her eyebrows furrow, and she nods.

We walk a few feet and reach the bench. I drop a lingering kiss on her forehead, and she pushes off my chest slightly to look up at me with her big blue eyes. I can't imagine not looking into them every day.

"I've fallen in love with you," I whisper into her hair. "Every single part of you. You are good and kind and smart and brave."

"I love you too."

Her lack of hesitation causes my heart to clench. Maybe this can wait another day or two. Tonight has been perfect and . . . No.

I have to tell her. I search for words that will make it okay. Words that will explain why I didn't tell her and how I feel about her now, but they don't come. How did we get here? I stagger onto the bench, sitting before the weight of my confession makes me fall.

"Are you okay?"

I rest my elbows on my knees and scrub a hand over my head. "No. I'm not . . ."

She takes a step closer, and my gaze falls to her feet.

"Y-you're scaring me," she says.

Her wavering voice guts me. I take a deep breath and then flush out the words I don't want to say. "I'm not Mormon, Emmy."

Chapter Twenty-Six
Emmy

Écarté [ay-har-tay] a—Thrown wide apart

MY SHARP INTAKE OF BREATH cuts through the too-quiet night. "But . . . we met in Book of Mormon class," I hear myself say.

"Nonmembers are required to take Book of Mormon too," he whispers.

"You knew the answers though. And"—my eyes flick to his collar—"you wear—"

"An undershirt."

Several seconds pass, and I try to decipher his confession. "Why?" I ask.

"If you don't want to be a social pariah, you learn pretty quickly to look like you fit in."

I shake my head. "No. Why didn't you tell me you aren't . . . That you—" I can't get the words out.

"I didn't tell you in the beginning because I didn't think you needed to know. We were only study partners, and I had done my homework, so I knew I wouldn't hold us back. And I didn't tell you later because I didn't know how."

Okay. This is okay. We're going to be fine. He loves me. And I love him . . . and he goes to school at BYU. He's not a member yet, but . . . wait. "You are planning to be baptized, right?"

His jaw jumps under sudden pressure. "No."

"No?"

He looks up, completely destroyed. "No, I'm not a member. And no, I'm not planning to be," he whispers.

Everything blurs. My world crumbles beneath my feet, and I can't sort through the pieces fast enough to understand what they mean or how they fit together. Nausea and vertigo threaten my ability to stand. Rhys jumps to his feet with his hand outstretched like he means to steady me.

"No." I take a stumbling step away.

His shoulders sag, and he retreats.

"This doesn't make sense."

"I know." His voice shakes. "I'm sorry. I should have told you sooner."

Tears spring to my eyes, but I blink them back and blink and blink and blink, refusing to let them fall. And then I can't stop blinking and shaking, and strong arms encircle me, and it would be so easy to melt into his embrace, but I'm confused, so I push him away and take a step back and then another and another, and then I'm walking away and whispering no and trying to figure out what just happened. How in one sentence we went from I love you to over. Anger pools in my stomach, and I whip back around to face him. "Why?" I demand. "Why would you do this to me? To us? Why?"

"Please, Emmy."

"Please, w-what?"

"Don't walk away from me," he pleads. "I lov—"

"No." I hold up a hand between us. "Do not say you love me. I don't even know who you are."

He recoils as if I slapped him. "You don't know who I am?" He repeats each word, his voice reflecting more hurt than anger. "Because I'm not Mormon, you think you don't know me?" He rubs his neck and lets out a heavy breath.

I press my fingers to my temples to stop my racing thoughts. "Why did you let me think . . ."

"I wanted to tell you so many times, but then . . ." He shakes his head.

"But then?" There has to be some explanation that will make this go away. Like maybe this is some elaborate joke. Or a test or something.

"I fell in love with you," he says.

My heart breaks. And then breaks again. It breaks until there's nothing left except splintered fragments of him mixed with fractured pieces of me and tattered scraps of what our relationship used to be.

I press my eyes shut, wishing this nightmare would end.

I feel his trembling fingers lace through mine. "Please," he begs. "Say something."

It doesn't make any sense. Any of it. That he isn't a member. That he kept the truth from me. That he's the person I want to comfort me.

I don't know what to say because I'm not sure how I feel or what this means. "I have to leave."

His shoulders slump, and he bows his head to the pavement. He nods, keeping his gaze on the ground. I turn to leave.

"Wait." The desperation in his voice stops me before I can even take a step. "I'm worried if you walk away I'm never going to see you again," he says. "And that scares the snot out of me because I've never felt like this, and I can't imagine not feeling this every day."

Me neither. But I can't stay. "Go." My voice trembles.

"What?"

"Please leave. I can't . . ."

"Emmy, I'm not going to leave you here alone." His eyes scan the abandoned tunnel. "Please let me drive you home."

My mind jumps back to the last time he drove me home. When we sat in his truck and he told me about his mother's condition, about him attending UCAL . . . I think of the dozens of different comments he's made since that night that I should have put together. How he didn't go on a mission. Or answer when I asked what time he got out of church. All this time. How did I not know? I feel so stupid.

Every fiber in my body wants to run, but he'd follow to make sure I'm safe. Instead, I walk back to the bench and call Evie to come pick me up.

She pulls up ten minutes later. "Are you okay?"

I shake my head. Evie looks over my shoulder at Rhys and then protectively puts her arm around me as we walk back to her car.

As soon as we're inside, she starts the ignition and drives away. "What happened?"

How can I possibly explain what happened tonight?

"Em, you're scaring me. Talk to me."

"He's in love with me," I whisper.

"You don't feel the same?"

"Of course I do." How can I not?

"But you don't think you can be together because of ballet?" Evie guesses.

If only it were that easy. "It's not about ballet."

"Will you tell me what's wrong?"

I tell Evie about tunnel singing and the snow and how Rhys told me he loved me and how he ruined everything with his confession.

"What are you going to do?" she asks.

"What can I do? He's not a member . . . and I want to get married in the temple."

"Have you talked to him? Asked what he does believe?"

"No."

"Maybe you should."

"I don't want to end up like Lucy."

"You're not Lucy, and Rhys isn't Jeff. Rhys isn't what you thought, but . . . I saw you guys earlier. You've never looked so happy."

My throat constricts. As much as I'm hurting because of the truth he kept hidden, I still want him to be the one to hold me right now. My breaths start to hiccup, and Evie lays a soft hand on my shoulder. "It's going to be okay," she soothes.

Chapter Twenty-Seven

Rhys

*Choice and accountability [choys / and / uh-koun-tuh-bil-i-tee] n—The right
to make a decision and the responsibility to answer for it*

IT'S ONLY BEEN TWELVE HOURS, but it feels like a lifetime since I held her in
my arms. I have to make her understand how much I love her and that we
can make this work.

I get to class first and sit in our spot. She slips in right before class starts.
I'm not surprised that she doesn't sit by me, but it hurts more than I thought
it would. I finish the test quickly, then spend the rest of the hour staring at
her back.

"Brother Solario. Sister Jennings," Brother Clark says. "Time's up. I need
to collect your exams."

Emmy sets down her pencil, then chews her finger as she stares down at
her test.

I jump to my feet. "She's not done yet. You need to give her more time.
She's dysl—"

"It's fine." Emmy holds up a hand but doesn't look back at me. "I'm finished." She collects her belongings, hands over her test, and dashes out of the
room.

I run to catch her, shoving my test at Brother Clark as I pass. "Wait up," I
call after her. Already halfway down the hall, she stops, and I close the distance
between us. "Are you okay?" I ask.

With her back to me, she wraps her arms around herself, clutching the
lapels of her favorite pink coat. "No."

My heart stutters when she turns to face me. Her eyes are puffy and red
rimmed. I yearn to hold her in my arms and reassure her that everything is going

to be okay. But we aren't there yet. First I have to make her see how this will work. Resisting the urge to reach out to her, I stuff my hands in my pockets. "I should have told you sooner," I say. "It wasn't fair of me not to say anything, but will you let me explain?"

Her eyes search my face, and I hate myself for being the cause of the pain reflected in them. Finally, she nods.

"When I first moved here to take care of Mom, I didn't understand Mormon culture. I tried again and again to make friends and to date, but as soon as anyone found out I wasn't Mormon and that I had no interest in joining the Church, they disappeared."

Water pools in Emmy's eyes, and she lifts her chin, refusing to let the tears fall.

"But you were different. You got to know me for me and not for what religion I wrote on my application. I convinced myself that you were my study partner and my religion wasn't your business. But then I got to know you, and no matter how hard I tried not to fall for you, one thing led to the next, and—"

"It was too late," she finishes.

"Yeah."

"I understand, Rhys. Really, I do. I know you only wanted to be accepted for who you are. I'm not mad about that—"

"But you *are* mad."

"I'm hurt. And confused." Her chin quivers. "I don't know what to do."

I grab her hands and bend slightly to look into her eyes. "I know it will take time for you to trust me again—"

"This isn't about trust," she cuts me off. "I mean it is, but there's so much more to it than that."

"I know." And I do. But I also know the way I feel isn't like anything I've ever felt before, and I'm not walking away without a fight. "Emmy." I press her hand to my chest so she can feel my racing heart. "I know I messed up. Bigtime. But we have something amazing. Something that doesn't come around often."

"I think so too, but—"

"I meant what I said last night." I release her hand and place a finger under her chin, encouraging her to look at me. "I'm in love with you, Emmy. Tell me you don't feel the same, and I'll walk away."

She presses her eyes shut and drops her head to her chest. "I do love you, but—"

"All I'm asking for is a chance. To see what this can be. Will you give it to me?"

Chapter Twenty-Eight

Emmy

Cabriole [kab-ree-ohl] n—Caper

"DID YOU HEAR?" DAVID ASKS as soon as I walk into ballet Monday evening for rehearsal.

"Hear what?" My brain is so fuzzy from everything that happened last night and the midterm and everything Rhys said that even if I had heard, I'm not sure I'd remember.

"World's best dancer? Coming to BYU?"

I scrunch my nose in an I-have-no-clue-what-you're-talking-about face and drop my bag with a thud to the Marley.

"André Dupont is the visiting choreographer next semester," David says with a laugh. "It's been all over social media. You really didn't know?"

"I've been kind of distracted."

David smirks. "Having a significant other will do that to you."

I plop to the floor at the mention of Rhys.

"I thought you'd be ecstatic. This is huge."

I shrug and dig through my bag for my kit, trying to bury my thoughts in the familiar routine.

David frowns. "If you're worried about not having the solo this semester, don't be. Not having the lead this semester should only help your chances of getting it next semester when André is here."

"Yeah, maybe." I'd be lying if I said I didn't care about André coming to BYU. And I do want the solo, but after the slew of emotions I've gone through since last night—and honestly, the lack of sleep—I can't begin to think about ballet, let alone worry about André Dupont seeing me flounder around the studio.

David sits and pulls on his ballet slippers. He looks at me sideways several times like he's trying to gauge my hormonal levels, and I begin taping the hot spots on my toes. "Are you okay?" he asks.

"Fine. I just need to dance."

He nods, and I'm grateful that, unlike Rhys, David doesn't pursue the conversation.

I slide on my pointe shoes, lace them, and then walk to the *barre*. Piano music fills the studio, and my body goes into autopilot as we begin stretching. I don't think about the motions or what stretch comes next. I simply do. My body relaxes, and my brain clears.

The warm-up ends, and we come to the center. David lightly sets his hand on my waist in preparation for partnered pirouettes, but it isn't his hands I feel. It's Rhys's.

Ballet Master Miller counts the introduction, and I miss the first step, earning a quirked brow from David. "You sure you're okay?" he whispers.

I nod, but even I don't believe me. We rehearse the routine, and Rhys is there at every turn and with each breath, and no matter how many times I try to push him from my mind, he's there. I miss a count and then another, and though David doesn't say anything, I can tell he's frustrated, and so is everyone else because Ballet Master Miller makes us repeat the combination until we all get it right. Finally, I make it through the entire variation without any mistakes and we're released.

I don't bother showering before changing and hurrying to my car. I just want to get home.

When I turn down the street to our house, I'm surprised to see Q's truck parked in front and even more surprised to see him crouched on the driveway. I pull up to the curb, and he springs to his feet. I roll down the passenger side window, and Q jogs over. "Do you think she'll say yes?"

My heart stops for a second, but I manage to ask, "What do you mean, 'Say yes'?"

Q smirks at what must be a half-confused, half-panicked expression on my face because he points with his thumb covered in chalk dust to the driveway. "To giving me another chance."

Not to marrying him. I sigh in relief. "Yes. I think she'll give you another chance."

The tension in his face slackens into a sincere smile, and I catch a glimpse of the man my sister says she loves.

"I was going to play the guitar to get her to come outside and then apologize for being a less-than-stellar boyfriend. Is that too cheesy?"

Maybe Q knows Evie better than I've given him credit for. "Evie loves cheesy."

Q scratches the side of his head and looks back at the driveway. I follow his gaze over his shoulder to read the chalk message he's written on the driveway. It's a simple but sweet apology.

"You did good, Q. She'll love it."

He nods once and then steps away from my SUV so I can park.

I walk into the house and up the stairs, entering my bedroom just in time to hear Q strum his guitar. His voice isn't as deep or as husky as it was the night he sang at the party, but I like it better. More genuine, maybe.

A few minutes later, I hear Evie pad down the stairs. I hurry over to the window. Q says something I don't hear to Evie, and she replies with a nod. She swipes at her cheeks and then leans in to kiss Q.

I walk away from the window, giving them privacy, and sit on my bed.

Before last night, my world was black and white: I didn't date nonmembers. Everything was simple. Everything was easy. Everything was decided. But now? Colors are colliding and tumbling and morphing like I'm trapped inside a kaleidoscope. I'm confused and hurt and angry, but more than anything, I'm in love with Rhys. Rhys who isn't a member and doesn't plan to be.

I'm not sure where that leaves us. I didn't plan to fall for someone who doesn't believe what I do, but I did. Evie said I should give our relationship a chance, but I'm not sure that's a good idea because the reality is he may never accept the gospel.

I should pray about whether continuing to date Rhys is the right decision. But I'm tired and discouraged, and the truth is I already know what I'm going to do whether it's a good idea or not.

I'm going to give us a chance.

November

Chapter Twenty-Nine
Rhys

Repentance /ree-pen-tǝns/ n—Trying to make up for the past so you can move on with the future

I HAVE ONE SHOT, AND I'm not going to screw it up. Tonight has to be perfect. It's been almost a week since I've seen her, and the thought of doing it again seems impossible. I have to make her understand that we can make this work.

I run my hands through my still-wet hair, sending water droplets over the room. I pull some product through my hair and then tug on my coat.

Supe looks up from the TV when I walk into the living room.

"Going somewhere?" he asks.

"Date."

Supe's eyebrows shoot up. "So things went well when you told her, then?"

I shrug. "As good as could be expected, I guess."

"So tonight . . ."

"I'm taking her dancing again at Joe's." I'm hoping that will remind her why we're so good together.

Supe mutes the TV. "It's not a bad idea."

"But?"

"Is her forgetting why she likes you really the problem?"

No. The problem is that she thinks she doesn't know me. Taking her to Joe's is my attempt to show her where we first connected. Where I first tried to show her what I'm really like. To remind her I'm still me. But maybe Supe's right; maybe that isn't what needs to be addressed. "Maybe you're right. But I'm picking her up in ten minutes, and I don't have a backup plan." I sit on the arm of the couch and rack my brain to come up with a better date. "Any ideas?"

"Dinner? Walk around the mall?" His face crunches up, showing he's as unimpressed with his suggestions as I am. "Yeah. Not my best work."

I let out a heavy breath. This might be my one and only shot to show her that I love her and, even though I'm not a member, I support her. That's it. She needs to know that even though I'm not a member, no matter what my beliefs are, I support her in hers. A plan forms in my mind. "Can I borrow a white shirt and tie?" I ask Supe.

"Sure, man. Borrow whatever you want. Where are you taking her?"

"The mother ship." I go change, then hurry out to my truck. The streets to her house are familiar to me and are a blur. I leave the truck running so the heater will stay warm, and I smooth my coat as I walk to her door. I don't remember ever being as nervous as when I knock on her door.

"I don't want to talk about it," Emmy says as soon as she opens the door.

"Okay . . ." Not what I was expecting.

"Because I've been retracing every conversation we've ever had, and the thing is, I'm upset, Rhys. And not just because you didn't tell me—because I think I understand why you didn't—but because I'm in love with you and I'm not sure there's anything you can say or do that will make things work between us."

She's mad. Of course she is. I expected that, but she also said she loves me and that even though she isn't sure how things can work, she's here, so that means she *wants* us to work. I can't help smiling.

"Don't look at me like that," she says, her cheeks turning the same color as her pink pastel coat.

"Like what?"

"Like you know what I'm thinking."

"If I knew what you were thinking, I wouldn't be so nervous right now."

"You're nervous?"

"Aren't you?"

Her smile has never been so sweet. "Yes."

"So you don't want to talk about it. What do you want to talk about?"

She frowns. "I hadn't gotten that far."

"Can I take you to dinner?"

"Yes. But . . . this doesn't mean everything is suddenly okay. It's all still there. I just don't know what to do about it, and instead of tiptoeing around in awkwardness all night, I'd rather hold your hand and soak up whatever time we have. Okay?"

I take a step toward her and use a piece of hair that's fallen across her cheek as an excuse to touch her. My hands shake slightly as I tuck it behind her ear. "Okay," I say quietly. This can't be a good idea, but I don't really have the right to tell her what is or is not a good idea right now. I help her into the truck, and since we're ignoring everything, the second I sit down, I reach for her hand.

"So," she says. "How'd you do on your midterm?"

I chance a sideways glance at her. I expected things to be weird, but pretending like nothing happened feels *really* weird. "Okay, I think. You?"

"Fine. Considering I got stuck with the absolute worst-case scenario for a study partner."

Ouch. The jab is warranted but stings. "I think I held up my end of the bargain okay."

Emmy's nose scrunches up. "What? Oh. No. I was talking about you being a distraction. A very, *very* nice distraction."

"Am I?"

She pulls her legs underneath her and leans against the center console to kiss my cheek. "Obnoxiously so."

I squeeze her fingers, and she smiles.

"I'm not sure how I did. We might want to put in a little more study time the rest of the semester."

The rest of the semester. She pictures us being together the rest of the semester. My whole body relaxes a little.

The drive to Salt Lake goes quickly, which is good because it isn't awkward but bad because every second we don't talk about me not being a member is one less second I have to convince her we can work.

"I can't believe it took me this long to figure it out," she says as we exit the freeway in Salt Lake. "I know where you're taking me."

"Oh yeah?"

"Joe's, right?" She bounces in her seat a little.

I consider ditching the plan B date in favor of spending the night dancing in each other's arms, but I decide Joe's, as enticing as it is, would make it difficult to talk and impossible to convince her that I support her. "Nope. Guess again."

Emmy does this cute pouty thinking face. She even taps her index finger against her cheek. I turn the corner, and our destination looms in front of us. She sucks in a breath, and I glance over to see that her expression has become guarded. Almost guilty?

"Is that where we're going?" She points at the lit spires of the Salt Lake Temple and then looks at me.

"Actually, we're going there." I shift her index finger slightly to the right, pointing it at the Joseph Smith Memorial Building. "There's a nice restaurant on the top floor. Is that okay?"

She lets out her breath. "Yes. Perfect." She sounds relieved. Why does she sound relieved? The point of this night was to take her to the temple so I could prove how much I support her. That won't work if she doesn't want to be here.

"I thought we could walk around Temple Square after."

Her brow knits together. "You want to walk around Temple Square?"

She doesn't get it. She has no clue how into her I am. "Why wouldn't I? There's a visitors' center, right? Like, with statues and art?"

She doesn't answer right away, and I wonder what she's thinking. "Well. Yes, but . . . are you sure you want to go there?"

"You mean because I'm not a member?"

"Well . . ." She bites her lip. "Yeah."

I pull to the side of the road and park in a metered stall. "Will you do me a favor?"

"Okay."

"Try not to treat me differently tonight."

"I thought that's what I was doing."

"No. You're avoiding the subject."

Her gaze flicks up to the temple and then lowers to her hands wringing in her lap.

"And I'm okay with that . . ." I reassure her by folding her hand into mine. "For now. But we're going to have to talk at some point tonight."

"I know . . . I just . . . I'm not sure how to feel, let alone act."

"We have a lot to figure out. I get that, but you don't have to think about how to act, okay? I'm still me."

"I know. That's why I'm giving us a chance."

* * *

"Thank you for dinner," Emmy says as soon as we exit the Joseph Smith Memorial Building. "It was delicious."

It *was* delicious: prime rib, au gratin potatoes, rolls to die for. We were even seated next to the window with a perfect view of the temple. I caught her looking longingly at it more than once, but she tried to hide it when she noticed me staring. "You're welcome. So . . . visitors' center?"

"If you're sure."

"I am."

We walk into the temple courtyard through a tall black gate. There are several buildings, the most majestic being the temple. To our left, Emmy points out the South Visitors' Center—apparently there are two. In front of that is a darker gray building that looks like a smaller version of the temple, though not as white and not as tall. There's a domed building she calls a tabernacle and, next to that is the other visitors' center—the North Visitors' Center. It sits in front of a courtyard and is the most modern of the buildings. We walk inside, and though I can tell she's trying to contain her excitement, it still shows.

Girl missionaries meet us at the door. They look about our age, maybe younger, and I wonder if Emmy considered going on a mission. Supe went on one, but I remember him saying girls didn't have to. "Welcome to the North Visitors' Center. Would you like a tour?"

Emmy looks up at me. "Do you want . . . ?"

"Why don't you just show me?"

She nods, and the missionaries walk away. We look at several large pictures of Jesus Christ. They're . . . large. And . . . nice, I guess, but all I can think about is that we still haven't talked and we really, really need to. We walk to the next painting—a picture of Christ in all white surrounded by white puffy clouds and angels.

Emmy squeezes my hand, and when I look at her, her eyes are filled with tears. I can't say I understand her reaction, and I don't feel what she does, but that's not important. She just needs to know I support her in this, so I rub her knuckles with my thumb and smile. A tear rolls down her cheek. I wipe it away.

"Do you want to see the other visitors' center?" she asks hopefully.

"Okay."

She tells me about the temple as we walk to the South Visitors' Center. Bits of trivia I won't remember by the time we get to the next building.

A grandma missionary, Sister Kerns, meets us at the door this time. She also asks us if we want a tour. This time Emmy says yes.

"This is my boyfriend, Rhys. It's his first time here. He isn't a member."

I'm not sure why Emmy feels the need to introduce me this way or why it makes me uncomfortable, but it does. I do my best to let it go, and luckily this center is more interesting than the last, so it's easy to distract myself. The first exhibit is about the pioneers—Emmy's ancestors who walked across the plains and built the temple. I enjoy learning about her history because it helps me understand her better.

"It's incredible," I say.

"It is," Sister Kerns agrees. "Would you like to see a model of the inside of the temple?"

Emmy bites her lip, waiting for my response.

"Sure." It's probably the closest I'll ever come to going inside.

Emmy's hand tightens around mine as we walk deeper into the room. Sister Kerns shows us a paper model of the temple surrounded by glass. It really is amazing.

"It took forty years to construct the outside but only one to complete the ornate interior."

"Wow."

"Do you know why they persevered despite so much opposition?"

I can guess at the answer, but I'd rather she just tell me so Emmy and I can get back to what's important—me convincing her I support her.

"Because they understood the necessity of covenants in creating forever families."

Emmy holds her breath.

"What if I told you you could be with your mother and father and siblings forever? Would you want to learn more about that?"

Every muscle in my body freezes. No. I do not want to learn more about that.

Sister Kerns ushers us to a video before I can answer. I catch bits and pieces about forever families and the plan of happiness. Both Emmy and Sister Kerns are so happy and so touched, but the only thing I think is that my family doesn't look like that, and while I love Mom and Cami, I don't want to be with my entire family forever.

The video ends. Sister Kerns smiles warmly, and her eyes are misty. "I want you to know we will all have the opportunity to accept the gospel. To be eternal families."

"Everyone?"

"Yes."

I roll my shoulders. "Is there something I can sign to opt out?"

Emmy's eyes widen in shock, and I regret asking the question. Not because I don't mean it but because whatever ground Emmy and I had advanced tonight is now lost. She deserves to know how I really feel but not like this.

The smile on Sister Kerns' face slips. "I'm not sure I understand."

"Like if I don't want to be sealed to my family. Can I sign something so you won't use my name?" They have every right to believe whatever they want to believe, but I don't believe it, and even on paper, I don't want to be attached to *him*. If there's even a chance that the man who calls himself my father can worm his way back into my family—I can't let that happen. I have to protect Mom and Cami.

Sister Kerns looks at Emmy confused. "I'd better go check on my companion." She excuses herself. "It looks like you two have a lot to talk about."

We do, but now that I'm finally getting a chance, I'm not sure I want to have the conversation. Though I know we have to.

Emmy looks up at me. "I don't understand what just happened."

"I'm sorry. I was just caught off guard. I thought all that stuff, the temple and forever families and getting sealed, was just for members of your church, not for people who didn't believe in it."

Emmy bites her lip and nods but keeps her eyes down like she's trying not to cry. "Have you tried to believe?" Her voice shakes, and she looks almost as uncomfortable asking the question as I feel answering it.

"I went to church with Supe a few times. And I've read the Book of Mormon."

"D-did you pray about it?"

I've prayed two times in my life: once when Mom got sick and again when Dad walked out. Didn't change anything then, and it won't change anything now. "No. It's a nice idea, forever families. But it isn't for me." A person shouldn't have to try to believe something. You either believe it or you don't. And I don't.

"If you would pray, I know He'd answer."

She's not getting it. Tonight wasn't my attempt to prove to her that I could become a Mormon but rather that we could be good together despite it. "I'm not going to become a Mormon, Emmy."

She nods, but it's more of an I-hear-you type of nod than an I-accept-you type of nod. "Is there any chance that one day maybe you might?" Her eyes are so hopeful.

Everything inside me wants to tell her there's a chance. That I'll learn to believe. Think deeper, pray harder, read longer, but deep down, I know none of that will make a difference. God, even if He does exist, has never been concerned about me. A god like that isn't someone I want to put my faith in. "I'm sorry, but no."

Chapter Thirty

Emmy

Spot [spot] n—Focal point

I TRY NOT TO PANIC as we walk out of the visitors' center, but it's hard not to. Rhys has been to church. He's read the Book of Mormon. And he's not interested. Why? There has to be a reason. "Can I ask you a question?"

He stops walking and turns to face me. "Anything."

"Why wouldn't you want to be with your family forever?" My question is bold and seems to catch him by surprise, but the whole point of going out tonight was to explore if this relationship could work, and I'm worried that it's not going to. I owe it to both of us to voice my concerns.

Rhys swallows hard. "Mom and Cami, I do. My father I don't."

His father. Of course. "Were you ever close?"

Rhys works his jaw. "Once."

"What was he like?" Despite Rhys's obvious discomfort, I need to know.

He takes a moment before answering. "He worked a lot."

"When was the last time you saw him?"

"My eighth birthday. He bought me a bike."

"Did he teach you to ride it?" The bike doesn't matter. Whether he learned to ride it doesn't matter. But how Rhys feels about his father *does* matter.

"Yeah, he did."

I reach for Rhys's hand, hoping the contact will help him relax, and he intertwines our fingers. "I didn't know how to balance very well, but somehow I got myself going. I made it a few feet and then crashed." He chuckles. "Skinned my knee, started crying, the whole nine yards.

"I got back on the bike and pedaled as hard and as fast as I could, but I kept falling. Eventually Dad went inside, but I kept at it. I thought that if I could just learn to ride that bike, somehow, things would get better. Mom would smile, Dad would be proud, they'd stop fighting, and everything would be okay. It sounds so stupid now."

"It doesn't," I say.

"It took forever, but I finally got it. I rushed inside to tell Dad and found my parents fighting. They fought frequently, though, so I wasn't bothered by it. But then he turned around and we locked eyes, and even though I was young, I knew something was different about this fight.

"He told me I was the man of house now and to take care of Mom and Cami. That was the last time I saw him."

"I'm so sorry."

"Don't be. He's gone, and we're all better for it. Last I heard, he has a new family now."

I'm not sure what I was expecting, but it wasn't this. "So I'm guessing you don't hear from him often."

His eyebrows rise and then fall when he lets out a breath. "Once a year he sends a me a birthday card."

Rhys reads my pained expression and squeezes my hand. "I want you to know I'm nothing like him, Emmy. I would never abandon my family."

"I do know."

"I've made a few big mistakes, but I promise I'm willing to do everything I can to prove that you can trust me. We may have differences in religion, but I support you. I'm in this, okay? I love you, Emmy. I want this." His voice is as desperate as I feel.

Rhys is a good man. A great man. My man. He says he doesn't want forever with his family, but I think that's just because he hasn't seen what a forever family looks like and doesn't understand how happy one can be. But if he did, if he saw my family, maybe he'd have a change of heart. "I know it's just one weekend and that you're probably supposed to work, and of course I know you like to stay close to your mom, but Evie is taking Q home and . . . I'm not saying this right. That makes it sound like I'm asking you this because Evie is bringing Q home, and that's not what I mean. I'm asking because I want you there . . ."

Rhys looks like I've shot him with a stun gun. Features frozen. Eyes wide. I'm not making any sense. "Are you asking me to come home with you? For Thanksgiving?"

"Yes," I say quickly and then bite my lip. "Will you?"

He blinks several times like he's trying to come out of a trance. "You're sure?"

I barely have time to nod before he pulls me into his arms.

"I promise you won't regret this."

Chapter Thirty-One

Rhys

*Family home evening (FHE) [fam-uh-lee / hohm / eev-ning] n—A program
that gives groups of students an excuse to gather for social activities*

MONDAY NIGHT AFTER WORKING AN eight-hour shift, I kick my shoes off and
sink into bed. Emmy should be getting home from FHE soon. I want to call her,
but I need to call my sister before she goes to bed. It rings several times before she
answers.

"To what do I owe this unexpected pleasure?" Cami says.

I laugh. "It hasn't been that long since we last talked."

"No. But it's been a long time since *you've* called *me*."

As sad as that is, it's probably true.

"What's up, big brother?"

Instead of answering right away, I let out a breath. I should be able to handle this without having to ask for help, but Mom needs assistance, and Emmy
wants me to go home with her, and there's no way I can do both—not without
Cami. "I need help with Mom."

"Is everything, okay? Is she getting worse? What's going on?"

"Mom's fine, Cam. She's had a few setbacks, but she's all right."

"Be honest. How bad is she?"

Telling Cami the truth about Mom is not something I want to do, but she
should know. "She's relapsing," I admit. "But she's been taking her meds again
for about a month now, and she's able to get around with a wheelchair, and
most of the feeling is back in her hands and feet."

"Do you need me to come home? Is that why you called? I can move there—"

"No." I cut her off. This is exactly why I didn't tell her about Mom sooner.
I do need Cami's help, but I don't need her to move home. I'm the man of the

family; it's my job to make sure Mom is taken care of, not Cami's. "I've been invited to go to California over Thanksgiving, but Mom needs someone to be nearby 24/7 in case—"

"I'll come. When do you want me?"

"It's a holiday. Do you need to ask for time off?"

"I'll figure it out. You shouldn't have to take care of Mom on your own."

"And you shouldn't have to drop everything to care for her either."

Neither of us says it, but I know we're both thinking it. Mom doesn't need me or Cami; she needs Dad. Not the guy who walked out on us but the guy who vowed to stay by her side in sickness and in health. But he's not here, and luckily he's never coming back.

"Is it time we consider assisted living homes?"

"No," I say, my voice sharp. "I'm not giving up on her."

A moment passes before Cami says, "It wouldn't be giving up on her. It would be giving her more."

I snort. "You sound like an adoption commercial."

She laughs, though I wasn't trying to be funny. I can't remember the last time I heard her laugh like that. The last time *I* laughed like that.

"I can't abandon her, Cam." That would make me like Dad. And I'm not like him. Never have been. Never will be.

"At some point, you may have to. She may need more help than you can give her." I hear what she's saying, but I don't accept it.

As if she can sense my growing frustration, she changes the subject. "So what inspired a road trip to California?"

A smile replaces my scowl. "I have a girl, Cam. And she's asked me to go home with her to California and meet her parents."

"What? A girlfriend? When did this happen?"

"We met at the beginning of the semester."

"And you're already meeting her family? That's fast. You haven't converted, have you?"

"Not even close. Things just move quickly in Provo."

"Sounds like it. What's she like?"

"Amazing."

Cami giggles. "You're in so much trouble."

"Shut up."

"Do I get to meet her when I come to Utah?"

"Of course."

"I'm happy for you, Rhys. Really."

"Thanks."

"All right." Cami yawns. "I've gotta get to bed. I'll see you in a few weeks."

We hang up, and I sit smiling at my phone for a second. For once, things are looking up.

"Girlfriend, huh?"

Startled, the phone pops out of my hands, and I fumble to catch it before it falls to the floor. "How long have you been eavesdropping, brother?"

Supe walks into the room and sets his backpack down on his desk. "Long enough to know that things went well on your date."

"So well." I set my phone on my night stand. "I'm going to meet her family over Thanksgiving."

Sup looks up. "That's a big step."

"Your point?"

"Is that a good idea?"

"Why wouldn't it be? *She* asked *me* to come home with her, knowing where I stand with the Church stuff."

Supe sits at his desk and unlaces his shoes, then tosses them into his closet. "And she's okay with you not being a member?"

"I'm not sure I'd say she's okay with it, but we're figuring it out."

"Figuring it out, how? Are you taking the missionary lessons? Going to go to church?"

"No." I stare at him hard. "I don't see how this is any of your business."

"You're my friend. I don't want to see you get hurt."

"Kinda late for that."

"You're meeting her family, Rhys. It's serious for her."

"And it isn't for me?"

"I didn't say that. Marriage is kind of a big deal for us, if you hadn't noticed."

"I have noticed, but just because I'm not Mormon doesn't mean I can't commit to forever. It just means I don't need a fancy building to do it in. I appreciate your concern. But we're going to be fine."

Chapter Thirty-Two

Emmy

Glissade [glee-sad] n—A traveling step

RHYS'S KNEE BOUNCES UP, DOWN, up, down, up, down as we sit waiting on my couch for Q to arrive so we can leave for California.

"You're not nervous about leaving your mom, are you?"

His knee stops bouncing. "Not to leave my mom. No."

With Cami home from New York to take care of their mother I didn't think Rhys would be so worried. And I especially thought this after meeting her when we picked her up from the airport yesterday. Cami is kind and smart and funny; he has to know his mom will be well taken care of. His mom is still feeling blue about relapsing, though, so maybe . . . "Are you worried about leaving your mom with your sister?"

"No. They'll be fine."

"If you need to stay here—"

"No way. I'm not giving up this time with you for anything."

Q's truck rumbles up the street and stops in front of the house, ending our conversation. Evie runs down the stairs past Rhys and me on the couch, flings open the door, and throws herself into Q's arms.

Rhys stands from the couch and pulls me to my feet, kissing my forehead. "Ready?"

"To spend the entire day driving? No."

"Well, I've been looking forward to this for the last week. Ten hours with you in my arms is going to be heaven." He grins.

"Remember that when you wake up with drool on your shirt."

He picks up both our backpacks stuffed full of everything we'll need for the weekend and opens the front door for me.

We walk down the brick path, and Rhys stops dead in his tracks, our arms pulling taut between us. I look back at him. "Everything, okay?"

He hesitates. "Yeah . . ."

"What's wrong?"

His chin falls to his chest, and then he points at Q's truck. I stare at the truck for a second, trying to figure out Rhys's negative reaction to it, and it hits me. It's *the* truck. Black. Ford F-150 Raptor. Everything he'd saved for and then had to sacrifice to care for his mom. I was so excited about spending an entire weekend with him that I didn't put the two together.

Rhys drops my hand and walks over to the truck. He runs his hand over the metal lines of the body, leaving a foggy handprint on the waxed paint.

"It's nice, right?" Q says to Rhys.

"Yes, she is." Rhys steps away from the truck and shoves his hands in his pockets. "What does she tow?"

Q grunts. "This beast doesn't tow anything but ladies."

I roll my eyes. Despite the somewhat pleasant conversation Q and I had the day he apologized to Evie, when he makes comments like that, it's really hard to want to get to know him. Evie and Q climb into the front seat, and Rhys opens the back passenger door for me. His eyes bounce between the bottom of the truck and the ground. "Should I help you up?" He laughs.

I shake my head and climb in. Taking either mine or Evie's SUV would have been more comfortable, but Q insisted we take his truck. I wish I had insisted we didn't. Rhys hands me his backpack, and I set it next to mine on the far side of the seat.

"I see what you're doing here." He points at our luggage as he sits beside me.

"Oh yeah? What's that?"

"Taking up all the leg room. I'm on to you."

I pretend-punch his arm, and he catches my fist and pulls me to his side. A wave of his clean scent drifts past my nose as I snuggle into him.

Q revs the engine, and the floor vibrates. Music blares out of the speakers. I cover my ears, and Rhys ducks.

Q turns down volume. "Ready, baby?"

"Ready."

Q speeds down the street, his tires screeching against the asphalt.

"We might be safer in my truck," Rhys says.

"True, but then we couldn't do this." I kiss his lips.

"I guess we'll have to risk it, then."

"Guess so."

"So, baby," Evie says to Q. "How long is this drive?"

The question bothers me for several reasons, but mostly because she knows how long the drive is. We've done this exact route at least twenty times.

He rewards her with a lopsided grin. "Ten hours, but we're going to make it in eight."

Rhys rests his hands on the back of Q's seat and leans forward. "Help a guy out." He motions to me with his head. "Make it ten."

Q looks in the rearview mirror at me, then nods to Rhys in a boys'-club kind of way. "Ten hours it is."

Rhys leans back in his seat and dips his mouth to my ear. "He may not care about getting his girl to LA safely, but I sure do."

I snuggle back into Rhys. As we merge onto the freeway, Q turns to Evie. "How's traffic?" He nods to his in-dash navigation screen. I'm pretty sure he doesn't care how traffic is but more about how his new GPS system looks.

"Oh, I forgot to program the address in." Evie touches the screen and programs our parents' Hollywood Hills address into it.

"Not that we need it," I mumble to Rhys. One interstate will take us all the way to California.

Evie studies the screen, then turns to Q. "Traffic looks good, baby."

Q glances back at Rhys. "I had this put in last week."

"Cool."

"Cost me nearly $800."

"Steep."

Q puffs up. "Everyone should have one."

"Too rich for my blood."

"Nah. It was worth every penny, right, baby?" Q says to Evie.

Evie flips down her sunshade and readjusts her Chloe sunglasses. "Sure, baby. It's great."

I lean toward Rhys and lower my voice. "If I have to hear the word *baby* one more time, I'm going to lose it."

"Sorry about that, *bebé*." Rhys winks.

"*Bebé?*" I ask.

"*Bebé.*" His accent covers my skin with chills. "You remember I'm Mexican, right?"

"Vaguely, sometimes. Honestly, I never think about it. But I'm loving it right now."

He chuckles and drops a kiss on the crown of my head, and we settle in for a long drive.

Q drums a beat on the steering wheel, and Evie reads a magazine.

"Are you okay with this?" I look around Q's truck so Rhys knows what I'm referring to.

His mouth slopes down into a tough-guy frown. "I made a choice to put my family first, and I would do it again. Junky truck and all." He laughs disparagingly.

"You're a good guy, Rhys."

His knee starts bouncing, and he looks out the window.

Wanting to take his mind off the truck, I search for a new topic of conversation. "Oh! I forgot to tell you. André Dupont, this incredible choreographer, is visiting BYU next semester. I'm going to audition for the solo."

Rhys smiles. "You'll get it."

"How can you be so sure?"

"Because I've seen you dance."

Chapter Thirty-Three
Rhys

Grand (grahnd) a—Big, massive, overwhelming

EMMY HUGS HER ARMS TO her body, and her heels click against the Las Vegas pavement as we walk along the Strip. Had we known Evie and Q were going to ditch us for several hours, we would have worn jackets.

"Did you know this tower is half the size of the real one?" Her chin tilts up to look at the faux Eiffel Tower.

"You've seen the real Eiffel Tower?" I ask. "In Paris?" My eyes trace the criss-crossed metal slats that make up the impostor tower. This is the closest I will ever get to Paris.

She nods. "Yeah. My parents took Evie and me when we graduated high school. Don't get me wrong; this one is pretty cool, but the real thing is much more impressive."

I squint up at the tower. The sun is setting behind it, casting pink and purple hues across the desert sky.

Emmy taps another text to Evie. She waits for a response, but when nothing comes, she shoves her phone back into her pocket. "She must not have reception. Maybe we should look for her."

"Just a guess, but I don't think they want to be found." Two hours ago, we were all so excited to be out of the car and stretching our legs that we didn't think to state a meet-up place or a return time. Something I regret now that we're ready to get back on the road and complete the second half of our car ride to LA.

Emmy sighs. "Yeah, maybe."

Across the street, a loud explosion sounds, and Emmy all but jumps into my arms. Music blares over loudspeakers, and her head whips around to look for the source. She giggles when she sees water dancing thirty feet above the large lake in front of the Bellagio. Her eyes light up, and she grabs my hand and pulls me across the walkway that leads right to the show. "Come on!" she says. "We can still make it!"

I couldn't fight her enthusiasm if I wanted to.

When we get across the street to the large fountain, which is at least the size of half a dozen Olympic-sized swimming pools, there are so many people walking on the sidewalk that I have to pull Emmy close to squeeze to the front so we can see. Wrapping her in my arms, together we watch the mechanically choreographed arcs of water explode into the air in sync with an old Sinatra song. Emmy sways in my arms and sighs contentedly.

My stress melts away as I realize I have an entire weekend free of responsibility. I don't have to worry about Mom or making money or school. For one weekend, I'm free. All I have to do is enjoy my girl. I let my muscles relax around Emmy, and she leans her back against my chest.

A slight breeze catches her hair. The silky blonde strands tickle my cheeks, and her sweet blueberry-coconut scent touches my nose. I brush her hair to one side, resting my check against hers. "Dance with me?"

Emmy glances side to side like she's trying to find a sanctioned dance floor. "Here?"

I pull her close, and we sway under the sunset. Everything falls away: the music, the dancing waters, the crowd passing us by on the street, everything except Emmy and me and this perfect night.

I know things won't always be as good as they are in this moment. We'll have to compromise on many things. Little things like paper or plastic. And big things like what religion we raise our kids in. It's just that none of that matters anymore. Not even the big stuff. Because I know—this is the girl I want to spend the rest of my life with. This is the girl I want to wake up next to in the morning. This is the girl I want to tuck into bed each night. This is the girl I want by my side for the rest of my life.

The music swells, and all the doubt I've felt since talking with Supe clears. I can see mine and Emmy's future. The family I want to be ours. Little girls with Emmy's blonde hair. And rowdy boys. Christmas mornings and Easter Sundays.

The song ends, and the fountain turns off, bringing our dance to an end. I press a gentle kiss to her cheek. "I'm in love with you," I whisper into her ear.

Her mouth lifts into a smile against mine. "I love you too," she says. "So much."

We seal our confessions with a kiss. Once, twice, and then again. We're in love. I couldn't be happier if I were dreaming. This is the girl I want to be my wife. I just have to convince her how committed I am to her.

* * *

As the iron scroll gates open like a red curtain revealing a game-show prize, I realize I've vastly underestimated the type of wealth Emmy comes from.

At the end of a cobblestone driveway sits a house so large it can hardly be described as a house. An estate, a mansion, a plantation even, but not a house. I laugh under my breath. I probably have more in common with the people Emmy's parents pay to keep this place up than I do with Emmy's family. How will I ever get her father's permission to marry her?

The cobblestone driveway leads to the front steps, but Q has to stop much sooner because a fleet of luxury cars prevents us from going any farther.

I look down at Emmy sleeping in my arms. A wet stain grows on my sleeve; apparently she wasn't lying about drooling. And my khaki's, which I was already uncomfortable in, are now hopelessly wrinkled. So much for making a good impression with Emmy's parents.

Q shuts off the truck, and without the sound of the engine to lull her in her sleep, Emmy blinks awake.

"We're here." I reach for the handle and push the door open. Since Evie and Q disappeared for a few hours, we hit LA traffic, so it's much later than we intended to arrive.

"You could have told me you lived in the most expensive part of Hollywood," I whisper to Emmy as I help her out of the car.

"I don't. I live in Provo."

"You know what I mean."

She laces our hands. "I do. And it doesn't matter. It's just a house."

As we walk up to the door, it feels like I'm shrinking by the second.

Emmy squeezes my hand. "My parents are going to love you. Trust me. You have nothing to worry about."

Somehow I'm not sure about that.

* * *

When we get to the front door, Emmy takes out a key. The house is unusually dark. It's late but not so late that everyone should already be asleep. Maybe they went to a movie or something.

Emmy pulls me inside, and as soon as my feet hit the hardwood floor, I know I will never fit into Emmy's world. The ceilings are high, the hallways wide, and the spiral staircase hugging the far wall is like something out of a movie—the kind of movie where a butler waits at the door and offers to carry you up the stairs.

I look over at Q, hoping for some clue as to how to act in this kind of world, but find he's more worried about kissing his girlfriend than making a good first impression on her parents. I'll give the guy credit for confidence, but he's lacking a brain. I would never kiss a girl like that in her parents' home.

Emmy lets go of my hand and feels for a light switch on the far wall. I nearly jump out of my skin when I spot a guy crouched at the base of the stairs, trying but failing miserably at being inconspicuous. I nudge Emmy, and she follows my gaze. She giggles and then cups her hand over my ear and whispers, "Ghosts in the graveyard."

"I have no clue what that means."

"It's like hide-and-go-seek but in the dark." She points at the ripped guy at the bottom of the stairs. "That's my brother Jason."

Jason touches his fingers to his brow and then salutes me.

Before I have time to process the fact that I'm being introduced to the guy who is probably the next Heisman trophy winner, the lights turn on and a younger version of Jason jumps out in front of us. "Gotcha!" he shouts. His eyes flash from me to Emmy. "Dang it!"

Jason saunters out from behind the banister. "You lose again, baby brother."

"And that's my younger brother, Drew." Emmy motions to the younger kid.

Drew shoots a cold glare at Jason. "I always lose when you're around."

"Things have apparently not gotten better between the two of them since Evie and I went away to school."

"Boys!" a woman scolds, abandoning her hiding spot in the kitchen. "We have guests. Control your feud for one weekend, please."

"Nice to meet you. I'm Jason."

"You too."

Emmy's brother Drew rolls his eyes and stomps up the stairs. Jason laughs and then walks into the kitchen.

The woman, most likely Emmy's mom, straightens and walks to where Emmy and I stand in the foyer. "You must be Quinton. Evie has told me so much about you."

Can she not tell her own kids apart? "Actually, ma'am, I'm Rhys."

Her mom looks at me, confused, then at her daughter. "Emmy?"

I shift side to side.

Emmy leans into my side. "She's kidding."

Her mom smiles. "I'm sorry. I couldn't help myself. Emmy told me about how you mixed them up when you first met. I've been waiting to do that since I heard you were coming."

"She told you about that, did she?"

"She did, but I'm sorry to say I don't know much about you. It's Rhys, right?"

"Yes. Rhys Solario." I extend my hand.

She shakes it and then smiles at Emmy. "Oh, this is going to be fun."

I glance at Emmy, unsure how to react.

"She's kidding again. I've talked her ear off about you."

"Right." My voice wavers.

"She has," her mom says, dropping her act. "I'm pleased to meet you, Rhys. I'm sorry for giving you a hard time."

"Where's Dad?" Emmy asks.

Her mom points to the family room, where Mr. Jennings stands behind the couch. Evie and Q now sit a respectful distance apart. Judging by Mr. Jennings's pinched eyebrows and clenched fists, whatever spot he was hiding in gave him the perfect view of their kiss.

He clears his throat, and Q jumps to his feet. Mr. Jennings watches Q like an angry Doberman ready to defend his territory.

"Hello, sir. I'm Q." He trips on the edge of the rug as he walks around the couch to meet Emmy and Evie's dad.

"That's not a name, that's a letter. What is your name?"

Q pales. "Quinton, sir. Quinton Walker."

Her dad's head remains still as he assesses Q. "Quinton, you can take the guest room next to the master bedroom at the end of the hall."

Q nods sheepishly.

"Evie, we'll talk about this later." He replaces his hardened frown with a welcoming smile as he walks into the foyer. "And who is this young man?" he asks Emmy.

Emmy pulls me closer. "Dad, this is Rhys. And, Rhys, this is my dad, Stephen Jennings."

Mr. Jennings shakes my hand with a firm grip. "I trust you've been looking out for my little girl?" her father asks, but what I think he means is "I have a bullet with your name on it; do I have a reason to use it?"

I swallow hard. "I have, sir."

He smiles at Emmy adoringly, approvingly even, then turns back to me. "Nice to meet you, son."

Emmy squeezes my arm. "See. I knew they would love you."

They do seem to. Odd. I expected them to hate me. Has Emmy not told her parents I'm not a member?

Chapter Thirty-Four

Emmy

Renverse (rahn-vay-say) v—To reverse

"WHAT'S THE PLAN?" MOM TOSSES the football to Jason, and we all lean into a huddle.

"Score a touchdown," Jason deadpans.

"Obviously, smart aleck." Mom flicks Jason's ear. "Anything more specific?"

"Just run downfield and get open. I'll do the rest."

We break from our huddle with a clap and spread out on Mom and Dad's sprawling lawn, facing the other team.

This is the last play of the annual Jennings family day-before-Thanksgiving game. It's me, Mom, Jason, and Q against Dad, Rhys, Evie, and Drew. We're winning since we have Jason, obviously, but not for lack of effort from Drew—who is playing like it's his life goal to beat Jason. Without Lucy and Charlotte and their husbands, our family is incomplete, but it's their year to be with their in-laws, so I can't be too sad.

Rhys stands in front of me, and I make my best tough-girl face: narrowed eyes, pinched mouth. He chuckles, and I try not to let my game face slip.

Jason calls out an official-sounding play, though not one of us knows what it means, and Q hikes him the ball. We run as fast as we can down the field, but I don't make it very far because Rhys won't let go of my waist or stop tickling me.

"I think that was holding," I say.

"I think you're right." Rhys winks at me.

We get back into position a few yards from where we started, and Jason calls another play—this one just as ambiguous as the last. Something about blue and red and numbers. Whatever. Jason throws the ball to Q, who takes his

offensive position a bit too seriously and sprints to the end zone for a touchdown.

Evie joins him in celebrating, despite the fact that they're on opposing
teams.

Dad checks his watch. "Should we start the movie soon?" he asks Mom.
"We have to get up early to start the turkey tomorrow, right?"

Mom raises an eyebrow, and Dad not so subtly looks over his shoulder
at Evie and Q.

"Right," Mom says. "The turkey. We should probably start the movie soon."

Dad nods, pleased.

We start to walk inside, even Evie and Q, but I hold back Rhys on the
wraparound porch. It's cold in Utah, but here in California, it's unseasonably
warm. Mom says we can thank the Santa Ana winds—the warm front blowing
over from the desert—for that.

"I used to come out here to stretch sometimes," I tell Rhys. "Silly, but
after long hours in the studio, it felt so nice to be outside. It was Evie's idea,
actually." I smile. "Want to watch the sunset?"

"I'd love to."

We sit on the wooden porch swing. I curl my legs up, and Rhys lazily
rocks us. Today has been perfect. Exactly what I had hoped it would be. The
football game was fun. Even Jason and Drew behaved. Mom and Dad were
cute together. There's no way Rhys doesn't understand just how great having
a forever family can be.

"Your family is great," Rhys says, confirming my thoughts. "Thanks for
inviting me. I've never had a Thanksgiving like this."

"They like you too." A warm feeling fills me, and I'm so happy I could
burst. "Have you talked to your mom?"

He nods. "Last night and this morning. She said I'm worrying too much
and she's going to block my number."

I smile. "Your mom is awesome."

"I'll tell her you said so."

Rhys continues to lazily rock us using one foot. The other is propped on
his knee, relaxed. We enjoy the warmth, the lingering light, and each other in
silence for a moment.

"I've been wondering something," Rhys says.

"What's that?"

"Have you told your parents I'm not Mormon?"

The moment evaporates. "No," I say quietly.

"Why not?"

"Because . . . because . . . I wanted them to get to know you first."

He nods, but his gaze drops below the horizon, and his jaw sets. "Okay."

I've never seen Rhys upset before, but he definitely looks it now. He must think I'm ashamed of him. That I'm embarrassed of him. But I'm not. I only wanted Rhys to have a glimpse of what being part of an eternal family felt like because I knew if he saw it, if he felt it, he would want it. I love Mom and Dad, but I'm not sure they could have put aside what they want for me—a temple marriage to a returned missionary—to give Rhys a real chance.

"Are you going to tell them?"

"Of course. Yes. I am."

"When?"

"I-I'm not sure. Not because I'm putting it off but because I wanted this weekend to be perfect. I wanted to introduce you to my family without having to explain your beliefs. I wanted things to be perfect so that you . . . wanted to be a part of this," I admit.

He looks up, and our eyes meet, any trace of hurt in his gone. "You want me to be a part of this?"

"More than anything." How does he not know?

He reaches for my hand, laces our fingers, and stares down at them. "I want this, angel."

Chapter Thirty-Five
Rhys

Patriarch [pay-tree-ahrk] n—Father of the family

WE SIT ON HER PORCH until the sun dips below the horizon and the stars appear one by one in the night sky. The temperature drops, but we stay snuggled in each other's arms until we can't feel our fingers. We walk inside, and her family is watching a movie. Everyone is in their pajamas, eating Chinese takeout out of red containers with chopsticks. Thanksgiving Eve tradition apparently. We join them, and when the movie is over, we say good night at the bottom of the stairs. She walks upstairs to her room, but instead of going to the guest bedroom downstairs where my bed is, I walk toward her father's study.

I've known Emmy only a few months, but already I can't imagine my life without her. Don't want to. I've wasted too much time worrying about how different we are. But so what if we're different? The way we feel about each other is the same. Emmy believes in me. In us. And so do I. But she still isn't getting how much I love her. How much I want to be a part of her future.

She hasn't told her family yet, but I believe her when she says she will. I think she wants their approval but is scared about how they will react. Tonight, it occurred to me that maybe it isn't Emmy I have to convince; maybe it's her family. If I can just prove to her father that I'm able to support Emmy, to commit to her and love her no matter what religion I am, I'm sure he'll give me his permission to eventually ask Emmy to marry me. And then nothing will hold us back.

The light in Mr. Jennings's study is still on. I raise my hand to knock on the door frame before entering but hesitate. This is just a conversation, I remind myself. The hard part, the falling-in-love-with-her part, is over. I love her; she loves me. There's no place to go from here except up.

With a deep breath, I touch my knuckles to the door, and Emmy's father glances up from a stack of papers. "Rhys." He stands. "Come in." Standing well over six feet, Emmy's father is a giant. He waves me forward, and despite being nervous, I force my shoulders to relax. I shut the door behind me, and he motions for me to sit in one of the two large black leather chairs across from his mammoth cherrywood desk. The soft leather exhales as I sink into its embrace.

"I hope you're enjoying it here," Mr. Jennings says.

"I am, sir. Thank you for having me."

"My pleasure. Now, what can I do for you, son?"

I look around the room. Dark woods, fine leather, and a bay window with a view of his sprawling estate. Law books and picture frames line his shelves. Emmy and Evie with their arms around each other. Several of their family on various vacations.

"Well, sir. There's something I'd like to talk with you about."

He leans back into his executive chair, and I continue. "As you know, Emmy and I have been dating for a few months now."

He nods.

"And in that time, we've become close." That didn't come out right. "I care for her deeply," I amend.

He smiles as if understanding my anxiety.

"I've never met anyone so kind, so good, and . . ." All the words I had planned fly out the window. "She's amazing, sir."

"She is," he agrees and stands to his full height, then walks around the desk to a bookshelf behind me. He picks up a picture and hands it to me. It's of Emmy when she was a little girl, wearing a tutu, her bright-blonde hair slicked into a bun. The huge smile on her face reveals several missing teeth.

"That was taken right after her first recital," Mr. Jennings says. "It was the first time I'd seen her smile in over a year."

I hand back the frame, and he sets it on the desk in front of me.

"She's told you about her trouble with reading, yes?"

"She has," I say.

"And about that boy in first grade?"

I nod. First grade or not, I would like a word with the kid.

"After that incident, Emmy all but caved in on herself." His head levels, and his jaw clenches. "Every morning, she woke up crying and came up with some excuse about why she couldn't go to school. Hurt tummy, headache, anything she could think of to stay home. We did everything we could to help her." He sighs. "But nothing helped. For months, I dropped her off in the mornings because she thrashed so wildly her mother couldn't get her out of the car and into the classroom. It broke my heart to have to see Emmy like that. I gave up. I let her cave. We let her stay home, hired private tutors, saw doctors. We took her to therapy. Speech therapy. Behavior therapy. Even the bishop. But as the months went on, her nightmares got worse. She'd wake up screaming, and it would take hours to coax her back to sleep. It was the most horrible experience of my life."

My heart breaks for both Emmy and her father. Emmy's dad stands from the desk and walks back to his chair. "We went to the temple every week, sometimes more, pleading for answers. Finally, one came: ballet. We didn't understand how that was an answer, but her mother enrolled her in the best ballet school we could find. Emmy took to it immediately. Her nightmares dwindled, and she decided to return to school the next year with Evie." Mr. Jennings pauses for a moment. "Do you understand what I'm saying, son?"

I try to figure out what he means with his line of reasoning. Emmy caved. Ballet saved her. But I don't see what it has to do with my marrying her. "Sir?"

Mr. Jennings leans forward with his elbows against the desk and fingers laced in front of him. "I'd do anything to save my little girl from any more pain."

It's not a threat, but it's a definite warning.

"I'd never hurt Emmy. I love her, sir."

"I know you do, son. I've seen how you treat my daughter."

"I can't imagine my life without her." I look him straight in the eye, determined to ask him the question that was my purpose in coming here. "I'd like your permission to ask her to marry me, sir."

He regards me carefully as the seconds tick by on his grandfather clock in the corner.

"I know it's too soon to ask her now, but I wanted to ask you in person," I explain. "But eventually I'd like to. And I would like your blessing."

"From everything Emmy's told me about you, you're a hard worker, and I'm sure you'd provide a comfortable life."

My throat tightens with emotion. This is the closest I've come to fatherly praise in a long time. His confidence in my ability to care for his daughter feels good.

"I'd be happy to give you my blessing as long as you can answer one question for me." His eyes lock on me. "Can you take my little girl to the temple, son?"

My insides clench, and a cold sweat leaves me weak. I'm unsure if he already suspects I can't or if he'd ask this question to any potential suitor. Either way, my answer is the same. "No, sir. I can't. I'm not a member of your church."

"I see." He rubs two fingers over his pursed lips, and even though he doesn't say it, I understand his meaning perfectly: I'm not good enough. Not worthy enough. Not *man* enough to marry his daughter.

He drums his fingers on the desk like a gavel delivering the final verdict. "I'm not naive enough to think you and Emmy won't make your own choice regardless of this discussion, but if you'd like my blessing, a temple marriage is my condition."

My future with Emmy erodes before my eyes, leaving me with nothing but flecks of wrought-iron dreams as I walk out of his study. Waking up is difficult when you forget you're dreaming.

Chapter Thirty-Six

Emmy

Soubresaut (sew-brah-soh) n—A sudden leap

THURSDAY AFTERNOON, RHYS SITS NEXT to me at the table, folding and unfolding the white linen napkin in his lap. I set my hand on top of his and give it a little squeeze.

Dad clears his throat as he drags his heavy wood chair across the formal dining room floor and sits down. Mom sets the last side dish on the table, completing our Thanksgiving feast. Evie and Q sit across the table from Rhys and me, and Jason and Drew are at the end, scowling at each other as usual. The table is full but feels empty without all my siblings.

Dad says the blessing on the food, and then Mom announces our annual family tradition: everyone says what they are thankful for.

"I'm grateful I got Holly's number last night," Jason says.

Drew rolls his eyes, and Mom frowns. "Can you please say something you're actually grateful for, Jase? Your family? Football?"

Jason points his fork at Mom. "Trust me." He sets his fork down and wipes his mouth with his napkin. "I'm thankful for Holly's number."

Mom sighs in defeat. "Fine. Evie, you're up."

Evie smiles at Q, who's lounging so far back in his seat he might slide right onto the floor. "I'm thankful to be Q's wife."

The world comes to a screeching halt, as if thrown off its axis.

"What did you say?" Dad asks.

"We eloped. Last night. In Vegas." She separates each bit of information like she's playing Clue and reciting who did what horrific thing and where.

Dad turns his head from side to side, his neck popping in short, angry bursts. His eyes narrow at Q, who now sits so straight he looks like a cardboard cutout of himself. He takes Evie's hand and pulls her closer like he intends to use her as a shield to block Dad's wrath.

Dad's steely gaze settles on Q. "Do you have anything you'd like to add, Quinton?"

Q swallows hard. "Uh. Well, it was a spur-of-the-minute decision." Q tries to excuse his behavior, but his words only make it worse. "I mean we . . . *we* decided it would be fun to get married in Vegas. You know, like a joke."

Evie pales.

Mom drops her fork, and it clatters to her plate.

"You think marrying my daughter is a joke?" Dad seethes.

"No, I just meant it wasn't real." Q cuts Evie a pleading look that slices her right in two. "I mean it was; we did it legally, had two witnesses, and got a marriage license and everything, but it's not like we got married in the temple or anything." Q grasps for the right words but fails.

"P-please stop," Evie stutters, pulling her hand out of Q's.

In a sudden burst, Dad rises from his seat, and the heavy wooden chair crashes to the floor.

Jason jumps up and puts himself between a furious Dad and a cowering Q. "Careful," Jason warns.

I look at Rhys, unsure what to do. Evie is about to break down, Dad's close to losing it, and Mom can't stop sniffling.

Rhys takes in my expression and then sets his napkin on the table, stands, and walks over to Q. "Come on, man." Rhys tugs Q's arm. "I think maybe we'd better take a drive."

Q, who is pale white, glances at Evie, but she won't look at him. "I'm sorry," he whispers and then follows Rhys past Dad's and Jason's threatening glares.

A moment later, Q's truck roars down the driveway, and Evie dashes from the dining room and up the stairs. Dad walks out of the room and slams his study door closed behind him. Mom crumples in her chair.

"Well, that was epic," Drew says.

I run up the stairs after Evie. Her duffel bag is already unzipped on the bed when I walk into her room.

"Evie, are you—"

"Don't."

"I just—"

"Seriously, Em. I can't handle being judged by you tonight."

No matter what crazy choice she may have made in Vegas, there's no justification for the way Q treated her tonight. I'm on her side. Always. "I'm not judging you. I promise. Please talk to me."

Evie jams her clothes into the duffel, and I sit at her desk. She swipes at the tears streaming down her cheeks, then wipes her hands down the front of her jeans.

There are a million things I want to say to Evie right now, but I'm so afraid I'll say the wrong thing and she'll think I'm judging her that nothing comes out.

She shoves her belongings into her duffle bag and then walks to Q's room down the hall and does the same with his things. She hefts the overstuffed bag onto her shoulder and then walks out of the room and down the stairs. I follow. "Where are you going? Should I pack?"

"No." She walks into the living room, where Jase is playing Xbox. Evie steps in front of the TV, and he glares at her.

"I was winning."

"Can you give me a ride to Q?"

Jase looks at the clock hanging on the far wall. "Now?"

"I'll go pack," I say.

Evie glances at me and then lowers her voice to address Jase again. "Please. I need to talk to him."

Jase's eyes bounce back and forth between us. "I'll get my keys." He stands and leaves the room.

Evie turns to me, her whole face wet and puffy. "I know you want to come with me, but I need some space, okay?"

"No. Not okay." I shake my head. "I don't understand. Why?"

She stops in the entryway, right outside Dad's closed study door. "Because despite how much you may dislike it, I'm Q's wife, and we need to figure out how to be married by ourselves."

Wife. Married. I was supposed to throw rice and catch her bouquet. Ever since we've been able to walk, we've planned to go wedding-dress shopping together and pick out flowers and eat samples of cake. How is this happening?

Jase jangles his keys when he walks back into the living room. "Ready?"

Evie nods.

I grab the strap of her duffel as she walks past me to leave. "Don't go, Eve. You deserve better than this."

"Better than *him*, you mean." She frowns. "You've been judging him from day one. You didn't bother to get to know him, even though you said you would."

She shrugs the strap out of my grasp and then strides to the front door behind Jase.

"Evie!" I call after her, but she doesn't acknowledge me.

Both car doors slam, and then Jase's Porsche starts up. Before they can make it down the driveway and out the gate, I run back inside to Dad's study. He's standing at the window, watching Evie leave.

"Aren't you going to stop her?"

Dad lets the curtain fall closed and walks to his chair. "No."

No? "What do you mean, *no?*"

"I mean, no." He sits and rest his elbows on his desk.

"She got married in Vegas, Dad. Vegas. To a guy who . . ." I shake my head, too upset to finish my sentence. "You have to stop her. Please. She's—" My sister.

"Believe me, if I thought it would change anything, I would stop her." Dad picks up a pen and taps it against the desk in a frantic beat.

"You can't give up on her!"

"I would never give up on Evie. On any of my children," Dad says, looking at me. "Promise me that before you make any serious decisions about marriage, you'll carefully consider your choice."

"What do you mean?"

"Sit down for a minute. Let's have a talk."

My heart pounds as I sit facing Dad.

"Rhys and I spoke last night."

"Y-you did?"

"We did. He asked me for permission to marry you."

I feel the blood drain from my face. And my hands and feet tingle like they're going numb.

"He also told me he can't take you to the temple because he isn't LDS."

I nod.

"It surprises me that you'd date a nonmember, Emmy. Especially after everything we've seen Lucy go through."

I explain how Rhys and I were partnered in Book of Mormon class and how things grew between us. I tell him how I fell in love and about our date at Temple Square and about Rhys's father and how I brought Rhys here, hoping to show him what an eternal family is like—to get him to want one with me.

Dad listens attentively until I'm crying more than I'm talking. He hands me a tissue and then says, "He seems like a nice young man. Respectful, and he obviously loves you, but in the end, being with him will require sacrifice. You don't go into marriage hoping to change the other person. That is as kind as it is wise. I hope that before you progress in your relationship, you'll ask yourself what compromises you're willing to make in order to be with him. If you're willing to make them, that's your decision, but if not, you owe it to Rhys and to yourself to be honest."

I run out of Dad's study and straight up the stairs.

Jason returns a little while later with Rhys. Evie and Q have already started the drive back to Provo.

All night I toss and turn. By morning, I'm more tired than when I got into bed. After breakfast, we search for plane tickets back to Provo. Tickets are expensive because of the holiday, and the only flight available isn't until tomorrow evening, and it has two layovers. Dad offers to buy Rhys's ticket, but Rhys declines. Guilt eats at me, knowing he doesn't have the money to spare.

When we finally get to Provo, I rush right home and go straight up to Evie's bedroom, needing to reconcile with my twin. I don't know why I expected her to be here, but she's not. All of her clothes. Her makeup. They're gone. Her room is completely abandoned. Just like me.

Chapter Thirty-Seven
RHYS

Equally yoked [ee-kwuh-leel yohk-d] a—Term used to justify a decision made about a marital relationship—or lack thereof

WE CHOOSE TO MEET ON campus in front of the JSB, where we have Book of Mormon class . . . or, rather, had. Finals are this week, and our test is at the testing center, so Book of Mormon class is almost officially over. I'm not sure why we chose here. Maybe because this is the only place that belongs to *us*.

She's already waiting when I walk up, and she doesn't see me right away. She rubs her hands together and then blows into them. I watch her for a moment, trying to figure out what I can possibly say that will convince her to stay with me despite her father's not giving us his blessing, but my mind is blank.

She looks up, and my heart skips a beat. I don't want this to be over. I slow my steps, drawing out what may be the last of our time. And before we sit, I gather her into my arms and kiss her, giving her every part of my soul. Every hope, every dream, every wish I have for the future I want to share with her. I give her every part of me I can find to give away and silently beg her to accept me for who I am. When I'm done, I rest my forehead against hers. She opens her mouth to speak, but I shake my head. "Not yet. Please. Just . . . can we just be?"

Her eyelashes tickle my cheek, and she nods. I don't know how long we stand there, but it isn't long enough. We sit on the bench facing each other.

"I want to marry you," I say. "And I know that probably isn't the right thing to say, but I don't want there to be any confusion about where I stand or how I feel. I asked your father for permission."

"I know."

"He said no."

Emmy nods.

"I respect your father, and I don't want to go against him, but I think in time he'll understand. I still want to spend the rest of my life with you."

Emmy presses her eyes closed like the thought pains her. Like every other girl at this institution, Emmy was brought up on a steady diet of *Thou shalt marry an RM* and *Yea, verily, only in the temple*, but I love her, and she loves me, and what we have together is bigger than any rule. If she believes her God is all-knowing and all-loving, she should also believe He knows how much we love each other, and being together should be okay.

"Your religion is part of who you are, and I love that about you. I respect your faith. I know I'm not what you want me to be, but you have to know I love you."

"I do know."

Hope rises in my chest but then falls when she opens her eyes. Nothing in them has changed. "Then what is it?"

"Do you remember when I told you about Lucy?"

"Yes." It was that conversation that convinced me Emmy was different, that she thought marrying a good guy was better than marrying a Mormon guy. It's what made me believe we had a shot at a relationship.

"Every Sunday Lucy wakes up early, gets the kids ready, and drives to church. And every Sunday she sits alone. She's the one who reads all the scriptures, writes every Primary talk, and says every prayer. She's married, but she's alone. I don't want to be alone, Rhys."

"You think you'd feel alone if we got married?" Is that what this is about? She's scared I'll leave her? That because I'm not a Mormon, I don't have the ability to commit to forever? "I would never let you feel alone. I swear it."

She bites her nail.

"Emmy." I pull her hand away from her mouth and press it to my chest so she can feel my heart beating. "I don't want you to feel alone as much as you don't want to be alone. I will never abandon you. For better or for worse, come what may, I'll be there. Marriage isn't something I take lightly. I'm in this. Every day of every week. Even Sunday."

She tries to pull her hand out of mine, but I hold it tight. "Please don't make this harder than it already is," she says. "I thought we shared the same beliefs, that we wanted the same things. But we're not equally yoked."

I have no idea what yoked means, but I don't like the sound of it because obviously in her eyes, I'm not yoked enough. "You say you don't want to feel alone, and you don't have to." I wrap my arms around her, and she relaxes into my embrace. "If you'll let me, I'll always be here for you," I say.

"It's not enough," she whispers. "I want you forever."

"You have me."

She shakes her head. "The only way I can have you forever is if I marry you in the temple."

I don't believe that, but if she needs to get married in a certain building to have her forever, then, "Fine."

Her eyes widen. "We can't—not unless you get baptized."

"I'll get baptized, then. Problem solved. We can marry in whatever temple you want."

"No—"

"Why not?"

"Because you don't believe it." Her voice wavers, and she clears her throat like she's preparing to say something I don't want to hear.

"I love you," I say. "Religion and all. You don't have to be afraid I won't support you in your faith."

"I believe you."

"Then what is it? Just tell me what you want me to do, and I'll do it. No drinking. Church every Sunday. All three hours. I'll even sing the songs with you. Loudly."

Her eyes fill with tears. "You drink?"

"I used to."

"Do you still?"

"Jeez, Emmy. Give me a little credit. I signed the same honor code you did."

Her shoulders round, and she seems to sink into herself, her eyes falling to the floor.

"No, angel. Please don't be sad. Listen to me." I level my eyes with hers. "You want me to take the plunge? Fine. Temple? You've got it." My words are desperate, but I don't care. She needs to know what I'm willing to do to be with her.

"If I let you do those things, Rhys, you'd resent me for it one day. I love you too much to do that to you. Our home would be a constant struggle. How we raise our kids, what we allow . . ."

"I wouldn't regret anything. Not so long as I have you. Just tell me what you want."

"I want you to believe."

I'll give her anything else. My whole heart. Every penny I'll ever make. Every breath I'll ever take. They're hers. I'll do everything. But I can't do that. "I can't give you that."

"I know."

I reach out for her, wanting to be near her, but she doesn't take my hand.

"I know you're worried our relationship would become like your sister's. But I would never let that happen. Nothing has to change."

"It already has." She touches my face and says, "I will love you forever," but all I hear is good-bye.

Before she can walk away, I plead my case with a kiss. "Don't do this." Another kiss. "Please. I'm begging you. Don't give up on us, angel."

She puts a hand to my chest and steps away. "I'm sorry. Sorrier than you will ever know. But you can't believe it, and I can't not."

Winter Break

December

Chapter Thirty-Eight
Emmy

Sans [sahns] a—Without

THE FLAT SCREEN HANGING OVER Mom and Dad's fireplace reflects the lightning flashing outside. One one thousand, two one thousand, three—the thunder sounds again. It's not far. I pull the quilted Christmas blanket up around my neck and close my eyes. The last time I sat on this couch, Rhys was next to me.

"You doing okay, Em?" Lucy startles me as she sits on the couch next to me. I pull the blanket over my head without replying.

"That good, huh?" Lucy tugs the blanket off my face. "Want to talk about it?"

"Don't know what I'd say."

"Anything you want. Let it all out. Tell me what you're feeling." Therapy speak. Lucy and her husband must be seeing a counselor again. This only reminds me I made the right choice to separate from Rhys. No matter how much it hurts.

Lucy nudges me with her knee.

"I'm feeling sad."

Like a good therapist, she nods knowingly. "What else?"

"And upset. It's like he took my favorite puzzle and replaced half the pieces. Nothing fits. Nothing makes sense."

Lucy listens intently. The thing about my older sister is that she's completely comfortable with silence until she finds the right words to express what she means. This probably comes from having to choose her words so carefully for so many years. "Evie said Rhys was nice. I'm sorry about how things ended."

Evie. Since she married Q and moved out, I've tried to give her space like she asked. I've wanted talk to her every single day, but I've decided she will reach out when she's ready. I just need to be patient. But at the same time, it's been a month now, and I've never felt so far away from my sister.

"I feel so stupid. I thought he was the one, Lu. Everything was so perfect. Too perfect, I guess."

"Trust me; I understand." While I'm sure she's been happy at times, Lucy's life appears to teeter on the edge of constant battle.

I let my head fall back against the couch. Coming home for Christmas was supposed to help me feel better, not worse.

"Did you talk to Rhys about what you want?"

I nod. "I told him I wanted to get married in the temple. That I wanted forever."

"What did he say?"

"That he'd get baptized."

She laughs. "Seems like an easy solution."

I frown. "You of all people should know it isn't that easy."

Lucy's face falls. "I do, but I wish it were that easy."

"Me too. I know I can't be with him, but I can't forget him either. There are no good options."

"So what are you going to do?" Lucy is so much like Mom. Fun but not afraid to get straight to the heart of the problem.

"What *should* I do?"

Lucy draws her knees up to her chest. "You know I can't answer that for you."

"It's not fair."

"Life never is. I think the key is to remember who you were before you met Rhys," she says. "What you liked to do, what your dreams were before you lost yourself in him."

It's hard to remember my life before Rhys. Life before him was just waiting for him. I let out a sigh.

"It'll get easier," Lucy says.

"I don't think so." The sting might not be quite so sharp one day, but the scar will never go away. I'll always carry him with me, comparing every relationship to him.

"It may seem like that right now—"

"I know you're trying to help, but this is different from you and Jeff. I made all the right decisions."

She lifts her head off my shoulder. "Yeah. You're right. Of course."

"I didn't mean it like that."

"Doesn't make it any less true though. I made my bed and all that." She waves a hand in the air.

I wince. "Jeff is great. If you hadn't married him, you wouldn't have the kids."

Lucy smiles a sad sort of smile. "It's okay, Em. What I meant earlier is that if you've decided not to be with Rhys, then maybe you should remember who you were before you met him. Start over."

"I don't want to start over."

"I know, but humor me for a second. What did you love before you met Rhys?"

"Ballet." That's not something I even have to think about. It's natural. A part of me.

"Then do that."

Dancing ballet was difficult without Evie this past semester, but I worked hard to rehearse for the recital that happened right before break, and it went really well. Being up on stage, even though I didn't get the solo, filled my soul and quieted my mind—just like ballet always has. It felt amazing to relax into the choreography and let my mind forget everything for a brief moment. Ballet has always been the one constant in my life. What takes away all my pain. Of course. Ballet.

Chapter Thirty-Nine
Rhys

Adversity [ad-vur-si-tee] n—Continued difficulty

"I want to get baptized."

Elder Scott elbows his companion, and a grin spreads across his face. The other missionary, Elder Marsden, tries to hide his excitement, but it still bubbles through. I know what they're thinking: golden contact. I let them think that. It'll be easier that way.

"So, um . . ." Elder Scott fumbles for the right words. "Why have you decided to be baptized?"

Why shouldn't matter so much as *when*. "I'd like to set a date. I have to go to church a couple of times and have a few interviews, right? So maybe just before school starts again?" The timing will be perfect. Inviting Emmy to my baptism will show her how serious I am about making things work.

Elder Scott inches to the edge of the couch—he would dunk me now if he were allowed, but Elder Marsden sits completely unmoved in his seat. "What's made you want to be baptized, Brother Solario?"

"It's Rhys. And I've attended BYU for three years now. I've studied the Book of Mormon, I've gone to church, and I want to be baptized."

"That's great!" Elder Scott digs a three-inch binder out of his bag and sets it on his lap. "Let's see. We can't do it over break, but maybe sometime in Jan—"

Elder Marsden holds up his hand, stalling Elder Scott's words. "You haven't answered my question. Why do you want to be baptized?"

"Isn't it enough to want to be baptized?"

"No," Elder Marsden says. "It's not."

Elder Scott's eyes snap to Elder Marsden's. "Elder, uh . . . could we have a word outside?"

Elder Marsden ignores his companion. "Level with me, Rhys."

What is it with these guys? Do they have lie detectors implanted in them at the MTC?

"Isn't it your job to baptize people who want to be baptized?"

Elder Marsden's face remains unreadable. "No. Our job is to baptize people who are *ready* to be baptized."

"Great. I'm ready."

Elder Marsden appraises me for an uncomfortable moment. "I'll make you a deal. You answer my questions, and I'll baptize you myself."

"Ask away." I'll pass their test, no problem. I don't drink or smoke. I haven't crossed one line since signing the honor code. Pure as snow.

"Do you have a testimony of the restored gospel?"

The only thing I have a testimony of is my relationship with Emmy. "I want to get baptized."

"Do you have a testimony of Jesus Christ? God the Eternal Father?"

"I want to get baptized."

Elder Scott's eyes bounce back and forth between his companion and me.

"What's her name?" Elder Marsden asks.

Human. Polygraph.

"Look, Brother Solar—"

"Rhys."

"Right, Rhys. The gospel of Jesus Christ isn't something you join because of a girl. It's a lifestyle. An eternal commitment—"

"I know all that. And I agree. I'll sign the contract. Word of wisdom, law of chastity, whatever. I'm in. I want to be baptized."

Elder Scott's face falls, and he stuffs his binder back into his messenger bag. Elder Marsden smooths his pants as he stands from the couch.

"I know this isn't exactly conventional—" I say.

Elder Marsden shakes his head. "In Provo, it's too conventional. Guys join the Church all the time for a girl."

They both walk to the front door, but Elder Scott pauses in the frame. "If you want to know if the gospel is true, pray sincerely, and He'll answer you."

Been there. Tried that. I slam the door harder than I mean to.

As I walk back to the couch, my phone vibrates in my pocket with a text from Mom, reminding me to pick up a refill on her prescription and a bottle of lotion. Work has been insane with the Christmas rush, and between working overtime and trying to convert to Mormonism—unsuccessfully—I forgot. I grab my coat off my bed and stuff my wallet into my back pocket.

Snow starts to fall as I walk out to my truck, like the night Emmy took me tunnel singing. Emptiness swims inside me, sorrow threatening to drown me.

I pull into the drugstore parking lot, hurry inside, and head straight to the pharmacy.

The woman behind the counter types Mom's prescription into the computer. "How's your day going so far?"

"Horrible."

"I'm sorry to hear that. I'm sure this weather isn't helping." She laughs uncomfortably.

I grunt. I couldn't care less about the snow.

"It'll be $400."

There's no way the price has gone up that much since I last bought Mom's meds a few years ago. "I think there's been a mistake."

The pharmacist checks the amount again and then looks at me with pity. "I'm sorry. The price has increased."

I'm short.

By a lot.

"Could you check if there is a generic brand or something cheaper?"

"Sure." She types something into the computer. "Unfortunately, this is the cheapest option. The cost of many medications has gone up due to changes in the health-care system."

Now that Mom is finally taking her meds again, there's no way I'm going to jeopardize her health. I'll have to pick up more overtime, maybe unload boxes at Smith's or try to find a morning janitorial job on campus. I pull out my credit card and slide it across the counter.

She doesn't take the card. "It'll be done in about twenty minutes. You can pay then." She walks away to fill the prescription.

I look for a place to sit and wait but then remember Mom's lotion and head to the cosmetics aisle instead.

The first aisle is nothing but bottles. Shampoo bottles. Conditioner. Everything except lotion. I walk around the end cap and see tubes of lip gloss. The kind with bright-colored tops containing sparkly goo—the kind Emmy wears. The memory of her sweet blueberry-coconut scent hits me.

Emmy won't marry me if I'm not Mormon; the missionaries won't baptize me if I don't believe. Elder Scott said God would answer if I ask. I don't believe He will, but at this point, I'll try anything. Frantic to end the confusion, I brace myself against the shelving and close my eyes.

Dear Emmy's God, I pray silently. *The missionaries said—*
"Excuse me, sir?
My eyes blink open, and I turn to find a salesgirl staring at me.
"Are you okay?" she asks.
I glare up at her. "I'm fine."
Her eyes widen. "Oh-kay, then." She walks away. I drop my hand from the shelf and trudge back to the pharmacy. Mom's prescription is done, so I pay for it and then start back through the aisles to exit the store. As I pass the lip gloss, an empty feeling settles in my chest, and the memory of her blueberry-and-coconut scent haunts me all the way home.

Part II
Winter Semester

January

Chapter Forty

Emmy

Choreographer [kor-ee-og-ruh-fer] n—A person who creates dance compositions

HIS EYES ARE ON ME as I extend my leg into an arabesque. André Dupont. One of, if not the most talented classical ballet choreographers alive today. Here at BYU for an entire month to choreograph a routine we'll perform next month in BYU's Contemporary Dance in Concert. While I've always preferred classical ballet to contemporary, since dancing with Rhys, I have a newfound love for modern dance too.

This show will be a much smaller exhibition than last semester's recital showcase, but to me, it's more important. Since my talk with Lucy over Christmas break, I've mentally prepared for this moment, but I wasn't expecting someone as talented as André to be judging me. I can do this though. I will not repeat last semester's failure; I will earn this solo.

André walks slowly around the perimeter of the room, appraising each dancer as we warm up. I stand in the far corner next to David, like always.

Ballet Master Miller calls us to the center and demonstrates the simple combination that will serve as the audition piece. I watch her back, careful not to let my eyes rise to her reflection in the mirror so I don't reverse the steps. I run the combination in my head as I walk to the *barre* to wait for my turn.

I'm confident in my abilities as I watch dancer after dancer audition. I worked hard with David all last semester, and Rhys reminded me why I love ballet. Rhys.

My heart pounds when I'm called to the center. I begin the audition piece, and my head races. Rhys is there at every turn. Every time I leap and with each extension. I try to clear my head, but like my audition in the fall, I unravel. My confidence is replaced with melancholy. I'll never get this solo.

Not only was I not cast as the lead last semester, but I'm struggling to make it through each day now.

By some miracle, my technique carries me through the combination, even though my head and heart are with Rhys.

How am I supposed to go back to who I was before Rhys when he's still here? In my studio. In my head. In my dancing. I can't. It's not possible.

As soon as I complete the combination, I grab my bag and rush into the hall. By no means is this my strongest audition, but I put everything I had into it.

I don't make it three feet before a deep voice stops me. "What was that?"

When I turn, David is standing behind me with his arms crossed.

"What was what?"

David points to the studio. "You've always been good, but that was"—his eyebrows inch up his forehead, widening his eyes—"incredible."

"It was sloppy and emotional." Hardly incredible.

"Maybe, but it was also the most honest performance I've ever seen you give. André couldn't take his eyes off you."

Last semester, I would have been giddy to hear that, but now, without someone to share this victory, without Rhys, it feels incomplete.

* * *

In my last new class of winter semester, the second half of the Book of Mormon, I sit next to the door, wishing Rhys would walk in and somehow we'd be able to find a way to work through this. It's stupid. I know it's stupid. There are several sections of this class, and it's unlikely he'll end up in this one, but I watch the door for him anyway.

Fewer and fewer people walk in, and finally class begins.

No Rhys.

Syllabi are passed down the long rows. When the door opens a few minutes later, my heart jumps into my throat with hope that it's Rhys but then sinks when a guy with sandy blond hair walks in instead. He's tall and broad shouldered. By all means good-looking, but not Rhys.

"This seat taken?" The guy points to the open seat next to me, and I shake my head. He sinks low in his chair and kicks his legs out like Rhys used to do.

"I'm Nathan," he whispers. "You can call me Nate if you want."

I try my best to smile, but it feels more like a wince. "Emelia." I don't introduce myself as Emmy. Emmy belongs to Rhys.

"Nice to meet you." He grins, and it's a nice grin, but not as nice as—

I turn my attention back to the professor, who's discussing his expectations for the semester. Every task and assignment feels insurmountable. Not because I have dyslexia but because I don't have Rhys. It's hard to care about trivial things like homework assignments, midterms, and tests.

My cell phone vibrates with a text. I pull it out of my bag but keep it low in my lap so I don't anger the professor. It's a picture from David of the cast list. My eyes dart away from the screen, not ready to know whether I got the solo.

Nathan leans over. "Everything okay?"

I power off the screen and drop the phone back into my bag. I'll wait until after class, when I can break down in private. "Fine, thanks."

He eases back into his seat, and I try to concentrate on the rest of the lecture. When class ends, I stuff my iPad mini into my bag. I'm about to stand up when Nathan turns to me.

"Where are you from?" he asks.

"California," I mumble. "You?"

"Far-off, exotic Draper."

"You've traveled a long distance to get here."

Amusement lights his pale-blue eyes. "What can I say? BYU is worth the travel."

I hear myself giggle, though it doesn't feel real, like my body knows the script: giggle after cute guy makes a joke. But I don't feel it. I hoist my bag onto my shoulder, ready to make an escape.

"I know this might be forward, but do you have a boyfriend?"

I nearly choke on my fake grin. "W-what?"

"Boyfriend? Fiancé?" He searches my face for the answer.

"That *is* forward."

He laughs. "No one would accuse me of being subtle. So do you?"

"I just, uh, got out of something. It didn't end well."

"I'm mostly sorry to hear that."

"Mostly?"

A dimple appears to the right of his growing smile. "I'd be lying if I said I was completely sorry because that would mean I wouldn't be able to ask you out."

He cannot be serious. "Wow" is all I can think to say.

He winces. At least he's smart enough to show remorse. "I'm sorry. I'm not—I mean, I date a lot but not because I'm a player. I want to, you know, settle down."

"Nathan—"

"Nate," he corrects.

"Right, Nate. We just met, and you've already brought up settling down. I'm sorry, but I'm not looking for a relationship right now."

His face falls, and it's like I'm reliving my breakup with Rhys. Breakup. Ex-boyfriend. It's been a month, but it still doesn't feel real. "I'm flattered, but I'm not ready to date again so soon." Or ever.

"Yeah. I understand." Nathan's gaze falls to his desk. The transformation from cocky player to kicked puppy is so sudden that had I not experienced the confidence this guy had five minutes ago, I would never have believed this was the same guy. The dimple on his cheek is still there, but the smile beside it has turned into a grimace.

"I'm sorry," I say.

"It's okay. But promise me that if you're ever ready to move on, you'll let me take you to dinner."

Me getting over Rhys isn't going to happen. "It's a deal."

"All right, then," he says, and we both stand. "Where are you headed?"

We shuffle down the row toward the door. "The RB for ballet."

"A ballerina, huh?"

"Maybe one day. For now, I'm just a ballet dancer."

He holds the door open for me, and I follow him outside.

"See you next time," he says, and we start our separate ways. "Emelia," he calls out, walking backward. "Remember, you promised."

My head tilts to the side in question.

"If you decide to move on, I'm your guy."

Laughing, I wave good-bye and then hurry toward the RB, anxious to learn which role I've earned for the exhibition. I'm almost to the ramp behind the Maeser building when someone shouts my name. I turn and find Kennedy jogging over, waving her arms. My heart jumps, thinking Evie might be with her. I search frantically, but no, it's just Kennedy.

"You are one hard woman to chase down." She pants as she nears.

"Hi, Kennedy."

"Have you talked to Evie lately?" she says without bothering to greet me back.

It probably shouldn't bother me that Kennedy has obviously talked with Evie since Thanksgiving and I haven't, but it does. I'm dealing with a breakup, classes I'm in over my head with, and once again I've probably blown another solo. I'm depressed and overwhelmed, and I need my sister. I shake my head. "No. I haven't seen her." I haven't even talked to her. This is the longest we've ever gone without speaking. We've had fights before, but they've been nothing like this and never this long.

"Call her," Kennedy urges. "She *needs* you."

"But she *wants* Q." And space. And time. And not me. "I appreciate you trying to help—really, I do—but she asked me to give her and Q time alone, and I'm trying to respect that." No matter how hard it may be for me.

"But—"

I turn my back to Kennedy and hurry down the pathway to the RB without saying good-bye. It's rude, but seeing her is a painful reminder of everything I'm missing, and I'm anxious to leave.

My phone buzzes in my bag, notifying me of the text David sent with the cast list. As much as I want to walk into the ballet studio with my head held high no matter what part I got, with everything on my mind, I'm not sure I can. I miss my sister, I miss Rhys, and I miss ballet too much to be okay with failing again. Knowing what part I have now will help me be better prepared when I get to class in a few minutes.

Hand trembling, I swipe my thumb across the screen, then zoom in on the picture to search for my name. It doesn't take me long to find it because right there at the top of the list is my name next to the word *solo*.

Chapter Forty-One
Rhys

Relapsing-Remitting Multiple Sclerosis (RRMS) [ree-laps-ing / ree-mit-ing / muhl-tuh-puhl / skli-roh-sis] n—A disease characterized by clearly defined attacks of worsening neurologic function; these attacks—often called relapses— are followed by partial or complete recovery periods (remissions), during which symptoms improve partially or completely.

"THINK YOU CAN HANDLE CLEANING all these by yourself?" The head janitor of the JFSB motions to the row of toilet stalls. "The other guy didn't show."

"No problem," I say.

"I guess morning janitorial jobs aren't for everyone."

I don't think they're for anyone. Some people just need money more than others.

"You've got one hour before classes start."

"I'll get it done," I say.

He nods, then leaves me in the men's bathroom with a stocked cart.

I jam my headphones into my ears and turn the music up, trying to drive away thoughts of Emmy, who is forever dancing in my mind. Fifty minutes later, I've managed to clean every bathroom on the second floor. I pull the earbuds from my ears, stash them with my phone in my pocket, and then sign out at the front desk.

The sun is coming up when I walk outside. My phone buzzes in my pocket and buzzes and buzzes. I must not have had service inside.

I glance at the screen and see a long list of missed texts from Mom and just as many calls from Cami. I quickly scroll through Mom's texts.

911.

I fell. Hit my head. Lots of blood.

My fingers fumble to dial Mom's number as I sprint to my truck. She doesn't answer so I call Cami in New York.

Cami answers right away. "Hello? Rhys?"

"What happened? Is Mom okay? She won't answer." I jam my keys into the ignition and peel out of the parking lot.

"I don't know." She sniffles. "A paramedic called me trying to find some family member to talk to when they couldn't find you. They took her to the hospital."

I pull an illegal U-turn, redirecting my course from Mom's house in south Provo to the hospital southwest of campus.

Cami talks incoherently, switching between sobbing and shouting. Unable to make sense of anything she says, I cut her off. "Cam, are you okay?"

"I've been so scared, Rhys. Where were you?"

I pull into the hospital parking lot and take the first stall I see. "I was at work, earning money to pay for Mom's meds."

"Oh."

"I'm at the hospital, so I'm going to go find Mom. You don't have to worry anymore, okay? I'll handle everything."

She lets out a deep breath. "Call me as soon as you know anything. I can be on the next flight if you need me."

We hang up, and I jog into the hospital. A receptionist directs me to Mom's room on the third floor. She's asleep when I walk in, a bandage on her forehead.

A doctor motions me into the hall and explains what happened: Mom fell and hit her head trying to go to the bathroom. Luckily she was using her cell phone as a flashlight, so she was able to call for help. The doctor recommends installing a hands-free lighting system as well as handrails so this doesn't happen again. With such a fancy job, I'm sure he doesn't realize all of that costs more money than I have.

Because Mom sustained a head injury, she has to have a CT scan to ensure her skull isn't fractured. The CT reveals troubling results, so Mom also gets an MRI.

Several worry-filled hours later, the doctor walks into Mom's room to discuss her test results. "Good news," he says. "No internal bleeding and only minimal swelling. You have a urinary tract infection, but antibiotics will take care of that." Dr. Williams sits at the end of the bed. Not a good sign. He'll be staying awhile.

"And how are you holding up, young man?" he asks.

"Fine, thanks."

"Glad to hear that," Doctor Williams says, then turns to Mom. "I've reviewed your chart, and it appears you've had a decline in motor function over the last several years."

"Yes," Mom says.

Understatement of the century. Since moving to Utah, her health has taken a nosedive.

Dr. Williams laces his fingers in his lap. "Ms. Solario, your RRMS—relapsing-remitting multiple sclerosis—has developed into SPMS—secondary progressive multiple sclerosis."

When Mom was first diagnosed, the doctors said there were four types of MS. I rack my brain, trying to remember which type Dr. Williams is talking about, but nothing comes.

He turns to me. "Your mom has had a gradual worsening of at least one of her symptoms—in this case, mobility, over the last year."

Mom glances at the wheelchair in the corner of the room.

"Was she diagnosed wrong before?" I ask.

Doctor Williams shakes his head. "No. About 85 percent of people diagnosed with RRMS later develop SPMS."

Anger swells inside my chest. "Would this have happened if she had started taking her meds sooner?"

"It's impossible to say. MS is an unpredictable disease."

Frustration replaces my anger. There are never any answers. Only ambiguous facts. Mom deserves to know what to expect. To have medications that can offer her lasting relief.

Doctor Williams turns to Mom. "What we do know is that you're in what we call an interim period."

Mom adjusts the thin blue blanket covering her body. "An interim period?"

"Yes." Doctor Williams shifts on the bed again. "You'll still experience relapses, but the course of your disease has shifted. And you will have gradual worsening of your symptoms."

Not good news. "So what do we do? Change Mom's meds?"

"Unfortunately, no. With relapsing-remitting MS, we're able to address relapses by combating inflammation with steroids. But with secondary progressive MS, there are no treatments available to slow or stop its progression."

"What? No." Mom sits up in bed. "They said we could control flare-ups with meds." Mom curls and then uncurls her hands. "I thought . . . I mean, I've been taking my meds again; shouldn't I get better?"

"Not exactly. Taking the medication will help alleviate the severity of your symptoms caused by the relapse, but they won't prevent the disease from worsening over time."

Mom slumps in her bed.

"It's important to stay positive." Dr. Williams encourages. "Remember, you have MS; MS doesn't have you."

When Mom was first diagnosed, she said a variation of this phrase a million different times to Cami and me. And early on, MS didn't have Mom. But then she went off her meds, and over the last several years, it did get her.

Doctor Williams straightens a small stack of papers and then shuffles them into a large envelope. "I'm going to leave some material for you to read tonight, and we can talk about any questions you have tomorrow morning before you're released."

* * *

An hour before Mom is scheduled for release, a financial counselor appears at the door and leads me down the hall to her private office. My heart rate spikes as I sit at her desk.

She picks up a manila folder with Mom's name on it and flips through the pages. "Correct me if I'm wrong, but it appears you and your mother have been paying for everything out of pocket?"

Didn't see any other choice. I nod. So does the counselor. And then we both look at the bursting file of unpaid bills.

"You don't have to take all this on yourself, you know. There are other options."

Not with my schedule. I physically don't have more hours in the day to change anything.

"I printed these off for you." The counselor slides a file across the desk.

I pick it up and look inside. "What's this?"

"Help."

Call me cynical, but . . .

"Your mother is eligible to receive assistance."

"More than Medicaid?"

"With the *help* of Medicaid, much more."

Sounds good, but everything requires a price. "Go on."

"There are several assisted-living homes in Utah."

"I'm not going to drop my mom off at some home." That's what Dad would have done if he had stuck around. Put her in some dirty home with people who don't care about her.

"I'm not saying you should drop her off and never look back," the counselor says. "I'm only suggesting you help your mom search for a place where she'll be comfortable, happy, and safe."

Safe. Whether she means it or not, she's implying that Mom isn't safe living on her own with me as her live-out caretaker. Maybe she's right. I should've insisted on moving in. But even then, I can't be there all the time. "Even if she wanted to move into a home, I can't pay for it, and neither can she."

"Like I said. Help." She nods at the file clenched in my hand. "You don't have to make any decisions now. Just read the information and consider your options." She pauses for a moment and then hands me a smaller stack of papers stapled together at the top left corner. The bill. "There's help, Rhys. You just have to be willing to accept it."

As I walk back to Mom's room, the reality of the situation consumes me. Mom needs help. A lot of help. More help than I can give her.

Chapter Forty-Two
Emmy

Leçon [luh-SAWN] n—Lesson. The daily class taken by dancers throughout their career to continue learning and to maintain technical proficiency

"Ms. Jennings, can you stay for a minute?" André asks after class.

After watching me rehearse his brilliant ballet, I'm sure André's changed his mind about choosing me to dance the solo. My voice wavers as I say, "Sure."

All the other dancers take off their pointe shoes and walk out of the studio.

"Why are you here, Ms. Jennings?"

"B-because I love ballet."

"No. Why are you *here*?" André asks. "In Utah."

I readjust my duffel bag. "I'm not sure I understand your question."

André rests his hand on the *barre*. "You're extremely talented. You should be at least two years into your professional career already."

I know that. Ballet careers are short, especially for female dancers. But, "My dad—"

André holds up a hand. "I don't want to know what your dad thinks. I want to know what you think."

André's face stays blank, but somehow it squeezes the truth out of me. "I didn't want to leave my sister. We had always planned to go to BYU together. It was the safer option. I was afraid to go to New York and audition with the best dancers in the world."

"Last semester you were passed over for the lead. Why?"

My shoulders tense. "I don't know."

"Yes, you do. Why?"

"Because some lessons are best learned in the corps." I repeat what Ballet Master Miller said at the beginning of last semester.

"Was the dancer who got the part better than you?" André asks. "Were you not good enough?"

André's questions pile one on top of the other, and I don't know what to answer first or if I should answer at all. "Um."

"The truth, please."

"I'm better."

"By a lot," he agrees. "So let me ask you again. Why are you here?"

"I don't know."

"Me neither, Ms. Jennings." André studies me for a long moment. "What are your plans for the future? For your career?"

"I'm going to finish school and then—"

"How long do you have left?"

"A year and a half."

"That's too long."

He's right. It is too long. But I've come this far. I'm so close to graduating, and my technique is getting stronger. "I appreciate your confidence in my abilities, and you're an amazing choreographer, but getting an education is important to me."

"More important than being a professional dancer?"

I meet his gaze. "No." Ballet is all I have left.

"If dancing professionally is your dream, and I think it is, then you can do better than this," André says. "You should do better."

"I know," I whisper.

"I don't think you do; otherwise, you wouldn't still be here." André pushes off the *barre* and takes a step closer. "You have talent, but talent alone isn't enough. You have to fight for what you love. And the only person who will fight for your career is you. If you aren't willing to do that, ballet isn't for you. You have what it takes to make it in this world, and that is a rare gift. Fight for yourself, Ms. Jennings."

Chapter Forty-Three

Rhys

Secondary Progressive Multiple Sclerosis (SPMS) [sek-uh-n-der-ee / pruh-gres-iv / muhl-tuh-puhl / skli-roh-sis] n—One jerk of a disease that progresses without any certainty and at any rate it wants

SUPE AND I HAVE BEEN sitting at a table in the library all morning searching website after website, trying to make sense of all the information the doctor gave me last week.

"Okay . . ." Supe puts on his business face, brow slightly furrowed, head held high. It's the same look he gets when he studies. "So she has a new diagnosis; what now?"

Before coming to the library today, I read all the pamphlets on secondary progressive I was given at the hospital. The whole point of digging through online research was to prove Dr. Williams wrong about there being nothing we could do to alleviate Mom's symptoms. Unfortunately, there is nothing to find. There isn't a thing he or anyone else can do. "Secondary progressive MS isn't treatable. No matter what we do, her symptoms will gradually get worse over time."

"How worse, and how long?"

"No one knows."

"There's no time line?"

"Nope."

Supe blows out a breath. "That is . . ."

"Yeah." I log off of the computer and then tuck the pamphlets Dr. Williams gave me back into the manila envelope. The file the financial counselor gave me sits untouched. The stack of bills inside it is also too much to deal with right now. I know there are pamphlets in there about care facilities, but I'm not ready to admit defeat yet. This is my last semester. If we can hold on a little longer, I'll get a real job and be able to pay for decent in-home health care for Mom like a man instead of relying on the help of others.

"Thanks for going over all this with me," I say to Supe as we walk into the library lobby.

"Happy to help."

We stop to zip our coats before going outside.

"How's your mom doing with all this?"

"I think she's either in the anger or denial stage of grief. She's . . ." I sigh. "Depressed. Confused. Frustrated."

"And you?"

"Depressed. Confused. Frustrated." I snort. "Ready to get out of Provo."

"It hasn't been all bad, has it? Being here at BYU?" There's a hint of sadness in his voice I wish I didn't notice.

"Not all bad." I nudge him with my elbow.

"Right." He laughs. "You did luck out in the roommate department."

"That I did."

"I've got to get to class, but I'm around if you need anything," he says, and I know he means it.

"Thanks, man."

"Anytime." Supe takes off for class, and I walk toward the steps that lead down to the RB. Parking near the RB, hoping to catch a glimpse of her, is probably one of the stupider things I've done since the breakup. Seeing as how Emmy won't change her mind about us. About me.

I start down the stairs like always. And there she is. Walking up the stairs. Her cheeks are flushed like she's just come from ballet. I can tell by the way she bites her bottom lip when she checks her phone that she's in a rush. Probably late for her next class. She was late to class the day we met.

She continues up the stairs, and when she gets to the top of the third flight, she finally looks up, and our eyes meet. "Rhys."

I continue down the steps until I'm standing next to her. "Hey, Emmy."

"H-how are you?"

"Fine." One word answers seem the safest.

"Good. That's good." She pulls at her sweater and looks up at the sky. "This weather is crazy, right? Last week it was sunny, and now it's practically snowing . . ."

I didn't realize how much this moment would hurt. But of course it does. How could it not? The last time we saw each other, I poured my heart out to her, literally begged her not to give up on us. And now she wants to talk about the weather? I can't do it.

"I love the snow. It's a nice break from the rain and the sun, but I hate having to get all bundled up to go out. Everything ends up soaked and . . ."

I've missed the sound of her voice. Her sweet scent. My arms ache to hold her.

"Hopefully it will be a short winter though. There's nothing worse than when it's still snowing in May . . ." She continues to ramble.

It's too much and, at the same time, not enough. Being her friend, talking to her like a casual acquaintance isn't something I want to do. Not with her. "Emmy." I cut her off.

"Yeah?"

Her big blue eyes nearly bring me to my knees. "It was nice to see you again."

"You too."

It takes everything in me, but this time, I walk away from her.

Chapter Forty-Four
Emmy

Divertissement [dee-vehr-tees-MAHN] n—A diversion

Nathan is already seated, chewing on the end of a blue ballpoint pen, when I walk into class. I slam into the seat next to him. "Did you serve a mission?"

"Yeeeaaah?"

"And you're still active?" The question feels like a betrayal. Part of me says it shouldn't matter, but it does.

"Do you want to see my temple recommend?" He chuckles and reaches into his pocket.

"That won't be necessary." I wave him off. "Does your dinner offer still stand?"

Nathan raises an eyebrow, and all my confidence disappears. I don't ask guys out. I don't do this. Jumping into something with one guy only to forget another is wrong. Not even close to okay. "I'm sorry, Nathan." I shake my head. "I can't believe I—You know I just got out of something serious. Well, I ran into him. It's clear I have to move on, but it's hard because I loved him. But no matter how much we care for each other, we'll never—" The truth catches in my throat, and I can't finish the sentence.

Nathan leans forward and angles his face toward me. "I have no issue with being the rebound guy."

My head falls forward, and I bury my face in my arms. "I don't know what I was thinking."

"Trust me. It's nice being the one asked out for a change."

I spread my fingers and peek at Nathan through the cracks. "I'm sorry."

Nathan's dimple appears beside his smirky smile. "Don't be. I've heard of relationships starting crazier ways."

"Nathan, no. I'm not—"

"You're still in love with what's-his-face. I know." Nathan relaxes into his chair. "I'll take my chances though. I think you might be worth it."

I'm not so sure Rhys would think so.

"I'll pick you up tonight around seven?"

"Tonight?"

He nods. "I think if I let you sleep on it, you'll change your mind. So, yes, tonight."

Betrayal claws at my chest when I agree to the date and impales my heart as I program my phone number into his phone and slide it back to him.

* * *

My eyes cross as Nathan leans over the center console and puts a sticker in the middle of my forehead. He smiles a tragically beautiful smile. Beautiful because his teeth are straight and white and perfect. Tragic because all that perfection is wasted on me. I feel nothing.

"We're going Indian tonight." Nathan points at my forehead. "That's your third eye."

"Did you serve in India?"

"Nah. Anaheim, California. But there's a decent-sized Indian population there, and I fell in love with their food."

"I like Indian food too."

We get out of the car, and Nathan opens the restaurant door for me. A host leads us to a booth and hands us each a menu.

"On a scale of one to ten, how adventurous would you say you are?" Nathan asks.

"Seven?"

Nathan lowers his menu and looks over the top. "Trust me to order?"

"Sure, why not?"

He orders several things I've never heard of—not hard to do given that I've had only naan and chicken tikka masala before.

While we wait for our meals, we cover our families, his mission, our majors— him: graphic design, me: dance. I tell him about our upcoming show and how I got the solo. We cover all the obligatory first-date topics. I ask questions; he answers. He asks questions; I answer. Conversation is easy. He's interesting. Funny, even.

But he isn't Rhys. No one will ever be Rhys.

Eventually our food comes. Nathan's picked several things I like, a few I don't. I try a little of them all, and he gives me an impressed nod, like he's already formulating our next date in his mind. I look away, trying not to encourage him any more than I already have. This was a mistake.

I can't be with Rhys, but I also can't help the fact that I want to be. But coming out on a date with Nathan to forget Rhys? What was I thinking? Nathan's a nice guy; he doesn't deserve this.

"What's he like?" Nathan asks. "This dream guy of yours?"

I nearly choke on my tongue. "What?"

Nathan hands me a glass of water. "I'm only asking because I need to assess my competition."

I suck down some water, then set the glass on the table with a shaky hand. "I'm so sorry. I'm not ready for this. I should go." I unzip my purse and dig for my wallet. After dragging poor Nathan into the middle of my drama, the least I can do is pay for dinner.

"Don't be silly." Nathan motions for me to put my wallet away. "I knew what you were when I picked you up." He winks. "So come on; what's he like?"

"He's . . . kind and gentle and selfless and the most amazing person I have ever met." There are a million more things I love about Rhys, but all of them feel too personal to share.

"Hmm." Nathan studies my face. "I think I may have my work cut out for me."

"I'm not playing hard to get."

"I know you're not, which makes you that much harder to get."

I stare at the half-eaten piece of naan on my plate.

"I know we didn't meet under ideal circumstances, but I've had a great time tonight." He spoons another scoop of rice onto his plate and drenches it with sweet-tomato cream sauce. "Tell you what. No expectations. We can be friends. Maybe hang out and see where things go. If something comes of it, great. If not, I'll gain a friend, and maybe you can get a little distance from your past."

We finish dinner but decide to cut the rest of the date short. Dinner was hard enough. I felt like I was betraying Rhys the whole time. Even though the conversation was easy, the date felt forced. We had fun, and I can tell he hopes it will go somewhere, but I already know it won't. My heart is with Rhys.

Nathan walks me to the porch, staying a few respectful paces behind me as I unlock the door. We say a quick good-bye, and then I run up the stairs and sink to my knees in agony.

Heavenly Father, I can't do this. I don't want to do this. I want Rhys. I only want Rhys. I've done everything right. I waited to date until I was sixteen. I came to BYU. I've tried my best to obey every commandment. I know how important it is to marry in the temple, but I don't want to move on from Rhys. I know all things are possible with Thee. Please. Please give me Rhys. I'll do anything.

Even give up eternity? I don't want forever if Rhys isn't with me. What good would it be? To gain eternity but be separated from the person I love? Maybe I should take the time I have with him. Marry him. Let "till death do us part" be enough.

But what about your children. What about their eternity?

A wave of anguish hits me so hard it takes me under. Swimming in despair, I pray harder. Harder than I've ever prayed in my life. For me, for Rhys, for us. My face is damp with tears, my body wet with sweat. All I want is Rhys. The boy who gave up his dreams, his future, his desires to care for his mother. I want the boy who kneels in front of his mother's wheelchair and places slippers on her feet. I want the boy who works to pay his mother's bills. I don't want some Mormon boy who has all the right answers. I want the boy who makes me want forever.

My head throbs, and my heart collapses. How am I supposed to pick only one? Rhys or forever? *I can't do this. I can't do this. I can't do this. Take this away. I can't do this.*

Sobs wrack my body as I cry and cry and cry. *Please*, I whisper in a hoarse voice. *I'll do anything to be with Rhys forever.*

Would you give up ballet? a silent voice asks.

Yes. I'd even give up ballet.

My legs tingle as I rise to my feet. So hot, so white it blinds me. I know every reason I can't be with Rhys. Why I shouldn't. But tonight, the reasons aren't enough. Tonight, I just. Want. Rhys.

Chapter Forty-Five
Rhys

Eternity [ee-tur-ni-tee] n—A seemingly endless period of time

AFTER SEEING EMMY ON THE stairs today, it's like my mind is on this endless loop: Mom, SPMS, Emmy. Mom, SPMS, Emmy. For once, work was a welcome distraction.

It's a quarter after nine when I walk into the house. My uniform smells like burnt grease and is smeared with corn-bread batter. Supe is lying on his bed, tossing a baseball up at Helaman, smiling like he's just discovered ice cream. "Good night?" I ask.

Supe's grin widens. "The best." He rises to his feet and gets his shower stuff. "I don't know." He shakes his head. "I feel like I was supposed to meet this girl. Is that weird?"

"No weirder than all the other stuff you believe in."

He frowns. "I'm sorry, man. I didn't mean to rub your face in it. I know things have been difficult for you."

"Don't worry about it."

Supe goes to shower, and I sit at my desk and open the packet the financial counselor gave me on assisted-living homes. Since I didn't find the answers I wanted about controlling the course of Mom's disease, maybe it's time to open the other envelope and consider options for improving her quality of life. As much as I don't want to consider this option, I want Mom to be safe.

A moment later, a heavy knock sounds at the front door. I finish reading a sentence and stand. Before I can answer the door, the knock comes again.

Jeez.

I yank open the door. "Dude—"

Emmy bursts into the room, and before I know what's happening, her arms are locked around my neck and she's sobbing into my shirt.

I kick the front door shut and take a step back to make sure she's not injured. "Are you hurt? Did something happen?"

"He came to pick me up, and—"

"He? He who?"

She shakes her head. "After we talked on the stairs," she says, her voice muffled against my chest. "I couldn't—How am I supposed to walk away from you? I love you, and you love me." Her grip tightens around my neck. "I can't do it. Heaven wouldn't be heaven without you." She pulls back and looks up. Her face is wet and puffy, and mascara is smudged under her red-rimmed eyes. "I don't want eternity. Not without you."

My thumbs brush her cheeks, along her hairline until I'm cupping her face in my hands. I've dreamed of this moment so many times. The moment she realizes she doesn't want to give up on us. That we're bigger than everything she learns on Sundays. But that's not what she's saying. She's saying she wants all that, but she'll give it up for me.

It happens so quickly I don't see it coming. She rises to her tiptoes and presses her lips to mine.

I'm a good guy, but I'm not that good. I kiss her. With everything I am, with everything I feel. But then I pull back. I need to know what happened. "Talk to me."

"I w-went on a date. And he was nice. Everything I should want."

My jaw tenses.

"He was polite and funny and cute." She looks deep into my eyes. "But he wasn't you. No one will ever be you."

I pull her hands from my neck and entwine my fingers with hers. "I shouldn't say this."

"W-what?"

"That I love you."

Her mouth finds mine again, this kiss more desperate than the last.

The bathroom door squeaks open behind me, and Supe emerges in a cloud of steam, wearing his ridiculous bright-blue Superman pajamas. When he sees I'm not alone, he ducks his head and makes for the bedroom.

I look at Emmy and find her eyes haven't left me. Like she's afraid I'll disappear if she breaks the connection.

"Emelia?"

Emmy's head snaps up. "N-Nathan?" She turns ghost white.

"What are you doing here?" Supe asks Emmy.

Emmy's gaze bounces from Supe to me. "I didn't know."

"Didn't know what, angel?"

"Whoa." Supe drags a hand down his face. "Emelia. Emmy. I'm an idiot. The grainy picture. Blonde hair."

Emmy takes a step away from me. "I'm sorry. I shouldn't have come here. I didn't know you guys were—I'm so sorry. I shouldn't have come here. As much as I love you, nothing has changed. I want you, but we still can't be together. I'm a mess. I've only made things worse. I'm sorry. So sorry." Emmy bolts out the front door.

"What just happened?" I ask Supe.

"Emmy's the girl I took out on a date tonight."

Anger swells into a fierce rage deep inside my chest. I charge Supe, stopping just short of slamming him into the wall. My fists tighten around his collar, and he holds up his hands. "We didn't know."

I want to pound him into next week, but I don't have time for that. I grit my teeth and drop my hold on him and run out the door to find Emmy. I'm just in time to see her taillights disappear around the corner.

Cursing under my breath, I turn back to the house to get my keys. My hand is on the doorknob before I stop. If I go back inside right now, I'm going to bloody my best friend. I sit on the frozen cement steps until I've cooled down. Emmy is probably home by now. What am I going to do? I can't keep chasing her, hoping she'll accept me for who I am.

Emmy said she didn't want eternity without me, but as soon as she saw Supe, she retracted everything. She doesn't want to get back together, and she isn't going to give up her version of eternity. She misses me. She loves me. But deep down, she still wants a Mormon guy. Big wedding, white temple. Forever and ever.

All the lights in the house are off when I finally go inside. It's late, and Supe is in bed.

I kick off my shoes but don't bother changing out of my clothes. This day needs to end.

"I swear I didn't know," Supe whispers. "I never would have gone out with her."

"I know," I say. Supe is quiet for a few minutes. "I tried," I finally say.

"Tried what?"

"To feel it. That burning feeling you guys talk about. Even met with the missionaries and asked to be baptized. I prayed too."

Supe's bed frame squeaks as he shifts. "And?"

"No answer."

He doesn't hesitate. "Maybe you weren't asking the right questions."

"I don't think that was the problem."

"Were you asking because you wanted to know the truth or because you wanted Emelia, er, Emmy?" He sounds like that lie-detector missionary, Elder Marsden. Sometimes I forget my best friend is an RM trained in the art of conversion.

His question hangs in the air, but the answer doesn't matter, so I say what does. "Treat my girl right."

Chapter Forty-Six

Emmy

Choreography [kor-ee-og-ruh-fee] n—The art of composing

NATHAN IS WAITING OUTSIDE WHEN I walk up to class Monday morning. It's blustery cold, and his nose is bright red. "Wasn't sure you were going to show," he says.

"Me neither."

"How are you?"

"You don't have to be nice to me, Nathan."

His eyebrows pull together. "Why wouldn't I be nice to you?"

I wouldn't be nice to me. He took me out. We had fun. And then he found me in his living room kissing his roommate. *Nice* shouldn't even be in his vocabulary. "I can think of a few reasons."

"You warned me." He shrugs. "I've been thinking about it. There are over thirty thousand students here at BYU. Don't you find it odd that you happened to date my roommate, break up, and then go on a date with me?"

Odd. Uncomfortable. A cruel twist of fate. "Umm—"

"Yeah. Me too," he says. "So it made me think, you know. Why, out of all the girls on this campus, did I have to meet you?"

I wince.

He shakes his head. "That didn't come out right. What I mean is I think we met for a reason."

I stare at him, still confused.

"I want to help you guys."

"Y-you do?"

"Of course I do. Rhys is my best friend. There aren't many guys like him."

"None," I say. This is not how I expected this conversation to go. Something more along the lines of him sitting on the opposite side of the classroom and ignoring me was what I imagined. "Why do you want to help? I don't understand."

"I've seen Rhys struggle for the past three years. His stress load was Rocky Mountain. I thought if he dated casually, he'd like it better here. I was worried he'd leave Provo with a bad taste in his mouth." Nathan pauses. "I never meant—" He clears his throat. "I convinced Rhys to take you out."

I let myself process his words for a moment before I speak. "And you feel guilty," I guess. "Because of how things ended up between Rhys and me."

"A little," he admits.

"Please don't." I wanted to date Rhys. No matter how badly it hurts, loving him is worth the pain.

"Still feel guilty," he says.

A gust of wind interrupts our conversation, and we walk into the building.

"Why does Rhys call you Supe?"

Nathan grins. "Super. Nathan Super. I don't remember how the abbreviation happened."

"Ah. Well then, *Supe*, tell me about this plan of yours?"

Nathan grins and opens the classroom door for me.

"You're a ballet dancer, right?"

I nod.

"And you guys have a show coming up?"

I set my bag on the floor next to my desk. "Yeah, why?"

"Step one of the plan is for you to invite Rhys to your show—"

"I can't do that." I interrupt. "I've already made a mess of things. Going to your house and saying things I had no business saying, even if I was hurting . . ." I should have been stronger. "I can't yank him around anymore than I already have. Asking him to come to my show would only make things worse."

Nathan lets out a breath. "Okay. New plan. *I'll* get Rhys to come to your show."

"How do you think you're going to do that?"

"Easy. I'll tell him I still want to date you." He holds up his hands as if to ward off my glare. "Just to get him to come to the show. I don't date girls my best friend is in love with."

"Nathan—"

"Trust me." He slings a brotherly arm across my shoulders as we walk into the classroom. "Rhys will be so jealous he won't be able to help himself."

"I'm going on record that this is the worst plan in the history of plans."

He laughs like I'm joking. "You're probably right, but do you have any better ideas?"

"Can't we buy him a box of chocolates or something?"

Nathan's face winds into a knot. "How is that going to convince Rhys to join the Church?"

"How is making him come to my show going to get him to join the Church?"

Nathan's brow furrows as he thinks over my question. "Well, if Rhys knew you were moving on, he might work a little harder to do what he needs to do to be with you."

It's not that Nathan's reasoning isn't there; it's just flawed. "It's never going to work." Making Rhys jealous won't convert him. At least not for the right reasons.

"You want to be with Rhys, right?"

"More than anything."

"Then let me try to help you." His voice is soft and sincere.

"Okay." I have nothing left to lose anyway.

Chapter Forty-Seven
Rhys

Preordination [pree-or-duh-nay shun] n—Fate, but not.
Mormons don't believe in fate

"YOU STALKING ME NOW?" I ask Supe when I walk out of class Monday morning. I've somehow managed to avoid him since the episode with Emmy last weekend, and I didn't expect him to wait outside my classroom.

"If that's what it takes to talk to you, then, yeah, I guess I am."

I continue walking.

"Come on, man. Don't be like this. We've gotta talk it out."

Slowing my stride, I turn to face him. "I don't know what to say. I get that you guys didn't know, but—"

"I'd like to keep seeing her," Nathan says. "But I wanted to make sure you're cool with it."

Nothing good could possibly come from this conversation. I'm not cool with it. I'm not even close to cool with it. I don't respond.

"Listen," Nathan continues. "I know you liked her—"

"I don't like her. I *love* her." Present tense. *Love.* Probably always will. She'll always be the girl who got away. Or rather ran away.

"Right. Love," Supe says. "Here's the thing. I think there's a reason you guys dated."

Yeah, we dated because we're perfect for each other. "And that would be what exactly?"

"So she and I could meet."

I shove my hands in my pockets to stop from strangling my best friend. "I thought Mormons didn't believe in fate."

Supe grunts, then falls in stride beside me. "We don't, but she's incredible, man. It feels like I've always known her." He glances sideways at me as if trying to gauge my reaction.

My jaw tenses. "I do not want to hear about you and Emmy."

"She has a show coming up."

That's right. We talked about the visiting choreographer and this semester's solo briefly on the ride to Los Angeles. "Did she get the solo?" The words fall out of my mouth before I can stop them, but I don't have any pride left to be embarrassed.

Supe grins, though I can't imagine why. "Come to her show and find out."

"I don't think so."

"She'd love to have you there."

I pause midstride and face him. "I get what you're trying to do."

Supe stops short. "You do?"

"Yes. I do. You want to date her, and you still want to be friends with me. But I can't pretend I'm cool with you guys being together when I'm not." And quite frankly, I can't believe Emmy is already ready to date. Do. Not. Get. It.

"I'm going. You should come with me."

"So I can what? Watch you make a move on my girl?"

Supe lets out an exasperated groan. "That's not what I meant. You're both miserable. Talk it out at the show. Friday night, seven o'clock."

I jam my thumbs under my backpack straps and brush by him. My shoulder catches his and knocks him off balance.

"Classy, man. Real classy," Supe says as I stomp up the hill away from him.

February

Chapter Forty-Eight

Emmy

Ballerina [bal-uh-ree-nuh] n—A principal female ballet dancer

I PULL THE RED VELVET curtain back an inch and survey the audience. I scan the rows and spot Evie sitting next to Kennedy a few rows back and off to the side. Evie's hair is up in a messy bun, and her sweats are anything but appropriate for the night, but I'm so glad she's here. Mom and Dad would have been here too if Dad's client weren't still being tried in court.

I spot Nathan sitting toward the top in the middle. The seat next to him is empty.

It's been a week since I last saw Rhys. I hoped it would get easier, but it hasn't. I still check my phone a few dozen times a day, wondering what he's thinking, hoping he's okay. And my head is on a constant swivel every time I walk through campus wanting to catch a glimpse of him.

"Full house. Pretty exciting, huh?" David stands behind me and peers over my shoulder at the audience. "Ready?"

I let the curtain fall closed. "Absolutely."

David returns a sympathetic smile. "You okay?" I nod unconvincingly, and David reminds me, "Leave it on the stage."

"Places," André calls.

David follows me to the middle of the stage, where two pieces of neon-colored tape mark our spots in the dark. He rests his hand on my waist as I settle into position in front of him.

The overture begins, and the curtain opens. The world is dark. Nothing but a bright spotlight, classical music, and the stage exist. The music takes over and erases everything. Every hurt, every pain. Better than any drug, any therapy. I get into the flow. The air swirls around me as I turn in a pirouette, David's strong hands around my waist, assuring my balance.

The initial adrenaline gives way to a steady high. My muscles flex, pulling my body up, up, up until I'm flying. I lose myself in the magic, and for a brief moment, the agony of losing Rhys subsides.

Before I know it, the music swells, and then I'm bowing, and the curtain closes. And then I'm standing in the dark in the middle of the stage again. The swish of tulle and the hollow patter of pointe shoes sound as the corps rush off stage behind us. The moment forever gone. Rhys rushes back into my thoughts full force, but determined to enjoy this night, I push him away.

Once backstage, I change out of my tutu into street clothes and then check my cell phone. A few texts from Evie and Kennedy telling me what a great job I did and that they're waiting in the lobby. Seeing my sister's name on the screen, her congratulating me on a great performance, makes my mood soar. I can't believe she came. I'm so happy I could burst. But then another text comes in from Nathan. One word: *Sorry.* And my elation deflates. Rhys didn't come.

Willing myself not to cry, I grab my bag and press open the stage door that leads into the lobby.

"You were great out there."

Goose bumps cover my arms like a warm blanket fresh from the dryer the moment I hear Rhys's voice.

"You came."

A sad smile shadows his face, and he takes a step closer, but then, as if thinking better of it, he stops. It kills me that he's right here but so, so far away.

"You got the solo," he says.

"Yeah."

"You deserved it."

"How have you been?" I ask, not caring about the solo but wanting only to know about him.

He bounces his keys in his hand. "I've been better."

"How's your mom?"

His eyebrows raise and lower in one quick motion. "She's been better too." He holds my eyes with his. They're so intense it's hard not to look away. But I don't. I don't want to waste a single second of him. This may be all we have left.

"She fell," he finally says. "Cut her head and had to get stitches. But she's— We're surviving."

They're always surviving. Never living. I wish I could help. But it's not my place anymore. No matter how much I want it to be.

"I didn't think you would come," I say.

"I probably shouldn't have."

"I'm glad you did." I regret the words as soon as they leave my mouth. I've hurt him enough already; saying things like this will only make it worse. "I'm sorry I came the other night. I didn't mean to hurt you. It was a mistake." I did not say that. Face on fire, I look at the floor.

"Kinda figured that out when you ran out of my house and I didn't hear from you again."

Mortified, I tug on the hem of my cardigan. "Yeah. I, uh . . ."

"There you are!" Nathan drapes his arm around me, and a muscle in Rhys's jaw jumps. I squirm away from Nathan's embrace, and Evie and Kennedy join us.

"You were amazing!" Kennedy gushes.

"You really were," Evie agrees quietly.

"Thanks." An invisible rope wages war on my emotions. I'm tugged toward Evie. She came. For me. I want to wrap my arms around her, tell her I love her, and ask all about her new life. But then I'm pulled back to Rhys. If I take my eyes off him, he may walk out of this lobby and I may never see him again.

"Dessert?" Nathan asks the group.

Kennedy readily agrees and, with a nudge, gets Evie to agree.

"What about you guys?" Nathan asks Rhys and me.

"Nah. I'm good," Rhys says.

A wave of disappointment crashes over me.

"I, um . . ."

"Dessert is to celebrate *your* magnificence. You have to come." Nathan winks conspiratorially.

Rhys's glare intensifies. "I'm going to go," he says. "You did great, Emmy. I'll see you around."

Around. Around where?

Rhys walks away, and it feels like my heart is on the verge of collapse again.

"Maybe a box of chocolates would have been a better choice," Nathan says.

"Wait," I call after Rhys and run over to him.

My mouth takes over as soon as I reach him. "It's like I'm in this loop where I keep hoping something will change, but it doesn't. I try to focus on ballet, but you're always on my mind. I think about you constantly. I'm no closer to moving on than the day we broke up."

His eyes flash to where Nathan stands. "Doesn't look that way."

Right. I close my eyes, wishing I could go back in time and talk Nathan out of his stupid make-Rhys-jealous plan.

"I'm destroyed without you, Emmy. You said I'm always on your mind, that you keep hoping something will change, but here's the thing—I don't want anything to change. I love you for who you are. You just can't love me for me. *We* didn't break up. You broke up with me."

His words punch me in the gut. "That's not fair."

"But it's the truth." He takes a step closer, close enough that I can smell his clean scent. "You walked away, not me."

"Rhys—"

"You want a clean break? You want to forget me? Fine. Here it is. Move on, Emmy. I'm done. You can have your forever; you just can't have mine." His strides are quick and sure. He slams his hand against the glass door. It swings open and hits the wall with reverberating force. Surprisingly, it doesn't shatter, but my heart does. Into a million pieces.

The dull hum of voices fades away, and dozens of pairs of eyes settle on me. My humiliation is complete. I didn't ask for this. I didn't want to hurt him. All I want is him. Forever.

Nathan walks up behind me and puts his hand on my shoulder.

I turn into him and let my eyes empty onto his pressed white dress shirt.

"Come on." He rubs my back, quieting my cry. "Let's get you out of here. You did amazing tonight. You deserve to celebrate."

I shake my head. I don't want to celebrate. I want to hide, shrivel up, sleep until it doesn't hurt anymore. "Go after Rhys," I tell Nathan.

"Pretty sure he needs to cool off alone."

Another tear drops down my cheek.

"It'll be fun," Nathan says. "You'll see."

I don't have any fight left in me tonight. "Fine."

The four of us walk outside: Nathan, Me, Evie, and Kennedy.

"Creamery on Ninth?" Nathan says as we walk to his car.

"No!" My head snaps up, and I slip down a stair. Nathan reaches out a hand to steady me. It snowed all day yesterday, heated up, then froze again and turned it all to ice. "Anywhere but there." Too many memories.

"Yeah," Evie whispers. "It is freezing outside." The threads on the rope pull me toward Evie, trying to tie us back together, but I'm too frayed to be moved.

"O-kayyy. What about hot chocolate, then?"

"Too bad," Kennedy pouts. "Ice cream sounds good."

Nathan's head pops up. "Yeah?"

"Totally. Rain check?" she asks, not so subtly veiling her date request.

"Definitely," he agrees. "Hey, I've got an idea. Why don't we race? Whoever gets to the address last has to buy."

"You're on," Kennedy says.

"And you're with me," Nathan says to Kennedy.

As he and Kennedy pile into Nathan's car, Evie and I slide into mine.

"You okay?" Evie asks.

The most I can manage is to lift one shoulder.

"I'm sorry about Rhys. I wanted to call, but after the way we left things, after how I treated you . . . I didn't know what to say or if you'd even want to talk to me at all."

I'm happy Evie's here. But I'm physically exhausted from my performance and emotionally drained from Rhys's leaving; there's nothing left inside of me to give her right now. Maybe tomorrow we can talk and I can figure out why she married Q and understand her need for space from me, but tonight, I'm too consumed with Rhys to think about mending things with Evie. "No matter what's happened, I love you, Evie. Thank you for coming, but would it be okay if we talk about this later?"

She nods. "Whenever you're ready."

Nathan pulls up beside us and gives us an address of a bakery in Lindon—apparently they have hot chocolate to die for. Evie punches the address into her phone and pulls up directions.

"Ready. Set. Go." Nathan peels out of the parking lot, and I step on the gas pedal. Adrenaline kicks in and erases every thought of Rhys as all five hundred horses under the hood sprint toward the goal. The more I press the pedal to the floor, the farther I am from my problems.

I manage to keep up with Nathan and speed through every green light between here and the freeway. And as soon as we get to I-15, I floor it.

It starts to snow, and Nathan maneuvers into the right-hand lane. I decelerate to follow him, but find as soon as I start to slow, everything catches up to me, including Rhys, so I accelerate again. My SUV momentarily loses traction. I ease my foot off the gas pedal but only just. Tonight is about forgetting. Evie's hand comes up in sudden panic, and she points frantically out the windshield. I look into the dark night and see headlights rushing toward me.

Chapter Forty-Nine
Rhys

Angel [ayn-juhl] n—Heavenly being

MY PHONE WON'T STOP VIBRATING. Can nobody take a hint? Leave. Me. Alone.

I yank open my dresser drawer, throw my phone inside, and slam it shut. I tug my sweatshirt over my head and toss it to the ground. Kick off my shoes and sink into bed. With the covers pulled over my head, it takes only a few minutes to fall asleep.

Her perfect body glides through the air as she floats across the stage. Black lashes, red lipstick, her hair piled on her head like a crown. Her performance is flawless. The perfect ballerina. The crowd applauds. So do I.

After the show, she runs to find me. Throws her arms around my neck. Nuzzles into my embrace. My hands tangle in her hair. My lips touch hers. So soft. So sweet. I pick her up, swing her in my arms.

"I love you," she says, smiling.

My heart melts.

"Promise you'll never leave me," she says.

My smile slips. "You already left."

"Promise me," she pleads, her eyes holding mine.

This isn't real. She walked away.

"It's going to be hard," she says, her words rushed as if she already knows she's leaving. Already fading back into reality. Everything becomes fuzzy, fades in and out. I hold her tighter. Not yet. I kiss her again, but instead of kissing me back, she pushes away from me and bends down. She fumbles with the pink ribbons around her ankles and then pulls off her pointe shoes. "It will be hard, Rhys. But don't leave me."

"What's going to be hard?" My head is filled with this dark cloud, and I'm trying to focus, to listen, but the fog is too deep and her words too muffled, and I can't understand. "I would never leave you," I say.

"Promise me."

"I promise."

She sets her ballet shoes in my hands. "I choose you."

My fight-or-flight response kicks in as I'm yanked from the dream.

"Rhys! Wake up!" Supe kneels above me, shaking my shoulders, and reality slams into focus.

I sit up and push him off me. "What is wrong with you?"

His hands claw at his hair, and he paces the floor. "I tried to call. I called, and I called, and I called. But you didn't answer. And so I left her there. And she's—it's bad. Real bad."

I jump to my feet. "What happened? Where's Emmy?"

"It all happened so fast. We were driving, and the roads were slick, and then it started to snow. I got in a different lane. When I looked to make sure she was still with me, I saw that a car in front of them had lost traction and done a three sixty and—"

I sink to the floor, find my boots, and yank them on. "And what?" I yell. "Is she okay?"

"I don't know." He sits on the bed, cradling his head in his hands, crying. "There was so much blood, and it took forever for the ambulance to get there."

I grab my keys and sprint out to my truck. Supe climbs into the passenger seat, and we drive to the hospital. We hurry to the front desk and ask where Emmy is.

The nurse ushers us down the hall, explaining Emmy's condition. I only get bits of information. "Bad shape. Pulverized tibia and fibula. Intensive care. Can't operate. Too unstable." Her words blur together as we walk down the endless hall.

We aren't allowed inside her room but can look through a window at her. Everything I said in the lobby of the theater floods my mind. I didn't mean any of it. I was upset, and I wanted to change her mind.

What have I done?

A red line jumps erratically on a monitor next to her bedside. White bandages cover her face. Her crushed left leg is elevated. The nurse informs me that there will be scars. Big ones. Inside and out.

That doesn't matter. "Will she dance?"

"She might never walk again."

My eyes shut, and I rest my head against the cool glass window. "You have to fix her," I whisper.

"We're trying," the nurse says.

"Try harder. She has to be able to dance."

The nurse turns away to leave, and I stop her.

"Wait. Where's Evie? Her twin?"

The nurse relaxes. "Next door, resting. She's been given a sedative to calm her."

"Thanks."

She nods and then walks back to her station. Hospital policy or not, I walk into Emmy's room. I pull over a chair and gently kiss her swollen knuckles. She doesn't react. Not a single twitch. "Don't leave me, angel. Not again."

The nurse comes back a few minutes later and pushes me out of the room and into a blue chair in the lobby, promising to keep me informed.

Emmy's in surgery when the majority of the Jennings cavalry arrives a few hours later: Mr. and Mrs. Jennings, Jason, and Drew. It's been four hours since the accident, but I have no news to report. Mr. Jennings presses the nurse for information.

My eyes well up, and my head drops into my hands. I should have been with her tonight.

Chapter Fifty

Emmy

Vole [voh-lay] v—To fly

"You're awake," Rhys whispers. His velvet lips brush the back of my hand.

"I love your lips," I say.

He presses them together as if to hide them from my view. "You're drunk. High on pain meds."

"You're hot. And I love you."

The blush I adore so much colors his cheeks. He leans forward and whispers in my ear, "I love you too, angel."

The edges of Rhys blur. He's too soft, too beautiful to be real. I'm dreaming. "You're not real," I say.

"I'm very real."

I try to shake my head, but it doesn't move. Sleep paralysis—another indicator this is a hallucination.

"Is she awake?"

Dad's voice.

Rhys nods, the movement creating an arc of color. I get lost in the colors. Rhys stands, then moves aside. Dad sits. Tears pool in the corners of his eyes. I don't like this part of my dream.

"Rhys," I demand.

Dad's face falls. "He's right here."

Dad backs away, and Rhys reappears. My hand flutters toward him. His fingers are gentle as they lace with mine.

"Can we pretend this is real? That you still love me—"

"I'll always love you," Dream Rhys murmurs.

"You only love me because I'm asleep. Clean break. Done. Just not when I'm dreaming."

"You're not dreaming."

"Let's pretend you asked me."

"Asked you what?"

"To marry you."

Rhys's eyes flick to the end of the bed. To Dad. Except Dad isn't actually here. He's back home in California in a trial. "Aren't you supposed to be in court?" I ask "Dad."

"I had a partner take over the case so your Mom and I could be here with you."

Of course, even in my dreams Dad has all the answers. I turn back to Rhys, determined to make Dad disappear. "And I said yes," I continue. "Maybe we can run away like Evie did. I wish I were more like her. Carefree."

"I don't."

"How many kids should we have?" I ask. "We never talked about that. I want at least three. And they better all have your eyes. I love your eyes."

A throat clears.

I frown. "Go away, Dad. You're ruining my dream."

Rhys's Adam's apple bobs as he swallows.

"How many?" I ask again.

Rhys ducks his head closer to my ear. "However many you want," he whispers.

I smile. "I want to make out with you."

Rhys's eyes flit toward the foot of my bed again. "We should call a nurse. Maybe they gave her too much medication?"

"Kiss me before I wake up and you leave again."

Rhys's gaze flashes to my mouth and then up to my eyes. "I can't do that, angel."

Footsteps tap against the floor. A door squeaks open and then clicks shut. Dad's gone. Finally. Rhys seems to deflate with relief.

"Kiss me."

His thumbs caress my cheek, but he doesn't move any closer. He isn't even going to kiss me in my dreams. "I wish I wasn't me," I say.

"Don't say that."

"It's true. If I weren't me, I could have you."

Rhys bows his head. "If I hadn't walked away from you, if I had gone with you guys after the show, maybe you wouldn't be lying here right now." He swipes at his eyes.

Darkness crowds my vision and then nothing.

Chapter Fifty-One
Rhys

Power [pow-ur] n—Ability to do or act; authority

WHILE EMMY'S ASLEEP, I RUN to Mom's to check on her. Once I've confirmed she's okay, I hurry home to change clothes and then rush back to the hospital, hoping Emmy hasn't woken up yet.

"Rhys!" Emmy's shrill scream echoes down the hospital hall. I scramble off the elevator and sprint to her room but stop at the door, unsure what to do. She thrashes in her bed, yelping in pain as each wild movement jostles her battered body. Mr. and Mrs. Jennings watch helplessly as a nurse fiddles with her IV and gives her another dose of something. Jason and Drew stand at the foot of the bed, their eyes wide with concern.

"Emmy," Mr. Jennings coaxes as if she were a small child when the nurse moves away. "It's okay. You're okay. Everything is going to be fine."

She's not okay, and everything is definitely not fine. Mrs. Jennings reaches toward Emmy, but Emmy bats her hand away.

"Rhys! I want Rhys!"

I step into the room. "I'm here."

Whether it's me or the drugs they're pumping into her system, I'm not sure, but she finally settles and reaches out for me as if I'm her lifeline.

The left side of her face is bruised a mottled blue-green. I smooth her blonde hair, careful to avoid the angry black stitches hidden beneath its veil. "What's wrong? What happened?"

"They said I'm never going to dance again." Emmy sobs.

I look at her parents standing on the opposite side of the bed. Her mother's face is buried in the folds of her father's shirt, but her father nods.

I attempt to steady my voice. "Who said that?"

"The doctors. All of them."

I brush my thumb across her cheek, wiping away her tears.

"I have to be able to dance, Rhys. I have to. It's who I am. I'm not anything if I can't dance. I h-have to—" The monitor beside her bed blinks like a strobe light, and alarms sound.

Mr. Jennings walks to the other side of the bed. "Emmy."

Emmy wildly shakes her head, and the bandage on her face loosens, revealing a deep laceration along her left cheek. I move to help her, and she pushes my hand away. "No. No. No. This isn't happening. I don't want this. This isn't my life." She claws at the IV on her hand.

Mr. Jennings stops her before she can rip it out and then looks at his wife. "Hand me my keys." His voice is gentle but authoritative.

Mrs. Jennings grabs his keys from her coat pocket and holds them out to Mr. Jennings. Mr. Jennings toys with his key ring with one hand but doesn't release Emmy as she continues to squirm. I move the hair out of her eyes but can do little else.

"Jason, I need your help." Mr. Jennings motions him to his side. Jason straightens but doesn't move forward.

"Now, son."

Jason takes a step back. "I can't."

Mr. Jennings' gaze turns lethal. "Then find me someone who can."

Jason looks from his father to Emmy, regret clouding his eyes.

"Now," Mr. Jennings orders, and Jason dashes out the door.

"I can help, sir," I say, my voice unsteady. "Tell me what to do."

Mr. Jennings shakes his head. "I wish you could, son."

A moment later, Jason walks back in with Supe. "I'd be happy to assist if needed," Supe says to Mr. Jennings.

Assist with what?

Mr. Jennings nods, and Supe walks over to where I stand and pats me on the back. Mr. Jennings takes something off his key ring—a small silver vial. He unscrews the cap and then touches a drop of liquid to Emmy's head. He and Supe put their hands on top of her head. Supe says a short prayer, and they readjust their hands.

Mr. Jennings prays now, and the instant he says "Emelia Jennings," her anguished cries lessen and an unseen power enters the room. It's thick and warm and fills me from head to toe. Her father whispers a prayer, sweet and soft, making promises I'm not sure are wise but that somehow feel right. She'll walk again. Dance again. Be happy again. Everything will work together for her good. When he says amen, I open my eyes.

Mr. Jennings thanks Supe as their hands fall from Emmy's head.

There's power here.

Whatever they did, whatever that was, it was real.

Mrs. Jennings leaves the room to check on Evie next door, and Drew goes with her. Supe walks out behind them. Her father sits in a chair next to the window, and within minutes, he's snoring.

Feeling wholly inadequate, I do nothing but sit at her side. Gradually she drifts to sleep, and her hand falls from my shirt, leaving it wrinkled. I pull her covers up, making sure she's comfortable and warm.

Exhausted, I rest my head on the edge of Emmy's bed, allowing sleep to claim me too.

* * *

Her fingers are like ice on the back of my neck. I startle awake. My chair screeches across the floor as I sit up. Her eyes are still bloodshot, but they're dry. "You're here."

"Of course I'm here." I rub the sleep out of my eyes with the heel of my hand and find that the chair Mr. Jennings fell asleep in last night is now vacant. "How are you?"

She points to a cup sitting on a rollaway table beside her bed. I hand it to her, and she takes a long drink. When she's finished, I take the cup from her trembling hand and set it back on the table.

"Take me away from here," she whispers.

More than anything, I wish I could. But her leg, all the stitches . . . "I can't."

A tear slips from her eyes, but luckily, her crying is nothing like before. I move as close to her side as I can without hurting her and gently fold her in my arms. She whimpers quietly until she falls back asleep.

Finally, her breathing evens out and her muscles relax. She's so helpless like this. Her hair is down but in knots, not soft waves. She's kicked off her socks, exposing her bruised toenails and calluses—everything she didn't want me to see because she was afraid I would stop loving her.

Her lips, usually sparkly with blueberry-coconut scented goo are now chapped and split. With one arm in a sling, even the simplest things will be impossible for her for a while. I can't fix her injuries, but I can fix the little things.

I reach for the tube of lip gloss sitting on the table next to her bed. I unscrew the cap and then smooth it on her lips. In the bathroom, I find a hairbrush. I'll have to be careful of the stitches. Taking a small section, I brush the ends like Mom used do when she brushed Cami's hair. I try to be gentle, but it's difficult because of the dried blood. I manage to get out most of the tangles, but it's not perfect. When it's as good as I can get it, I twist it onto the top of her head into a bun like I've seen her do a million times and then secure it with a rubber band. But no matter how hard I try, strands keep falling out.

Finally, I move to the end of the bed and pick up the sock she managed to kick off her uncasted foot. I turn it right side out and gently pull it on.

"Rhys?" Emmy moans, and I hurry back to her side.

I sit in a chair beside her bed and rest my head next to hers. "Right here."

I touch my forehead to hers, and we both rest our eyes. That's how Mr. Jennings finds us: asleep, forehead to forehead.

"I only wanted to comfort her," I whisper.

"I know, son. I know." He hands me a bottle of water and then sits in a chair by the window.

"Is everyone still here?" I open the water bottle and take a sip.

"Diane is in the next room with Evie, but Jason and Drew had to go back home." Several minutes pass in silence, my discomfort rising exponentially. "Have you given any more thought to the conversation we had at Thanksgiving?" Mr. Jennings asks.

I've thought about that conversation every single day, his words ceaselessly replaying in my mind. Temple marriage. Temple marriage. Temple marriage. "Yes, sir."

"And?"

"And nothing has changed. I'm in the same place."

He rubs his chin with his fingers like a black-and-white movie detective cross-examining a witness. His gaze moves to Emmy and then back to me. "I'm sorry to hear that." He's quiet for a moment, then lets out an amused laugh. "You know, it's funny. The second you become a father, everything changes. The way you sleep, eat, think. Your whole life is different in an instant."

Like Emmy, Mr. Jennings talks in riddles. Emmy because she's nervous. Mr. Jennings because he's assertive. Emmy's rambling makes me smile, but Mr. Jennings' searching monologues scare me to death.

"We already had three children when the twins came, so I felt pretty confident. But after the first night home with them, I wasn't sure we'd survive. Evie screamed twenty-four seven, and Emmy . . . well, Emmy was an angel, but the two of them combined was . . . difficult."

My insides twist into a knot, unsure where he's going with this.

"Diane and I had many sleepless nights, some of which we didn't share the same bed. There were times I lost my temper, got upset. Times I think we both wanted to throw in the towel." His eyes cloud as though remembering some distant memory. "Like I said, it's funny. Love has a way of helping us see our true selves more clearly." Mr. Jennings sears me with a look. "Do you love my daughter?"

I look into his eyes, sure of my answer. "More than anything, sir."

"Then dig deep, son. Maybe you'll see in yourself what I do."

I have no idea what he means, but his words fill me with hope.

He stands from his chair and walks to the opposite side of the bed. He kisses Emmy's forehead. She rustles a bit and then settles again. Mr. Jennings straightens and then walks to the door.

I want to stop him and ask what he sees in me, beg him to help me see myself the way he does, but I don't. He told *me* to dig deep.

I look at Emmy lying calm and comforted. I can't give her this. I don't have the kind of power her dad does. She should be with someone like Supe, who can. If I loved her, really loved her, I'd step aside. I should let her get on with her life the way she always imagined it: marrying a white knight in her white temple, wearing a white dress.

And I do love her. So much. I love her enough to give her what she deserves. To be honest with her. I've tried to become what she wants, and I've failed. Now I need to man up and step aside.

March

Chapter Fifty-Two

Emmy

Echappé [ay'-shah-pay'] v—To escape

JUST LIKE EVERY TIME I'VE woken from a late nap the last two weeks, the first thing I see is Rhys. The setting sun's rays filter through the hospital window, bathing his face in warm golden light. I smile up at him, but he doesn't smile back. "You okay?" I ask.

His knee bounces against the side of the bed. "Since we broke up, I've thought a lot about what went wrong with us. Wondered if I had handled things differently, would they have turned out the same way."

The only thing worse than losing Rhys is never having had him in the first place. "Let's not talk about that."

"We have to."

"Can't we just let things be?" I reach out for him, and he tucks my hand into his.

He shakes his head. "When Supe told me about the accident, the only thing I thought about was getting to you. I wanted to save you." He smooths down the tape around the IV on the back of my hand. "But I can't do that."

My eyebrows pinch together, pulling at the sensitive skin beneath the bandages on my cheek. Wincing, I bring a hand to my face. "Can't do what?"

"Give you whatever that power was that helped you."

Confirming the truth is as pointless as denying it. We both know the truth of our situation; we've just been content to ignore it the past few weeks.

"When I saw you thrashing around in that bed the first night"—his eyes press shut like the memory physically pains him—"there was nothing I could do to help you. You were suffering, and I was useless. But your dad. Supe. They could."

"You were there. That's what matters. You stayed by my side and helped me through my darkest moments. Your presence has made me strong. I couldn't have gotten this far without you."

He searches my eyes, then swats at his own. "If I had been honest with you from the beginning, it's possible none of this would have happened." His eyes trace the scar on my face and then move all the way to the cast on my left leg. "I've been lying to myself," he whispers. "All this time. I didn't understand how you could ever need more than what we had. But after seeing them pray over you, I get it."

"That doesn't matter right now." Maybe it's selfish, but while we're in this room, I don't care about the real world or the choices we'll have to make once we're outside.

"If it mattered before, it matters now."

My chin quivers, and I turn away from him, unwilling to let him see me break any more than I already have.

"I promised myself I would never lie to you again. I know you're hurting, and I'd do anything to take away your pain, but staying here and pretending like things have changed would be a lie and would hurt you more in the end."

"I know once we leave here, we'll have to face reality, but I'm not ready to do that now. You're all I have left. My dreams are dead, Rhys. I'm a dancer who can't dance. You're the only thing holding me together."

"Your Dad and Supe said you would dance."

Tears cloud my vision. "Look at me. I'll never dance again."

"You will. And when you do, when you remember who you are and what you truly want, you'll regret the time we spent together."

"What are you saying?"

"I'm saying that I love you enough to give you what's most important to you. And it isn't me."

"Please don't leave me."

Rhys strokes the back of my hand with his thumb. "I'm trying to do the right thing here, angel. You deserve to have your forever exactly the way you want it. To have that power in your life. I'm sorry it can't be me giving it to you. I love you, Emmy, and I always will, but we can't do this." He starts to let go of my hand, but my grip on his tightens.

"I don't care if it hurts more later," I say in desperation. "Don't go."

"I'm sorry." He stands, and fear seizes me.

I search for any words that will keep him by my side. "You're a liar," I say. "You've always been a liar. And you're taking the easy way out like your father."

He flinches, and I want to take back my words. I didn't mean it. I just want him to stay. I can't do this without him.

"Can't you see that I'm trying to be honest?" he says. "That I'm trying—"

"If you walk out of this room, we're through." He won't leave. He can't.

"I know," he whispers. "But if I stay now, I'll never be able to leave." He drops a kiss on my forehead and untangles our hands. His boots scuff the floor all the way to the door. It creaks on its hinges as it swings open and then shuts with a final click.

Chapter Fifty-Three
Rhys

Truth [trooth] n—Fact or reality

THE BROKEN YELLOW LANE DIVIDERS blur on the road as I drive away from the hospital. Away from Provo. Away from Emmy. I floor it, daring God to do to me what He did to her. My tires slip all over the road, but I don't stop.

The street curves up a small hill, and taking the turn too fast, I veer onto the wrong side of the road. An oncoming car honks, and I jerk the steering wheel hard to the right. My heart pounds against my rib cage as I pull over.

I hit the steering wheel with an open palm and yank open the truck door. I slam it shut and then stop dead in my tracks at what looms in front of me. The Provo Temple.

A black wrought-iron fence surrounds the perimeter. A warning to anything unworthy to keep out. A warning to me.

Gripping the iron bars in my fists, I glare up at this ethereal thing keeping Emmy and me apart. Anger swells in my chest, and I curse at the sky. If we weren't supposed to end up together, why did He even let us meet? I kick the fence and then rest my head against the bars.

Emmy's voice whispers in my mind, *Don't you want to know?*

I'd give anything to know. To believe what she believes if it meant we could be together. Tears stream down my face as I turn my back to the temple, then slide down the bars until I'm sitting on the cold cement.

God, if he exists, has never answered my prayers before. No dove descended to cure Mom, and nothing brought Dad back to us. And Emmy. How could He let this happen to Emmy? She's lost everything, and He could have prevented it. Do I even want to know a God like that? I'm not sure.

I search myself for answers but come up blank. The missionaries said if I asked God sincerely if it was true, He would answer me. I can at least do that. If He doesn't answer me, I'll know. I fold my arms and bow my head. "If you're there. Give me some sort of a sign."

I wait for an answer, but nothing comes. Not a whisper in any kind of voice. Nothing small. Nothing still. *Nada.*

Ready to give up, I unfold my arms. I'm about to stand when Mr. Jennings's words play in my mind. *Dig deep, son.*

The words are as clear as if he were standing next to me, and I sink back to the ground. How much deeper can I dig? I've tried everything I know how to do. I've offered Emmy everything I have to give. I've read and prayed and gone to church. I've even tried to convert, and they wouldn't take me.

I ask myself the question Supe once did. Do I want to know the truth because I want to be with Emmy or because I actually want to know the truth for myself?

I can't deny the power that filled the hospital room when Mr. Jennings and Supe laid their hands on Emmy's head. It was unseen, but it was real. It came over me like a warm blanket and filled me up inside. It helped her when nothing else could. I want to feel that power again. So, yes, I do want to know the truth because of Emmy, but I also want to know the truth for myself. I want to feel that power again.

I clear away all the voices—Emmy's and Mr. Jennings's and Supe's—and try to focus on the question I so desperately want answered. I close my eyes, fold my arms across my chest, and bow my head.

"Dear God," my voice trembles. "Are you there?"

The question is simple, but as soon as I think the words, warm comfort floods into me, soothing, succoring, searing my soul. The same power that overwhelmed me during Emmy's blessing but magnified and meant for *me.*

Answers come so fast I can hardly process them. Every answer to every question I've ever asked surges into my mind. Like a deluge of water that has been held at bay, answers rush at me, and all I have is a paper cup to gather them.

My eyes fly open, and I expect to see something as brilliant as what I feel inside. Stars twinkle in the clear night sky. The mountains are illuminated in the moonlight, their peaks touching heaven.

The air is cool, but a fire heats me from inside. It's not unfamiliar. I've felt this before: with Emmy in the tunnel while we sang the hymns and in the car when I dropped her off when I told her about Mom's diagnosis and moving to Provo. With her dad and Supe. I know this feeling.

It's my answer.
It's true.

Chapter Fifty-Four
Emmy

Soutenier (soot-nenir) v—Support

It takes twenty minutes for the nurse to change me from a hospital gown into normal clothes. When I'm finally dressed, I lay back against the pillow, exhausted. The nurse reopens the curtain, and Mom and Dad are waiting on the other side.

I stare at the ceiling. In the four weeks I've been here, I've memorized every inch of this room. There are three cracks in the ceiling. A water stain by the window. Everything is blue, except the blanket. That's beige. A small flat-screen TV is suspended from the ceiling, but there's never anything good on.

The nurse goes over the discharge papers with Dad, and Mom busies herself with packing my things, carefully folding my clothes and placing them in a bag labeled *Patient Belongings*. She gazes for a long moment at my favorite coat draped over a chair in the corner of the room and then picks it up to inspect it further. Glass is embedded in the soft pink fabric, and a deep-red stain—probably blood—mars the black-and-white polka-dot lining. With a sad shrug, she lays it back on the chair.

Evie walks in pushing a wheelchair. She locks the wheels and then comes to my bedside. "Ready?"

I shake my head. Leaving without Rhys by my side feels like accepting we're over. I don't want us to be over. I'd rather wait for him to come back. He has to come back.

Mom walks to the far side of the bed and helps me sit up. The nurse untangles my leg from the sling and holds it up. Dad slips one arm around my back, careful not to jostle my arm and collar bone, and his other arm under my knees. The nurse lifts my leg, setting it on an outstretched leg rest as Dad puts me in the wheelchair.

"There. That wasn't so bad," the nurse says, out of breath.

Evie pushes me down the hall, and Mom carries my bag behind us. Dad goes to get the car and, a minute later, pulls up to the front door to get us.

"My car." It's the first time I've thought about it since the wreck.

"We'll get you a new one," Dad says.

I don't disagree, but I don't think I'll be interested in driving anytime soon.

With the help of a male nurse, Dad lifts me into the backseat of the car, situates my leg, then secures a seat belt around my waist and shuts the door.

Evie climbs in beside me, and Mom and Dad sit in front. Dad starts the engine, then pulls away from the curb.

Rhys didn't come back. I really thought he would.

"Emmy," Dad says after we've been on the road for a few minutes. "Your mother and I have been talking, and"—Dad pauses, and Mom gives him an encouraging nod—"we think it's best if you come home with us. At least for a little while. Until you're back on your feet."

It doesn't matter where I live; I'll never be back on my feet. But Provo is my home. "I want to stay here."

"We know you do," Mom says. "But with no one around to help you . . ."

"I'll move back in," Evie says.

"That's a nice gesture, sweetie, but Emmy will need round-the-clock care. You can't do that with school—"

"I've already taken the semester off," Evie cuts Mom off, and Dad's hands tighten around the steering wheel.

"It's okay, Eve," I say, trying to diffuse a suddenly tense moment. "I know you have a husband to think about now. Maybe we can hire someone?"

"No need, Em. Q and I are separated."

My gaze snaps to Evie, who sits silent and still. "Separated?"

Dad and Mom exchange a look, though they don't seem shocked by her confession like I am. Dad looks in the rearview mirror, and his gaze settles on Evie. "I thought we agreed back at the hospital not to discuss your . . . *situation* until after your sister healed a little more."

"We know you want to help," Mom says quickly, "but in a few weeks when Emmy's casts are off, there will be doctor visits and physical-therapy appointments. We just don't think it'll work."

"Emmy doesn't want to leave, and I'm offering to stay. What's the problem?"

"You have your own things to work through right now," Dad says in a hard voice.

Mom sets a soft hand on Dad's shoulder and then turns to look at Evie. "We feel it would be better for both of you if Emmy came home with us," Mom says more gently.

Evie's eyes narrow into a look I know all too well—the same look she got when we were in sixth grade and a boy told her she couldn't join the baseball team because she was a girl. She's not going to back down. "What do *you* want, Emmy?"

Dad glances in the rearview mirror at me and then back to the road. I don't want to let him and Mom down or make them worry, but I also don't want to leave Provo. I don't want to leave my sister, and I'm not ready to be so far away from Rhys, even if we can't be together.

"I want to stay in Provo with Evie."

We stop at a red light, and Dad looks in the mirror at me for a long time. "Okay," he finally says. "If this is what you need, your mother and I will support you."

"Stephen," Mom scolds, and they launch into an argument that lasts the whole drive home. Dad convinces Mom to let Evie move back in so I can stay in Utah on a trial basis. Mom doesn't like it, but at least she's willing to give it a chance.

* * *

At the end of the week, after Dad and Mom have made sure we have everything we could possibly need, they say good-bye. Without Mom constantly cleaning and Dad calling doctors and physical therapists, the house is instantly quiet. I miss them already.

Evie comes to my room a few minutes after I hear the rental car pull out of the driveway. "How are you?"

I look at my cast, the scars on my hand and arm, and then at her, with tears in my eyes. "I'm not sure I can do this, Eve."

She walks to the side of my bed and sits. "It's going to be okay."

I want to believe her, but the night of the accident was the first time I had seen her in weeks. We've hardly talked since she married Q, and now they're separated. How can she say everything will be okay? The lives we've planned for ourselves have fallen apart.

"I can't believe I almost lost you." She sniffles. "I've made so many mistakes. I'm sorry, Em. I'm so, so sorry."

Every part of me hurts, including my heart, but then Evie crawls onto the bed, lays next to me, and rests her head on my good shoulder like she used to do when we were children, and for a second, the pain recedes. In this brief respite, I realize something; I can't get through this trial on my own, but I can overcome it with my sister's help. And more than that, Evie needs me just as much as I need her. I have to be strong for my sister. "It's okay," I whisper.

"I should have been there for you." She cries.

"You're here now." I'm alive. She's alive. And no matter how much time together we lost last semester, we have the rest of our lives.

"I am. I promise I am." She snuggles into me, and I close my eyes. And then for the first time since the accident, with my sister next to me, I sleep soundly.

Chapter Fifty-Five

Rhys

Repentance [ree-pen-tens] n—Change that lasts forever

"I WANT TO BE BAPTIZED."

Elder Marsden looks at me, unconvinced. "What's changed?"

Supe nods encouragingly, and I turn to Elder Marsden. "Everything."

Elder Marsden leans forward. So does his new companion, Elder Barnes. Neither says a word, but both wait expectantly for my answer.

"Emmy was in a car accident."

Elder Marsden frowns, and I can tell he thinks I still want to be baptized for her.

I hold up a hand. "It's not like that. Right before I found out she was in a car accident, I had a dream." I shake my head. "That's not important either. Anyway, that night, my roommate came in, told me what had happened. I went to the hospital. She was a mess. Wild. Thrashing in her bed. Nothing would calm her. But then her dad gave her a blessing, and this power filled the room. And I . . ." I choke up. "I left her."

"You broke up?"

I nod and say again, "I knew I could never give her that, so I drove away and found myself in front of the temple. I prayed. Or yelled. I don't know. Is cursing heaven considered a prayer?"

Elder Marsden chuckles. "Prayer can take many forms."

I nod. "This one was angry. But then when I calmed down, I felt the same power that filled hospital room. And I think—I mean, I *know* I got an answer."

Elder Marsden smiles. "What was the answer?

"That it's true. And to call you guys." I laugh under my breath. "No offense, but I took my time with that one and had Supe teach me the lessons. I was kinda hoping you'd get transferred, Elder Marsden."

His companion laughs, and a smile lights Elder Marsden's face. "No offense taken."

"So what now?" I ask.

Elder Marsden laces his fingers in his lap. "That depends on you. Now that you have answers, what are you going to do with them?"

The answers I received were unmistakable. Mom needs more help. Thinking about putting Mom in a home fills me with dread, but it's the right decision. Emmy is harder. There's no way I will hurt her again. It would destroy both of us. To be able to be with her, I have to go to church. I have to read the scriptures and become the man she wants me to be. The man God wants me to be. I need to do this on my own before I can be with her.

I know what I'm going to do with my answers. "Follow them," I say.

Elder Marsden nods his approval. "That's good, Rhys."

"Actually," I clear my throat. "It's Brother Solario."

April

Chapter Fifty-Six

Emmy

Brisé [bree-zay] a—Broken, breaking

"IT HURTS."

"It's supposed to hurt," Pete, my physical therapist, says.

My eyes squeeze closed. "It *really* hurts," I clarify.

"No pain, no gain."

I pry one eye open to glare at him. "Who hired you?"

Evie chuckles from the couch behind me. True to her word, she hasn't left my side since I was released from the hospital.

"Okay, Emmy," Pete says. "We're going to try this again, but this time, I want you to put some effort into it."

"I am trying." My legs burn. They're shaky, and it feels like there's a knife piercing my shoulder blade. I'm trying, but there isn't much left of me to work with.

"You're not. You're trying to *look* like you're trying, but you're not actually trying. Again."

I grip the walker in front of me, awkwardly pull myself up using mostly my right arm and leg, and start to take a step forward.

Pete clears his throat. "You aren't fooling anyone. Use both arms and both legs."

A searing pain shoots from my left ankle all the way to my hip bone as I stand again. My knees start to wobble.

"Come on, Emmy. Don't give up," Pete says.

By sheer force of will, I press myself all the way up using both arms and both legs.

Pete claps his hands. "Yes! Thatta girl."

My eyes flick up to Evie's. She's sitting on the edge of her seat, giving me two thumbs up. My gaze wanders to Pete. A smile has taken over his face.

"Now I want you to step. Right foot first, then slowly onto your left."

Excitement takes over. I can do this. I'm going to stand up and walk. In six months, I'll be dancing again.

Right foot. Shift my weight. Left foot. It takes forever, and I stumble as I drag my left foot forward, but I do it.

Pete gets this crazy glint in his eyes as he nods. "Again." He scoots the walker a few inches forward. "Come on. One more time."

Right foot. Shift my weight. Left foot.

"One more time," Pete says.

I shake my head. "You already said, 'One more time.'"

"I lied." His persistence and optimism are infuriating, but that's what makes him good. He pushes me, and with his help, I will get better.

Evie smiles so wide not even Miss America could compete. I try to find the willpower to push myself one more step, but I can't. The burning in my muscles is now a fire. I have nothing left; every ounce of energy is exhausted. "I can't."

"You can," Pete says. "One foot in front of the other. Baby steps. One step at a time. Pick your motivational sentence, and it applies. Now come on. One. More. Step."

My heart pounds, and my legs tremble. The ache in my legs is bone-deep. It's excruciating. I move to obey—it's not like I could get back to the chair on my own, even if I wanted to.

"Right foot," I say out loud.

Pete nods.

"Shift my weight. Lef—" Suddenly I'm slipping, falling, and then I'm on the floor.

Evie and Pete kneel over me. "Are you okay?" they ask at the same time.

"Are you hurt?" Evie asks.

"Can you stand?" Pete offers me his hand.

Their overlapping questions disorient me as much as the fall. Everything comes crashing back down. The accident, my injuries. Rhys leaving.

I push Pete and Evie away, their nearness suffocating. "Stop!"

They freeze but don't move away. "Can I help you stand?" Pete asks somberly.

Sobs wrack my body. "No."

He sits next to me instead. "This is part of the process, Emmy. We knew this would take time. You've got to dust yourself off and get back on the horse."

"No," I say. "Don't you get it? I have nothing left. Nothing to fight for. Nothing matters anymore. No one cares if I walk. No one cares if I dance again."

"That's not true," he says. "You have your family. And you have a desire to dance that makes you want to fight. If you keep working, you'll walk again. Maybe even dance," Pete says. "Don't give up on yourself."

I look back at the chair less than twelve inches away. I'll never walk again.

Chapter Fifty-Seven

Rhys

Incidentals [in-si-den-tlz] n—Minor expenses

"It's called a spend down," the hospital's financial counselor says.

Mom fiddles with her magnetic bracelet.

"What's a spend down?" I ask the counselor.

"Exactly what it sounds like. In order to qualify for the full benefits Medicaid offers, your mother must spend down her excess funds."

"How am I supposed to live without any money?" Mom jumps in.

"Well, in order for Medicaid to cover your basics, such as housing, food, and medical expenses, you must not have the ability to do so yourself," the counselor explains.

Mom stops twirling her bracelet. "That's great that they will take care of the absolute necessities of life, but what about everything else?"

"You'll be given a small stipend each month to cover incidentals."

"How small?"

The counselor's eyes twitch almost imperceptibly. "Forty-five dollars," she says.

Mom gapes. "Forty-five dollars?"

The counselor nods. "I know it doesn't sound like a lot—"

"It doesn't sound like anything," Mom interrupts. "After this spend down, I'd be broke. What if I can't live like that? I'd be stuck."

"I'm not saying it wouldn't be an adjustment, but there are wonderful assisted-living facilities in Utah."

"You can't be serious?" Mom turns and searches my face. "In a home with old people? I'm too young to live in a place like that."

I want to tell the financial counselor she's crazy. That I will never ask my mother to spend all the savings she's worked so hard to earn and then live in some old folks' home, but I can't do that. This was the answer I received: get Mom help. But how can I put her in a facility? I can't abandon her like Dad did. My hands begin to sweat as my heart races. Eyes closed, I say a silent prayer, asking for clarity.

"I know it's scary to think about living on so little," the counselor says.

"You seem to know a lot."

The counselor sits unfazed by Mom's sarcasm.

"How would it work?" I ask. "The spend down?"

"It's pretty simple. You'd use the rest of your mother's savings to pay off all of her hospital bills and medications. Once the money is gone, you'll qualify for extra help." She pauses, but we don't say anything, so she continues. "You don't have to decide anything now, but I encourage you to think about it. Maybe tour a few homes and see what you think. You may be surprised."

A lump forms in my throat as the counselor pushes a stack of glossy brochures across her desk to Mom and me. Mom doesn't move to take them, so I do. On the cover are gray-haired people with big smiles. Mom has long brown hair and smooth skin. She's right. She's too young to live in a place like that. What if we can't find a home where she'll be happy?

Mom doesn't say anything as I wheel her down to my truck. Or as I walk her into the house. Or when I help her get ready for bed. But as I lift her into bed, she starts to sniffle. "I'm scared, Rhys."

"I know you are." I don't try to placate her fears. I'm afraid too. Everything is unknown. We could spend everything down and end up worse off than before. I cling to the feeling I had as I prayed. "I'm scared too, but we can't keep doing this. You need to be safe. And you're not here."

She nods, dabbing at her eyes with the edge of her floral comforter. "It should be me caring for you." She touches my face as I kneel at her bedside. "Not the other way around." She's silent for a moment. "If you feel this is the right thing to do, I'm okay with looking at some assisted-care homes."

"I promise I won't abandon you. We'll find a place that feels right, okay?"

She pats my cheek. "You're a good boy, Rhys."

I tuck her in and then flip off the light as I leave her room.

* * *

A week after our appointment with the counselor, I've set up several different tours at assisted-living facilities, and we're driving all over Utah Valley.

The first care center we visit is small. Two roommates in each room, a small living area, and an equally small kitchen. They call it cozy. I call it cramped. Having lived with Mom, I already know this won't work. She likes personal space and values independence. We keep looking.

The second and third facilities are nice, but the average age of the clientele appears to be ninety. Mom is half that. Our search continues.

The next several places are too dirty, the staff unfriendly, or just not right.

It's hard not to question the answer I received. This has to be the right decision though. I felt it. It's right. I know it's right.

Mom is exhausted. Getting in and out of the car only to see yet another no-go is wearing on her.

"Can you handle one more?" I ask as we pull into the driveway of a newer facility.

Mom looks out the window at the two-story building with a wraparound porch skirting the exterior—by far the nicest place we've seen so far. Mom nods, but I can tell even that takes effort. She needs food and rest. And so do I.

I'm not sure parking is allowed in the horseshoe driveway, but I see no sign posting otherwise, so I stop as close as I can to the front door.

An orderly appears at the door. He's older than me but still young. "Can I help you with that?" he asks as I take Mom's wheelchair out of the truck bed.

"Nah, I've got it." I help Mom into the chair and then follow the orderly up the ramp.

"So what can I do for you folks today?" the man asks.

"We're here for a tour," I reply.

"Excellent. I'd be happy to show you around."

The grounds are nice, and the building is a newer light-brick with white wood accents. Bright red flowers line the cement walkways. Inside there is an inviting fire with plush leather couches situated around it. A few women play cards at a round table, laughing. Our tour guide points out a bulletin board advertising the "clubs" offered to residents, special-guest lecturers, a driving service, and many other activities. Mom seems to perk at the idea of being able to have "wheels" again. But not half as much as when she finds out residents can have a plot to garden. For the next ten minutes, she talks about what she'd plant.

We're shown sample rooms. And a resident who looks to be only a few years older than Mom is kind enough to let us see her room as well. It's been painted yellow, and the woman's personal pictures hang on the walls. It's nice, not at all sterile like the other homes we've seen.

By the end of the tour, Mom has stars in her eyes. While the majority of the residents *are* over the age of eighty-five, a few are Mom's age.

The man asks if we have any questions.

I do. Several. I open my mouth to ask one, but Mom beats me to it.

"How's the food?"

The man smiles. "That's a common question. Why don't you let me treat you to dinner, and you can tell me?"

Before we even step inside the dining room, my mouth waters at the scent of garlic and butter. As soon as we sit at the table, a server takes our order. I select enchiladas, and Mom chooses vegetable stir-fry. Starved, we eat in record time.

The man continues to talk about the benefits of living here, and we feast on every word.

"So how's the food?" he asks as we push our plates away.

Mom wipes her mouth with a cloth napkin. "The best meal I've had in years."

He chuckles, not realizing Mom isn't exaggerating. I'm a terrible cook, and the vegetables she burns can't be considered a meal.

"How much does it cost to live in a place like this?" I ask.

"That depends," the man says. "Variables such as view, roommate, and amount of care needed all influence the final cost, but packages start at $2,300 a month."

Mom's smile falters. That is triple what her current living situation costs. Triple.

"I know it sounds like a large number, but when you think about the services we offer and the lifestyle we provide our residents, it's a bargain."

He sounds like a used-car salesman.

"I'm sure it is." I push away from the table. "Listen, a financial counselor at the hospital recommended we tour here, but I think she was mistaken about our ability to afford a place like this." The man listens politely as I try to back my way out of an embarrassing misunderstanding. "I appreciate your time, but—"

"Did this counselor explain Medicaid? Spending down?"

Mom shifts in her seat.

"She did," I say. "But I'm not sure that's something we're comfortable with."

"I know it can be scary, but our resident satisfaction rating is high, and in many cases, our residents are not only safer living here but also happier." The man hands me his business card. "Tell you what. You guys talk it over, and if you have any questions about our facility or spending down or anything . . . I'm happy to help." He stands, shakes our hands, and then excuses himself from the table.

Mom's eyes flash to me, hopeful as he walks away. And in that moment, I know we've found the right place for Mom to call home. It will be scary, but we'll spend down what's left of the money by paying her hospital bills, and we'll move her here. It feels right. She'll be happy. And safe. Things are going to be okay.

May

Chapter Fifty-Eight
Emmy

Temps lie (tahn lee-yay) n—A step to connect

SATURDAY MORNING, A WEEK AFTER the therapy incident, Evie fills a glass with water at the kitchen sink and then shakes a pain pill onto her palm. I've tried to hide my constant pain, but I must not be doing a very good job. It's been six weeks since I came home from the hospital, and I still can't stand without aid, let alone dance. Everyone says it will take time, but it already feels like an eternity.

Evie walks into the living room, where I'm pretending to watch TV, and sits on the couch next to me. She hands me the glass of water and medication, and I swallow the pill. She's been amazing since the accident. Not only has she taken care of my physical well-being, but she's also been my listening ear and shoulder to cry on. I've tried to talk to her about what's going on in her life too, but somehow she's managed to avoid answering. I can't let her do that anymore. We have to talk. I turn off the TV.

"What happened with you and Q?" I ask softly.

Evie looks down at her lap. "I don't know."

"You can tell me. I promise not to judge you. Let me be here for you the way you've been here for me these past weeks."

"It's not that I don't want to tell you," Evie says. "I just really don't know. Q had a lot of secrets." She brings her legs onto the couch and hugs them to her chest. "I think I may have been one of those secrets," she adds quietly.

"What do you mean?"

"He never introduced me to his family, despite the fact that they lived right here in Utah. We never hung out with his friends either. And even though we talked a lot about the future—our goals, our dreams, even what type of marriage we each wanted—we never discussed the past."

"Did you ask him about it?"

"Yes. I asked him about his mission and what he was like in high school all the time, but he never answered. He'd distract me with a kiss or make me laugh, and I'd forget. But it's not like I was worried about his evasiveness in the moment, at least not in the beginning. Things started off amazing. We could literally discuss any subject—the gospel, music, politics—and debate our viewpoints without getting into a fight. We almost always agreed. Being with him was easy. I think I was so blinded by my emotions that I never opened my eyes to see all the red flags."

I knew all too well what she meant. Rhys made small comments along the way that hinted at him not being Mormon, but I didn't pick up on them either. "It's much easier to see things looking back than when you're living through them, isn't it?"

She nods. "I knew he wasn't perfect—he said and did some obnoxious things—but he seemed perfect for me. There was never any pressure to be something other than what I already was. He didn't like me because I was a ballet dancer or because I was a twin or even because I was good at school. He liked me for *me*. When I was with him, I felt beautiful and intelligent. He was the man I always dreamed of marrying—smart, talented, fun—and I rationalized that all the answers to my questions would come in time."

"But they didn't?"

Evie shakes her head. "No. Two months into our relationship, around Halloween, things started to change. We saw each other less and argued more. He was often moody or withdrawn. I brought it up, but he always had a reason for being emotionally distant. He was stressed about school. His roommates were always home. A professor didn't like him . . . All those things made sense, so I didn't push him.

"November came, and I thought that if we could just get away, we'd be okay, so I invited him to come home for Thanksgiving. And it worked; the two weeks before that trip were some of the best weeks of my life. He took me on incredible dates, and we talked more about the future.

"On our way home to California, when we stopped in Las Vegas, Q and I came across this little chapel, and that's when he asked me to marry him," Evie says. "He could be spontaneous sometimes—I loved that about him—but I honestly thought he was joking. When I saw the vulnerability in his eyes and realized he wasn't kidding, I knew that if I didn't say yes and marry him right then, he would withdraw again and we wouldn't last another week."

I nod. "I understand not wanting to lose Q; really, I do. I felt the same way about Rhys, but how could you not wait to be married in the temple like you've always dreamed?" Growing up, we both had bulletin boards over our desks. On mine were pictures of ballerinas and pointe shoes. On Evie's were boys, wedding dresses, and temples.

"Because," she says, "I wanted to be married to him, Em. I wanted it so desperately that I didn't care where or when or even what the repercussions would be."

Evie has often made rash choices, like when she suddenly quit ballet this year, and part of me even empathizes with her marriage. The night I went on a date with Nathan, I missed Rhys so much afterward that I ran back to him. In that moment, there was nothing I wanted more than Rhys. Not even eternity. "What happened when you got back from our trip?" I ask, trying to fully understand.

"He filed for a divorce as soon as he got home from California. I've been sleeping on Kennedy's couch since Thanksgiving."

I feel the blood drain from my face, and a wave of vertigo washes over me. "Oh, Evie."

"You tried to warn me," she says.

We sit quietly for a few moments.

"Why didn't you move back here?" I ask. "Or at least talk to me?"

"I saw your face when I said Q and I got married. You were devastated. That hurt. I wanted so much for you to like him. I thought if you and I had a little space, things would cool down and you'd see how happy we were. But then everything fell apart, and I was embarrassed. About the marriage, the separation, the way I treated you. And you had Rhys and were happy . . . You didn't need me."

I *was* happy. But then I was heartbroken. Evie and I could have been there for each other.

"I wanted to be like you," she says after a quiet second. "To have a relationship like you. To be passionate about something like you are about ballet. I've always walked in your shadow, Em. Since the day we were born. Two minutes behind, you know?"

I struggle to make sense of her confession. She's always walked in *my* shadow? I shake my head. "You're better than me at everything. You're the pretty one. The smart one. The passionate one."

"You're wrong. You're the beautiful, mysterious twin. And you work harder at school than I ever could. I danced but only because you did. I've never been passionate about anything until Q. It was like one minute I was drifting aimlessly, following wherever you went, and then I met him, and instantly, I had this intense passion. I thought he was the one. I *wanted* him to be the one. And I believed what we shared was enough to overcome anything. I was wrong."

Evie drags a finger under her eye, smudging her eyeliner, and I do the same.

"Look at us." Evie sniffs. "Didn't we make a pact never to cry over boys?"

"This isn't first grade," I say. "And Q isn't a boy. You loved him."

The humor fades from Evie's eyes. "I *do* love him, but love wasn't enough."

She's right, but I wish she weren't.

"When did you tell Mom and Dad?" I ask.

"The night of the accident. They knew something was wrong when he didn't come to the hospital."

"I wish you would have told me sooner too."

"I wanted to, but I was afraid," she says. "Kennedy said she saw you one day and told you to call me, but then you never did. And then after your show, when you didn't want to talk, I thought you were mad at me."

"I wasn't mad. I was hurt." Hurt that we had grown apart since she'd quit ballet. Hurt that she had gotten married without me there. Hurt that she had packed her belongings and left without saying good-bye. But . . . hurt only because I love her. "How could you think I wouldn't be here for you? You're my sister. I'm always on your side."

"I know, but sometimes guilt can make a person believe things that aren't true. I messed up big-time, and I didn't see any way to make it right."

"Do you miss him?" I ask.

"Despite everything, I do."

"I miss Rhys too," I say. "What are we supposed to do with our lives now?"

"Pick out matching rocking chairs and buy a couple dozen cats," she deadpans. She lets out a long breath. "I don't know what's next for me. I'm only worried about you. Will you be okay, Em?"

She hasn't asked me that since the accident. No one has. I think we're all pretending things will go back to normal. "I'll be okay. Eventually."

"What if you can't dance professionally?"

"I don't know. I'm just trying to focus on the blessing Dad gave me in the hospital. It wasn't specific, but he promised I'd dance in some capacity again one day. Maybe not professionally like I planned, but I will dance again. I have to rely on that."

"See? That's exactly what I'm talking about. You've always known what you wanted to do with your life. Since the first time you walked into the ballet studio, you've lived, breathed, and bled ballet. You're so passionate."

"Ballet is part of who I am. But in the last year, I've learned there's more to life than dancing." My mind drifts back to Rhys and the night he told me about his mother's disease. He gave up his own dreams to care for her. I remember how it felt to be in his arms. The night he held me and sang with me in the tunnel so I wouldn't be alone. There's more to life than ballet—so much more. And even though I can't have more with Rhys, I will always love him. "You'll find your passion too," I say to Evie. "One that doesn't rely on anyone else to make you happy."

She bites her lip. "How can you be so sure?"

"Because, like you said, I'm older than you, and that makes me wiser."

Evie laughs.

"What do you say we eat a pint of salted caramel ice cream and finally have our Ridge Dashly movie marathon?" I ask.

"I'd say there's nothing Ridge Dashly can't fix."

Now I giggle. Evie hurries into the kitchen and grabs a tub of ice cream and two spoons and then walks back into the living room and pops the movie into the Blu-ray player. A moment later, Ridge appears on the screen, and we both sigh. It's been way too long since we've had a sister day.

Chapter Fifty-Nine
Rhys

Immersion [ih-mur-zhuhn] n—Concentrating on one course of instruction or subject to the exclusion of all others for several days or weeks

JEN LOOKS AT THE BAPTISMAL font and then turns to me. "You're a moron."

Supe bumps me with his elbow. "That's what I said."

"Me too," Mom says.

"I think the word you're all searching for is *Mormon*. I'm a *Mormon*." Jen rolls her eyes.

"Don't worry; they're commonly confused," I reassure them.

Mom shakes her head as Supe wheels her to the front of the room.

Jen huffs. "First of all, you're not Mormon yet. And second, you *are* a moron for not inviting your girlfriend to your baptism." Jen reaches into her purse and pulls out her cell. "I don't care what you say. I'm calling Emmy. She should be here for this."

I place a hand on top of her phone. "Don't."

"I know you think your GF is going to forgive you, but this will hurt her. You'll be RIP'ing instead of DTR'ing. Trust me."

Jen might be right, but getting baptized isn't something I'm doing for Emmy. "Getting baptized is something I have to do for me. Regardless of how she may feel or whether or not we get back together." I want to be the man she wants me to be, but more importantly, I need to be the man God expects me to be.

I can tell by the way Jen's forehead scrunches that she still thinks I'm a moron. Maybe I am.

"Thanks for coming," I say to Jen. "Even if you think I'm a moron."

"I wouldn't have missed this for anything."

Elder Marsden and Elder Barnes stand on either side of the font, ready to serve as witnesses, and Supe leads me through the door to the font. Gripping the metal handrail, I step onto the submerged stairs. Even though we've practiced how the dunk will go, Supe still has to place my hands correctly on his forearm.

"Ready, Brother Solario?" Supe asks.

I nod, and he raises his right hand to the square and utters the first words of the baptismal prayer.

My heart races. Pounds. And my brain fuzzes out. This isn't right. Brother Clark would have referred to this as a stupor of thought. Not right. Get out now. "Stop."

Supe's words cut off, and the whole room seems to hold its breath.

"Somebody's missing."

Supe releases my arm, and I climb the stairs out of the font. Water drips down my pant legs and pools at my feet on the tile bathroom floor. My hands shake as I grab my keys off the counter next to my folded clothes. I pick up my jacket and stuff my arms through the holes and then dash outside to my truck.

Chapter Sixty

Emmy

En avant [ahn a-vahn] a—Forward

AFTER THREE MOVIES IN A row, Evie decides it's time for a dinner break. She rifles through the cupboards, the fridge, the pantry, and then declares there's nothing to eat and that she's going to get takeout. "Need anything before I leave?"

"Actually, I do." While Evie spent the last hour watching Ridge fall in love, I was thinking about ballet. Listening to André's words ringing in my ears. *Fight for yourself, for your career.* Pete's voice also whispers in my ears. *Baby steps. You can do this.* "Will you get my ballet bag down from my closet for me?"

Evie doesn't waste a second running upstairs. My closet door squeaks on the tracks as it opens, and a moment later, she's back and sets the bag in front of me. "Need anything else?"

"My kit?" I've spent years toting my ballet bag and kit around, and I miss them. Maybe it's crazy, but I just want to see them, to touch them.

"Right. Of course." She jogs back up the stairs and returns a minute later with my kit.

"You good?"

I nod. "Great. Thanks."

"Be back in thirty with food." She grabs her keys off the kitchen counter and walks to the door. "Don't forget it's your turn to pick the next movie."

She's about to step outside when I call out, "Hey, Evie?"

She turns back.

"I know these past several months haven't been easy on you. Thank you for being here for me. I love you."

She smiles, but it doesn't touch her eyes. "Love you too, Em."

"Thanks." And then for the first time since the accident, I open my kit. The smell of resin and hair spray swirl in the air, beckoning me home. Back to the stage. Back to ballet.

My fingers caress each item. Pink thread, bottles of glue, moleskin, and tape. I've spent countless hours refining which items I carry in here.

I open my duffel bag next. My well-loved leg warmers and practice pointe shoes sit on top; beneath them are a new pair of pink tights and a pair of new pointe shoes. I've always carried two pairs. Pointe shoes are hardly more than papier-mâché slippers and don't last very long. These arrived in the mail the day before my last performance.

I stare at the satin shoes. The stitching is precise. Handcrafted to my exact specifications. What choreography might I have danced in these? How many hours of rehearsal would they have had to endure? What would I have learned with them on my feet? My vision blurs with tears, and instead of reaching for my pointe shoe, I pick up my cell phone to turn on some music. I power on the screen, and my wallpaper, a picture of Rhys and me, illuminates the screen. I can't bring myself to change the image.

My biggest regret of our relationship is the way it ended. I've tried calling countless times to apologize, but he never answers. I'd like to tell him I don't hate him—that I could never hate him—and that I understand his decision to leave.

I stare at the image of our foreheads pressed together. It's been nearly two months, but losing him still hurts. I love him. I will always love him. I'll forever cherish the memories of us. But that's all they will ever be. Memories.

I grab my earbuds and put them in my ears, then slide my thumb across the screen to open a music app. The last song I listened to pops onto the screen: "Divenire," by Ludovico Einaudi. The song I danced the pas de deux to with David the night of the accident. I played this right before going on stage.

Music flows from the speakers, and choreography invades my mind. I expect it to hurt, knowing I may never again dance like I did that night, but it doesn't. Instead, the music swells inside me, awakening hope deep within my soul. Last week I took a step. It hurt, but I did it. I will dance again too.

My heart races as I reach for the first pointe shoe. I don't know if I'll ever dance ballet like I used to, but if I don't try, I've already failed. I have to fight for myself.

Chapter Sixty-One

Rhys

Fear [feer] n—Opposite of faith

RAIN SHEETS THE SKY AN angry gray. The mountains hold up the clouds like a pole in the middle of a circus tent. I look at the brown paper bag sitting in the passenger seat, and my heart races. This is it.

Her house hasn't changed; it's amazing how much the life inside it has. I knock on her front door, but she doesn't answer, so I ring the doorbell. She probably moves slowly, most likely in a wheelchair.

I hold the bag against my chest with both hands so I won't be tempted to ring the doorbell again. But after a minute passes, I lose patience and ring it anyway.

Movement catches my eye through the window. Emmy. Her hair is up in her trademark bun. Her hands move gracefully in the air like she's dancing . . . but only with her arms. After a moment, she reaches into a bag and picks up a ballet shoe. She reverently touches the material.

She's right there, so close but so far away. She doesn't even glance in my direction. She isn't going to answer. She meant what she said. She hates me. I've lost her.

I turn to leave, but then stop. In Emmy's hand is a cased razor. She slides her thumb down the side of the plastic, exposing the blade. She holds up the ballet shoe and then drags the sharp end across the thick leather sole.

Panicked, I drop the bag and try the doorknob. It's locked. I ring the bell again and then check the window to see if she's moved or at least set down the blade. She has, but only to replace it with a lighter.

She positions one of the ribbons between her thumb and pointer finger. Clutching the lighter in her fist, she flicks her thumb against the strike, lighting a flame, then holds it to one of the silk ribbons.

Adrenaline kicks me in the gut, and I whip around to the front door. Whether she hates me or not, there's no way I'm going to let her literally light her dreams on fire.

I search the porch for a hidden key and find one under the mat. I quickly unlock her front door and stumble inside.

Emmy startles, dropping both the lighter and her ballet shoe. She pulls out the earbuds, and music pulses from the small speakers.

She didn't hear me knocking.

Chapter Sixty-Two

Emmy

Finale [fi-nahl-ee] n—The last piece

RHYS FALLS TO HIS KNEES in front of me and sweeps his arm across the floor, moving the razor blade and lighter out of reach. He checks my hand for injury. My pale white skin, once silky and smooth, is now sprinkled with dozens of small white scars. When he finds no obvious injury, his frantic eyes search mine. "Are you hurt?"

I shake my head, and he sighs with relief. His gaze travels down the length of the scar on my cheek, then back to my eyes. Embarrassed, I move my free hand to my bun to let my hair down to hide my face from his view.

"Don't." He reaches forward and covers my hand with his. "You're beautiful." His hand lingers against my cheek, his fingers lightly grazing the raised skin, sending a shockwave down my spine. His clean scent hits my nose, and I lean into him.

"Listen to me," he says, his voice is so earnest, concerned. "You don't have to do this. I'm sure things are difficult for you right now, but it's going to get better. I know it."

"Me too." He's here. Maybe enough time has passed that we can start a friendship. It will be hard, and I'll have to fight my feelings for him, but a friendship is better than not knowing him at all. And while we may not be able to be together, I have a renewed strength. I have my faith and my desire to work toward being able to dance again. It's not a lot, but it's something. And I know it will be all right. One day.

He presses on. "Things might not be like they were before, that you might not be able to—Wait . . . what did you say?"

His deep-brown eyes hold mine, and I remember the first time I ever saw him sitting in Book of Mormon class. As much as losing him hurts, I wouldn't trade our time together for anything. "I know it too. I'll be okay," I whisper.

His eyes flick behind me to the lighter and the razor blade. "Why were you doing that to your ballet shoes, then?"

"Doing what?"

His brow furrows. "Slicing them up and then burning them."

"I was preparing them."

"For death?"

I smile. "To wear. You can't use them right out of the box. I scored the soles for more grip and then *tried* to sear the ribbons so they won't fray."

He sits back as if realizing his break-in was a bit extreme. "Oh." His hand drops from my face, and I watch it fall to his side. "You're okay, then?"

"I'm okay."

Rhys shifts beside me, and I notice his jacket is damp and his white uniform pants are drenched, a small puddle growing beneath him. "I'd get you a towel, but I can't walk all that well at the moment."

He looks at his pants as if remembering they're wet. "I have to tell you something," he says. "But I need to grab something. Don't move."

"Okay . . ."

He hurries back to the door, grabs a brown paper sack, and kneels beside me again. "What you said in the hospital, about hating me if I left? Did you mean it?"

My hand lifts to his bicep as if physically trying to stop his sentence. "I don't. I couldn't. I was upset and didn't want you to leave." The apology feels so inadequate. "I wish I could unsay everything. You're the best man I have ever known."

"I'm not the same man you met at the beginning of last semester."

It goes without saying that I'm not the same girl either. We've changed each other.

"I didn't understand how you could walk away from us," he continues. "Your words made sense, but I didn't get it. There wasn't a thing in this world more important to me than you, so when you said we had to break up . . ." He presses his eyes shut. I reach out to him, but he shakes his head.

"I was so angry," he says. "With you. With God. I had prayed for answers, but He wouldn't give them. Silence. Something about that night was different though. Instead of praying because I wanted to be with you or to prove to myself that nothing was there, I prayed to confirm it was true. I wanted to feel the same power I felt during your blessing in the hospital." His eyes fill with tears. "And I did, Emmy."

It's like someone slams on the brakes and does a hasty U-turn, throwing my entire world off-balance. "W-what are you saying?" My eyes widen. "You're . . ."

"Getting baptized."

A million questions flood my mind, but only one escapes my lips. "When?"

"Now. Or I was about to be, but I stopped it."

My chin trembles despite my best efforts to stop it. "Why?"

"I thought I had to do it on my own to prove something to you. To myself. But then I realized that I'm doing this. I'm getting baptized whether you take me back or not. Either way, I want you there."

His velvet-like voice warms every inch of me. I've dreamed of this moment for so long. "Tell me this is real."

"It's real, angel." He looks at me for a long moment, then reaches for the brown paper bag next to him and sets it in front of me.

"What's this?"

"Open it."

I carefully unfold the top and pull apart the opening. My breath catches when I look inside. "My pink coat." I look up at Rhys, and he's watching me as if worried how I'll react. "How did you get this?" I ask and then immediately realize the answer. "You went back to the hospital."

He nods. "The next morning, but you'd just been released. I wanted to tell you I'd gone to the temple right after leaving you and how I'd prayed and that He answered me. I wanted you to know we could be together. But then I saw your coat, and it made me think about how much pain you've been through— because of the accident, because of me. And I realized something in that moment. I didn't want to cause you any more pain. The next time I saw you, I wanted to be a man worthy of you."

I pull the coat out of the bag and expect to see blood stains on the lining and small slices in the sleeve from the glass, but it's perfect. "How did you . . . ?"

"It took several weeks to pick out the glass, and I had to have the lining replaced, but I knew how much you loved it, and I wanted you to have it. I love you, Emmy Jennings. So much."

"I love you too." The simple words feel too small to describe the way I feel about Rhys.

He shifts to one knee. "I've spent the last two months trying to become the man you deserve," he says. "But I will never be good enough, strong enough, _man_ enough to deserve a woman like you. From the moment you stepped into

Book of Mormon class, I knew you were out of my league. Not only are you beautiful, you're strong and sincere and a thousand other qualities I will always fall short of. You're incredible, and I'm just me." He pauses for a moment to intertwine our hands. "But when I look at you, I want to try. If you'll let me, I promise I will spend every day for the rest of forever working to be worthy of you." He bows his head, takes a deep breath, and then looks up at me with pleading eyes. "Marry me, Emmy."

I tug on his hand, pulling him off his knees. "I need you to understand something," I say. "This is not about what we deserve. This is about what we choose. When I said that you are the best man I have ever met, I meant it. You are selfless and loving and kind. I love you, Rhys Solario."

He presses his fingers into the corners of his eyes. "I have nothing to offer you. No ring to put on your finger, no guarantee that our life will be easy or even close to what you could have if you married someone else. But I love you, and I want to spend eternity with you. Be my forever, angel. And let me be yours."

My answer is instant. "You already are."

Epilogue

Rhys

Forever [fohr-ev-ur] n—Emmy

One Year (to the day) Later

It's Friday afternoon, and the weather couldn't be any worse. Snow is coming down so hard it's comical. Except for the fact that I promised Emmy a perfect day, and I can't help feeling like I've let my bride down.

"Smile," the photographer says.

My smile is probably closer to a grimace, as is Emmy's. I carefully readjust her in my arms. Her white wedding dress swishes as I move her. "You okay?"

"I'm perfect, Rhys. Really."

She's been pushing herself too hard to walk today. She can only walk with a walker and even then only for a short distance. Her body is exhausted.

The photographer checks the camera display and frowns. We've been trying to get a decent shot for the last fifteen minutes. Judging from the frowns the photographer keeps giving her camera, I'm guessing none have come out.

"Why don't we try something different?" The photographer pulls a pink umbrella out of her bag and opens it as she walks over to us. She hands it to Emmy and then positions us under it, angling my face down to Emmy's. Another frown. "Okay, just . . . try to be cute."

Emmy presses her lips together as if trying to hide a smile. "We must not be very photogenic." She hides her scarred cheek in my lapel.

"I don't know what you're talking about." I give Emmy a toothy grin, meaning to distract her. "Have you seen this face?"

Emmy smiles and seems to forget her embarrassment.

The photographer takes a step away and then starts rapid-firing her camera. "Turn, maybe?"

I do. She takes more pictures. "Hmm. A little more."

I take another step, and she bobbles her head with a shrug.

Emmy giggles in my arms.

"You think this is funny, huh?"

"Maybe a little."

"I'll show you funny." I dip her back in my arms, careful not to hurt her. Her hair is in long ringlets and falls back into the snow. Her giggle turns into a full-blown laugh, and I can't help but join her.

"Good. Great!" the photographer says.

I secure Emmy back against my chest. "I'm sorry about the weather," I whisper. "I wanted to give you perfect."

Emmy's smile fades into something more somber. "I don't know. This is kind of perfect, don't you think?"

I glance at the photographer long enough to notice her furrowed brow and then gaze at my bride in my arms, not even able to walk. She deserves perfect.

Next, I look at our family. They're huddled together and shivering, but at least they're all here. Cami, Mom, and Supe. The only person missing is Jen, who's serving a mission in Peru. Mr. Jennings has had a smile stretched across his face all day. It feels good to not only have his blessing but to officially be his son now too. This day *is* good, but Emmy deserves perfect.

Emmy touches my cheek with a soft palm, forcing my gaze back to her. "Remember when we went tunnel singing?"

"You know I do." Never, as long as I live, will I forget that night. It was the night I told her the truth. The night I first told her I loved her.

"It was snowing," she says.

"It was."

"Just like today."

Despite the snow and the wind and everything that makes this day less than what I had hoped to give her . . . she's right; in a way, it is perfect. Today is the day our forever begins.

I touch my forehead to hers, her smile a mirror image of my own. My lips brush hers. "Forever," I whisper.

She kisses me back and then returns the promise. "Forever."

"All right!" the photographer calls. "I think that's a wrap. We'll get group shots at the reception tonight."

This day has been a blur. I can't believe it's already halfway over.

Everyone hurries to their cars. Supe wheels Mom to the Jennings's SUV, and then he helps her inside. He has been helping care for Mom all day and will check in on her at the care center while Emmy and I are on our honeymoon.

I tuck Emmy against my chest and curl my body around hers protectively as I speed walk to my truck. I gently slide her out of my arms and into the passenger seat and then hurry around to the driver's side.

She tries to hide her pain, but her breaths are shallow, and she can't stop rubbing her legs.

"How are you?" I ask.

"A little sore, but I'm okay." She closes her eyes and rests her head against the window.

I hate that she's in pain. Hate it. I wish there were something I could do. Wait. There is. "Emmy . . . may I give you a blessing?"

Her eyes flutter open. "Please."

I hurry to the home we'll be renting for the next year until Emmy graduates. It's a dark-red brick, one-bedroom house. We've spent the last month painting the walls yellow and hanging frames we mean to fill with wedding pictures. Judging by the photographer's less-than-satisfied expressions today, we may need only one or two frames.

I carry Emmy over the threshold and set her on the couch. Her fluffy wedding dress takes up most of the cushions. The second I set her down, she deflates.

"Do you need anything?"

"Just my husband to give me a blessing."

As I put my hands on her head, my wedding ring catches the light and reminds me of the promises we've made. Warmth spreads through me like it did the night I sat outside the temple and pleaded for answers. I say a silent prayer, inviting that same power to be my companion, and then place my hands on her head. My voice shakes as I utter the precious words I've waited so long to say, "Emelia Jennings Solario . . ."

* * *

Emmy
Forever [fohr-ev-ur] n—Rhys

"And for the first time . . . Mr. and Mrs. Rhys Solario!" The DJ's voice booms through the reception hall as Rhys carries me inside. "Let's have the bride and groom come straight to the dance floor for their first dance."

Rhys tries to hide it, but I can feel his arms tense around me and his steps slow. I haven't been able to dance since the accident. I'm doing better with walking, but he's still had to carry me nearly everywhere today.

"It's okay," I whisper to Rhys.

He nods, but I can tell he wants to tear into the DJ. We, as in Rhys, made it clear that there would be no first dance. "We don't have to do this . . ."

We are definitely doing this. I've been waiting for this moment for one whole year. "Set me down."

"Emmy—"

"Set me down, Rhys. I'm fine."

He looks around the dance floor as if unsure what to do.

"Do you trust me?" I ask him the same question he asked me the night he took me dancing at Joe's.

He slides me out of his arms and sets my feet on the floor.

Pins and needles prick my feet, and a deep ache radiates from my bones. I swallow back the pain. As much as it hurts to stand or walk, it *is* getting easier.

Rhys loops his arms around my waist, taking the majority of my weight. "Are you okay? Let me help—"

"I'm fine." I pull my gaze away from Rhys to nod at the DJ.

A second later, the man's voice on the recording rings through the reception hall. "Suavemente!"

Rhys's whole face lights up. "You didn't."

I smile up at him. I did. I so did. I never thought I'd want to hear this song again after I nearly kissed him and he stopped me by telling me what *bésame* meant. And now I can't get enough of it.

The words blend into the shrill whine of trumpets, the beat commanding us to dance, but Rhys doesn't move. "Are you sure?"

My legs are sore, and my body is tired, but I've been looking forward to this moment all day. "I'm sure." I've wanted to dance for weeks now, but I've waited for this moment to share it with him. My first dance for the rest of our forever. I'll never be the dancer I was before. More likely than not, I will never even go on pointe again. I'm okay with that though. I have a long way to go, but I'll get there with Rhys by my side. Dance will always be a part of my life. My goal is to open my own dance therapy center. Blend healing with dance.

Rhys grips my waist and takes a slow step back. Not in time with the music, not even close. He's tentative and careful, making sure I'm okay. The words of the song fade as he all but carries me around the dance floor. For a first dance, it's not exactly traditional, but then again, neither are we.

Playlist

THEME:

"Thinking Out Loud" by Ed Sheeran

EMMY:

"Arctic" by Al Lethbridge (Emmy dancing)
"The Blower's Daughter" by Damien Rice (Q playing guitar at the Village FHE)
"You Lost Me" by Christina Aguilera (after tunnel singing)
"The Heart Wants What It Wants" by Selena Gomez (date with Nathan)
"Dead in the Water" by Ellie Goulding (Emmy's prayer)
"Divenire" by Ludovico Einaudi (pas de deux)
"Ballerina" by Leona Ness (leaving the hospital)

RHYS:

"Dead Man Walking" by The Script (tunnel singing)
"Take Me to Church" by Hozier (Rhys's talk with the elders)
"Let It Go" by James Bay (after BOM final)
"Unkiss Me" by Maroon 5 (conversation on the stairs)
"Breakeven" by The Script (after Emmy's solo performance)
"With or Without You" by U2 (after Emmy's blessing)
"Awake My Soul" by Mumford and Sons (Rhys at the temple)

SCENES:

"You Are in Love" by Taylor Swift (ice cream)
"Suavemente" by Elvis Crespo (dance club and wedding)
"Turn Up the Night" by Enrique Iglesias (dance club)
"Everything Has Changed" by Ed Sheeran and Taylor Swift (first kiss)
"Say Something" by A Great Big World and Christina Aguilera (meeting on campus after Thanksgiving)
"Need You Now" by Lady Antebellum (after the date with Nathan)

About the Author

TIFFANY ODEKIRK BELIEVES COOKING SHOULD take less than thirty minutes, frosting is better than ice cream, and all books should end with happily ever after. After graduating from Brigham Young University with a degree in marriage, family, and human development, Tiffany completed an internship with LDS Family Services in adoption and then went on to work with homeless women and children in the nonprofit sector. Married to a Broadway star, Tiffany's days are filled with music, and her nights are spent writing the types of characters she hopes her children will one day marry. Tiffany loves to hear from her readers; you can find her at TiffanyOdekirk.com and on Facebook @ AuthorTiffanyOdekirk.